I0749323

TRUMPED

DAVID SPOHN

TRUMPED is a work of fiction. All characters, events, and dialogue are products of the author's imagination, and any resemblance to real people, business organizations or events is entirely coincidental and does not change the purely fictitious nature of this work.

First published by Corporate Connoisseur
7/01/2009

ISBN-13: 978-0-9820197-4-0

ISBN-10: 0-9820197-4-2

Printed in the United States of America

Corporate Connoisseur
3255 Lawrenceville-Suwanee Rd.
Suite P250
Suwanee, GA 30024
publishing@thecorporateconnoisseur.com
www.thecorporateconnoisseur.com

DEDICATION

to

Don Birmingham

A great friend who I miss every day.

WEDNESDAY

"Well, my friend, if Paul Kruger gets the promotion, you'll get thrown out with the morning garbage." Turning abruptly, Patricia marched down the aisle, her five foot, eight inch, well-proportioned and toned body rigid with exasperation.

Brent Shannon shook his head in disbelief and stared out the aircraft window to see dusk enveloping the Georgia landscape below. The day had begun normally enough but had transformed itself into a tsunami. A morning trip to Atlanta for quarterly financial reviews at Richmont's corporate offices then back to Charlotte the same day. Nothing to it. Today had been the seventh review in his almost four years with the division. But this review had ended with shock waves. His boss had been promoted to Richmont's chief financial officer and would be relocating to Atlanta.

People get promoted all the time but Brent knew that Marlene Wolff's promotion offered him an enormous opportunity. As director of marketing with a hell of a track record, he could compete for her job as general manager of Just For You, the 110-outlet store chain of Richmont Corporation.

His first job after graduating from the University of Wisconsin had been in brand management with The Pillsbury Company in Minneapolis. From day one his career aspirations focused on attaining general management responsibilities. Conquering "no-win" assignments that no one else would touch; long hours and merciless travel schedules became his norm in order to build his expertise and seasoning. He had endured the evening and weekend MBA program at the University of St. Thomas in St. Paul to better prepare himself. Now here it is within his grasp. He could feel it. However, there happened to be just one gigantic monkey wrench in Brent's wheel of ambition – his wife, Annette.

Annette had left him eight years ago because of Brent's consumption with work. He had left Pillsbury to work for a market research firm in Minneapolis as a marketing consultant. His only focus became making partner. His family had been on a far distant back burner.

Brent had been struck with the winds of reality when he arrived home from an out-of-town engagement to find his family gone. A brief note explained that his wife and children had gone to her parents in Albert Lea, Minnesota and planned to remain there for the foreseeable future. He had been devastated. Totally engrossed in his own career with his ego continually massaged by elevating stature within his business world, he had been blind to the deteriorating mental state of his wife and their crumbling relationship. Thankfully, over a period of time, his sister helped him comprehend the dysfunction of his misguided priorities.

This comprehension resulted in Brent's resignation from his consulting position and accepting a job with Richmont Corporation in Atlanta. Annette agreed to reconciliation with the non-negotiable stipulation that family would always trump career. She had been inflexible on this point for eight years and Brent becoming the general manger would not get favorable reviews in the Shannon household. In the taxi to the airport, he had decided that after all the pain and work he and Annette had experienced to resurrect their relationship, if offered to him, he would not accept this promotion. At forty-two, he had time to secure another general management opportunity. It would be foolhardy to play Russian roulette with his marriage. The decision had been straightforward and easy, a no-brainer, until he made the mistake of sitting with Patricia Bolivar on the flight home to Charlotte.

Patricia, Just For You's director of human resources and his friend and confidant, had conjured up quite a conundrum between wheels-up and 35,000 feet. Her assertion, delivered with great conviction, insisted that the candidate list for Marlene's job contained two names, Brent and Paul Kruger, Just For You's director of finance. And if Kruger got the promotion, one of his first acts would be to fire Brent. In his four years working with her, Brent knew Patricia to be no alarmist and he respected her opinion, especially on people issues. But she had to be wrong this time. Brent's record of contribution would secure him a place on a Kruger-led team.

Brent looked five rows ahead to see Marlene Wolff and Paul Kruger in animated conversation. Paul, a contemporary of both he and Patricia's, had the inclination to be arrogant and self-righteous. Not the type of guy you wanted living next door. Brent and Kruger had had some turbulent times emanating from business disagreements but nothing to signal that they could not work together. No, Patricia had made a flawed analysis.

The scent of subtle perfume signaled the return of Ms. Bolivar. Out of the corner of his eye, Brent could see her face outlined with shoulder length hair the color of bronze laced molasses as it turned to face him. One could only hope she had cooled down, he thought. A thought that immediately proved to be inaccurate.

"You can't take Marlene's job. I've got that right, huh?" Patricia squeezed the words through full, ripe lips drawn tight.

Brent ran a hand through thick, coal black hair while straightening his six foot, two inch wiry frame in the coach seat. "Correct. If it's offered, I can't take it." The lasers from her smoked glass-colored eyes began to unsettle him.

"Plus, you're way ahead of yourself. The new GM's probably coming out of Atlanta or the finance guy in the catalog division everybody thinks walks on water."

"No. It's between you and Paul. I'm certain of it. Marlene's loyal. She's not going outside the division and she's got Bible Ben's ear," she said signaling each point with one of her fingers. Richmont CEO, Ben Voorhees' nickname among employees was Bible Ben because of his strong Southern Baptist faith.

"It's not me. They'd have said something."

"You would get no heads-up. This is close hold. No. It's between you and Kruger. Ten to one, Voorhees wants Kruger because he's a finance guy and Marlene's in your corner."

Suddenly, his mind's eye returned to the quarterly review. The announcement caused the entire Just For You management team to be taken back – except Paul Kruger. He had been in complete control. Not shocked. Prepared! It had shown on his face. "Kruger knew. See him after the announcement?
Zero surprise. Who tipped him off?"

"I don't think anybody. But we're off point. Running this division should be the biggest thing in your world. We all need your leadership. Can't you comprehend that?"

"What I comprehend is my need to keep promises and priorities."

This conversation approached a subject that did not concern Patricia Bolivar, plus her verbal assault really aggravated him. Brent did not suffer being badgered by anyone. Even Patricia, with whom he felt a close business relationship.

"What promises and priorities?" she said.

"I made a promise to Annette I don't think I could keep if I became the general manager. And as Forrest Gump so aptly put it, 'That's all I care to say about that.'

"Patricia, what was the 'thrown out with the morning garbage' comment about?" said Brent in an attempt to distance the conversation from his relationship with Annette.

"You think you'd be part of a Paul Kruger team?"

"Don't test my survival instincts, Patricia. I don't appreciate it. Kruger can be a miserable human being but he's a competent manager who knows my marketing expertise and track record."

Patricia leaned close to Brent, her lips almost touching his ear. Her closeness made him very nervous. "He hates your ever-lovin' guts. Please hear me, Brent? You aren't going to be around. And I promise you, he'll be sure your career's in ruins when you go under the bus. See how your wife relates to that promise."

"Don't think you've analyzed this correctly. Your scenario isn't going to happen," Brent replied.

The pilot reduced power for their decent into Charlotte Douglas International Airport. The look in her eyes implored him to convince her he had not morphed into a categorical idiot.

"Hey, Paul and I've had disagreements but nothing we didn't work through," said Brent. Looking past Patricia, he could see they had broken through the cloud cover to reveal the lights of Charlotte. "And he knows I'm a hell of a marketing guy."

Patricia looked away offering no comment. When the aircraft stopped at the gate, she turned to Brent and said, "Get Annette's support and fight for Marlene's job. Or you'll have no job. Not with Richmont. I have no idea about your marriage, Brent, but I can tell you your career hangs on this."

Brent got up and retrieved his briefcase from the overhead. His brain was having a difficult time digesting this argument. "Well, I can't take the job," he said in a voice edged with equal measures of tension and uneasiness. "If it's offered, I'll turn it down."

They left the plane and walked up the jet way to the terminal. Walking along the concourse, Patricia put her hand on Brent's arm. "Please, Brent. Reconsider. Many people are affected by this – most significantly – you. And ... I don't want to lose you," she said gazing at him. With that, she squeezed his arm, turned and went into the ladies restroom. His stare followed her until she was out of sight.

Brent claimed his luggage, recovered his Audi and merged onto Airport Drive. What a day. This morning he controlled his world with self-assurance. Now conventional wisdom indicted it was in danger of imploding. He came to Charlotte four years ago to work at Just For You. They had been the most satisfying of Brent's career but that satisfaction might be coming to a screeching halt.

He didn't care what Bolivar said, Kruger knew. How did he get the word? Did his network reach into the inner circle?

One thing was a certainty, Brent thought as he turned onto his street. Regardless of the organizational dynamics in play, if he took the job, Annette would tell him to sit on a sharp fence post and spin.

On the flip side, if he didn't get the job, Kruger probably had it. In that case, Patricia foretold Kruger slicing and dicing him as quickly as making the case allowed. He shuttered in spite of himself. For the first time in his life, the glass might be half empty.

Waiting for the garage door to open, Brent noticed all the lights off in the house except the master bedroom. Annette had probably devoured at least one book waiting for him. He hoped the counselor possessed all of her faculties tonight. He needed her help sorting out this goat screw. He inched his way through the downstairs darkness, climbed the stairs and walked into the bedroom.

Annette looked up from reading in the chair by the side window. A light blue, terry cloth robe partially covered what was, in Brent's opinion, the finest forty-two year old female figure in the world. Her dusty blond, shoulder length hair had obviously been brushed and combed. She looked up at him with her saucer-sized, crystal blue eyes that had captivated him since the first day they met in an evening MBA class at the University of St. Thomas in St. Paul, Minnesota.

"Hi, honey," she said closing her book. "On time tonight, huh?"

Brent dropped his bag. "Yeah, can you believe it? On time out of Hartsfield." He moved over to his wife, leaned down and kissed her lightly on the mouth. The aroma of her freshly washed hair filled his senses and reminded him of the excitement she generated within him. As she softly touched the back of his neck, Brent felt himself responding to her sensuality but suppressed his desires. Not yet, he thought.

"Catching up on my reading after the kids went to bed. So how'd the review go? Marlene wow 'em as usual?"

"Review went fine. The surprise afterward stole the show."

"Which was?"

"Marlene's promoted to Richmont CFO. Wraps things up here till the end of the month and heads to Atlanta," Brent said going to his closet to allow his emotional temperature to return to normal range. He hung up his suit coat and came back into the bedroom pulling off his tie.

Annette pulled her feet underneath her on the chair. "Wow. Did you know anything about it?"

Brent paced as his stomach constricted into a tight ball. He turned suddenly and pointed toward her. "No. But that SOB Kruger knew. I know he did."

"Calm down honey," she said, her body giving a start of surprise at his sharp tone. "Kruger defines political animal. If anyone's going to know, it's him."

"Guess what upsets me most is Marlene not mentioning it to me."

Annette got up, walked over to the bed, and sat down. "Brent, Marlene was going to get promoted. She's too good to sit at this division forever. You've preached that."

"I understand that but–"

"Let me finish, Brent. Your male ego's overtaking your reasoning. So you didn't get told. So what? There could have been legitimate reasons."

"How come Kruger knew?"

"That's pure supposition. You're not sure."

"Yeah, I'm sure Annette," he responded while giving her a scorching look. He was starting to lose it and had to settle down. The situation was haunting him and he could feel the heightening pressure. But this dilemma hadn't been created by Annette. Also, her background did not give her a frame of reference for company politics. Her field was the law and she was superb at it. However, her experience with a family business, the law and as a Minnesota government attorney didn't make her politically savvy in a private, corporate environment. But she was very bright and he needed her help sifting through this potential crisis.

"On a more pleasant subject," Annette said, "Erik had a great soccer game today. They won two-to-one and Erik scored the winning goal."

Erik was their twelve-year-old. He and Brent were very close. "Sorry I missed it. He must've been on top of the world."

"Sure was. Would've meant a lot if his father was there."

"I'm sure it would have Annette. But you and the kids know I've got to attend the quarterly meetings."

"I'm just saying he's growing up, Brent. There won't be a lot more of these moments." Brent could feel his stomach clench. They had to get off of this subject. He always lost. "Annette, I'll talk to Erik in the morning. Back to the subject at hand. Need your help on what I should do."

"What you should do?" Annette parroted back. "What do you mean what you should do? People get promoted. Relax sweetheart. I know you like working for Marlene but the world's not going to end."

"No, but my job might if Kruger gets Marlene's job."

Annette rolled her eyes and looked at the ceiling. "Oh, please. That's absolute nonsense. What would be your basis for saying that? You and Kruger aren't best buddies but he knows your work and he needs you. He has no background in marketing."

Brent moved slowly across the room. Annette's nonchalant attitude was starting to grate him.

"Annette, wake up. Kruger can get twenty guys in here to do what I do. The only difference between me and them is he's observed my results. But if he doesn't want me around, that's a takeable downside risk."

Annette lay across the bed, put her chin in her hands and smiled. "Certain no women in those twenty?"

You're about to set me off, he thought. He didn't know the definition of feminist, but if it was looking under rocks for women getting a bum deal, Annette fit the bill.

"Don't go there. No feminist oratory tonight."

"Sorry," she said, the smile leaving her face. "I was just trying to lighten up the conversation a little."

"I know and I'm sorry I snapped. But there's nothing light about this."

"Okay. Okay."

Brent sat down on the bed next to her. "Look, Kruger doesn't like me. That's a fact. The feeling's mutual but I'd say that point is irrelevant. A different situation, I'd be right there with Kruger as a candidate for Marlene's job."

"A different situation," she said raising one eyebrow in a questioning slant.

Careful Brent, he thought. "I mean, if life balancing, if you and the kids, weren't the most important thing in my life."

"I see," said Annette. "You'd be a candidate if you didn't have a family."

There would be no give by his loving wife. No sir. She was going to be her predictable, inflexible self. He could feel it. His response had better be carefully worded. Years ago, he had accepted the truth that she was the brighter bulb in verbal sparring.

"Right. But he doesn't know that. There's a good chance my name's been brought up. With his network, he probably knows it. So answer me this. If I was a candidate, why would he keep me around? I'd be his potential replacement if performance slipped and Bible Ben got unhappy."

"But darling, you're ignoring your own philosophy. You've always said nobody succeeds over the prostrate form of the boss. They go down with him. If that's true, you wouldn't replace Paul if he couldn't cut it."

Brent reminded himself to never talk to her about his organizational philosophies again. "True. But for starters, he may not share my philosophy," he said with his voice going up an octave. "For finishers, the creep hates my guts. Why would he take the risk of holding onto a guy he has bad chemistry with?"

"There's no need to raise your voice."

"You're right. Sorry."

"So tell me. How do you know Kruger's got the inside track and hates your guts so bad?"

Brent recounted the highlights of his discussion with Patricia Bolivar. He knew there was big time trouble about to erupt when he saw Annette's body tense.

"Oh yes, I see," Annette said thick with insinuation. She sat up against the headboard. Her eyes darkened and became narrow blue slits. Her robe slipped open to show Brent more of her buoyant breasts than he needed right now. By the look on her face, he would do no anatomy investigations tonight.

"So Patricia Bolivar is your organizational consultant on this issue. Did she also advise you that she wanted you in bed with her?"

"You're being ridiculous. She has no interest in me. Got a boyfriend. Plus, she's cold as a fish. Half the office thinks the boyfriend's a sham. That she swings from the other side of the plate. But she's a competent human resource person."

Annette laughed, her nose wrinkling in disgust. "You are such a preoccupied, reforming workaholic. You have no idea when a woman wants you intimately – sensually – sexually. If Paul Kruger wants to kick you out of the company, Patricia Bolivar wants to kick you into her life."

"Well, that's really not the point is it, Annette?" he said fixing her with a level stare. "The point is she may be right. If Kruger gets the promotion and doesn't want me around, I'm out on my ear. Dammit, I like Richmont. We've a good future and I don't want to lose it."

"Well, husband of mine, in Patricia's case, my point's well taken. Why sleep with the director of marketing when you can do the general manager? I'd say there might be some opportunistic bias there. My god, Brent, you're great with people. Make peace with Kruger. Stroke the egotistical jerk."

"Not sure that's doable. I don't think you're grasping the drift of these winds of change, my dear. If the guy wants me on a skewer, stroking doesn't appear to be an option."

Annette threw her legs over the side of the bed. "Hold on, Mr. Shannon. I apologize. I missed the purpose of this conversation. You *want* Marlene's job." The veins in her neck stood out in livid ridges. He knew she was over the edge.

"I didn't say that."

"You didn't have to," she said, her voice becoming venomous. "All this love my job and security. Brent Shannon I'll tell you one thing. You go after Marlene's job and lose there might be a chance Kruger will throw you out the door. Go after it and win, you've got me to deal with. And that's no might, darling. That's downright certainty."

"Now Annette, settle—"

"No, sir. No deal, Brent. No way. No time." She was beyond rage. With her face flushed and pinched with resentment, she spat out her words. "You made a promise that I'm holding you to. I cannot abide it when you take me for a simpleton. You take that job and we go back to the hell we had in Minneapolis."

"Annette, listen to me."

"No. There is nothing to listen to, Brent. I didn't agree to come down here where they put coleslaw on hamburgers to see my marriage fail again. At least, in Minnesota there was family. No sir. I expect you to keep your promise."

Brent was unable to keep his temper in check. He stood up his voice rising to a shout. "Son of a bitch, Annette. I'm facing a crisis. At this particular time, I'm not concerned with your conjecture about Patricia Bolivar wanting to bed me but I am concerned about my job."

Annette's tone became icy. "Brent, please hold your voice down or we'll have children in here. Now I know you love your job and like Richmont. But I took you at your word. I trusted you when I agreed to come down here. It's time for you to validate that trust. Now I don't want to discuss this anymore tonight." She dismissed him with a theatrical wave of her arm and laid down in bed with her back to him. Brent knew when discussions with Annette were over. If he tried to press her, all hell would break loose. As he went toward the door, Annette turned in bed. "In fact Brent, there is nothing else to discuss on this subject. It's closed. Please don't bring it up again."

Brent walked downstairs to get a much-needed Wild Turkey. Maybe three or five turkeys. When he promised Annette that family would always trump career he never thought it would come to an either-or choice. He never considered the possibility of losing one because of the other. He drank the first Turkey in a gulp and while pouring the second thought his life glass looked emptier with each passing minute.

The dark blue Jaguar accelerated and merged into traffic on Airport Drive. It performed almost as well as its driver felt. He was buoyed by the events of the day. The 65-degree evening air cascading through the car's open window massaging his flaxen hair was invigorating. Paul Kruger felt better than good. He felt fantastic. Now everything could fall into place.

Marlene's promotion to Richmont's CFO came to pass just as his two-day advance warning had predicted. The early heads-up gave him time to outline his strategy. Now that strategy could shift into high gear. The next general manager would be Paul Kruger.

The heads-up had come from Wilson Rachet. Thank god for Wilson. As an attorney and member of the Atlanta law firm that enjoyed Richmont Corporation as one of its larger clients, Wilson specialized in labor law and a member of the three-attorney team that handled Richmont's work. His and Paul's friendship spanned twenty-plus years.

As Paul guided the Jaguar north on I-77, he recalled his motivation for accepting Marlene's offer to come to Just For You. One of Richmont's bright stars, she came to Charlotte for general management experience to prepare her for bigger things. She would be moving up; then it would be his turn. It amazed Paul she had stayed this long. He had been as patient and loyal to Marlene as he could without jeopardizing his solid network built around his mentor, Richmont's Controller Evan Roth, and Wilson. Now the division general manager job would be his – the first stepping stone to his destiny – the pinnacle of power. He was forty-four and his time had come. Nothing, or no one, would stand in his way.

Wilson had told him that he was not privy to the names of the final candidates but he felt they were internal. Any external candidate would require a background check carried out by his firm and none had been requested. Paul knew himself to be a prime candidate. But there were others or he would have already been promoted. When reviewing the possibilities, he had decided that the only other viable candidate in the division was Brent Shannon. Marlene liked Brent's work and management style. Much like hers, Paul had to admit.

It was he and Shannon from the division. No one else was remotely qualified. There could be someone from Atlanta. He had to call Evan in the morning to explore that possibility. Evan had been very upbeat today at the review. He seemed to be giving thumbs up without saying it.

Paul's mind accelerated to hyper-drive as he left the freeway. Yes, Shannon was the other candidate. Considering the performance of the business and Marlene's loyalty quotient, anyone from Atlanta would be a weak third. He mentally compared himself with Shannon. Marlene liked Shannon's work. Paul had to admit the guy did a hell of a job putting awesome dollars on the top line. If the need arose, Shannon could crunch numbers, too. In fact, he had a better working knowledge of the finance side than Paul had of marketing. He had to give him that nod. He was good. Conversely, as an uncultured blue-collar type, Paul considered Brent a social Neanderthal. His primary negative, however, had to be his past marital problems. They still governed his life. Marlene had tried to keep Shannon's problems under wraps when she'd brought him to Charlotte. Of course, she had to tell Voorhees about it. Ben brought Wilson into the conversation to discuss possible legal liability if Shannon did not work out. Wilson had provided Paul with every detail. The nagging, liberated bitch Shannon called a wife would not set well with Voorhees, either. Ben still got up in the morning shouting, me Tarzan, you Jane.

On his side of the ledger, Paul was recognized as one of the best financial minds in the company. Evan Roth had seen to that and Marlene had validated it with her performance reviews of his work. His expertise would never be challenged. That could be pivotal because Voorhees liked financial backgrounds running businesses and Ben had the deciding vote. On the negative, although he didn't think Marlene would block his candidacy she was close to Shannon. She liked Shannon's overall business acumen and could be pitching him hard. Even though a financial person, she was marketing-oriented.

That witch Patricia Bolivar could cause trouble. She would be a big Shannon supporter. God, she wanted Shannon. No way would she get him. He was tied to that mouthy wife. No, Shannon had never bedded Bolivar. However, her physical attraction to him was blatant to anyone with eyes. When they were together, her body language said, "please bed me." It was an issue that had potential for exploitation.

Yes, much could be used to advantage. In a covert way, of course. Information that could be funneled to Voorhees. The implications of Shannon's rocky marriage. The potential for organizational upheaval due to a concocted relationship with Bolivar. Even some missed budgets as fluff.

Yes, in the pecking order it was he then Shannon. It was going to stay that way. Nothing would be left to chance. Shannon's reputation and career had to be shattered. And, they would be.

Audra would be a huge asset, thought Paul as he pulled into the circular drive. He had married her because she had every skill to be the consummate corporate wife. Now he needed her political astuteness.

Paul left his car in the driveway, went through the front door, dropped his bag in the foyer and called for Audra.

"In the den," he heard her raspy but distinctly feminine voice say.

Paul walked across the entry foyer to the den. Audra was standing next to the built-in cherry bookshelves holding a brandy snifter. She wore a white silk, ankle length lounging robe with her light brown hair held back by a large silver clip. Her green eyes had that semi-dreamy look that signaled she should have stopped one cognac ago.

"Audra. You're up."

"Having a cognac and waiting for you, sweetie. How'd the review go?"

"Great. Marlene's promoted to CFO."

Audra ran across the room and hugged him. "Oh sweetie, does that mean what I think? That coming here's going to finally pay off?"

Paul smelled the sweetness of her cognac breath escaping between lips of deep cinnamon gloss. "It hasn't paid off yet. Voorhees didn't announce her successor."

"Well, it's you."

"If it was me for sure, Ben would've announced it."

Her eyes narrowed speculatively. "Who're the other candidates?" she asked moving away from him.

Paul followed her. "Marlene likes Shannon."

Audra spun around, her eyes probing. "Anyone from Atlanta?"

"I don't think so. Marlene's loyal."

"Anyone else in Charlotte besides Shannon?"

Paul laughed. "Are you kidding? Those imbeciles?"

"No, I'm not kidding. You're sure?" Audra's voice and body language made him uneasy. She topped the list of the few humans capable of intimidating him.

"Sorry, baby," he said. "I'm sure. I'm checking with Evan tomorrow to see if there's a candidate hiding in Atlanta. But, I think it's me or Shannon. Announcement's coming within a week."

"You're one up over Shannon. Good god. You came over here and helped Marlene stabilize this shit pile. Those dark days should cancel Shannon. Plus, you and Marlene have the same backgrounds."

"Think I have the upper hand. But Marlene likes Shannon's work. He's been the driver getting sales to grow the business. He's turned her into a strong marketing advocate."

Audra moved toward him. Her eyes were on fire.

"You *think* you have the upper hand," she hissed at him. Her face became crimson. "This's no god damned high school contest about who's taking the homecoming queen to the fuckin' prom. Got to be locked down. No margin for error. Now dammit! What's got to be done to take this son of a bitch out?"

"I don't know baby," he said backing away and looking at the floor. "There are some possibilities."

"Go on," she said closing the gap between them.

"Overruns in the ad budget," Paul said in a strangled voice.

"Oh, bull shit. He's a high performing top-line guy. Only people that budget overruns piss off are accountants. It's only icing. Where's the damn cake? What causes this guy to crash and burn? He's no boy scout."

"His marriage has a rocky past and it's still a huge problem. That can be brought up. If it's tied to need for increased commitment, heavier time requirements. Company doesn't want to ruin a marriage. Be other opportunities. It would have a big impact on Bible Ben if it could be whispered in his ear away from Marlene."

"Make it happen," said Audra softening her tone. "You have markers to collect in Atlanta. Don't leave them in your pocket. This promotion isn't a maybe thing, Paul. It has to happen. Don't forget, it's for your mother as much as you. She supported you against your macho, military prick father who thinks you're half a man. Long as we're on family subjects, has to happen to stick it up my pontifical father's ass. One who equates your background to a cut beneath his gardener. One who thinks my aspirations are bull shit. That I should spend my life on my back getting knocked up by some blue blood neurotic."

"I know baby," said Paul. "We'll make it happen."

"You're damn right we'll make it happen. What else can be gotten on this guy? Agree with your logic. Shannon's out of the way, we're home free."

"The killer would be if Shannon and Bolivar were making it together."

"Oh, damn. Ole Bible thumping Ben would hang them off the corporate yardarm."

"But they're not."

"How do you know? Puppy dog look she has for him. Does everything but give him a lap dance. They are or not isn't important. Voorhees only has to think they are. If he does, on top of the rocky marriage, Shannon's dead meat. Ben won't only kick him out of Richmont but make sure he has a hell of a time getting employment anywhere. Wow. Talk about being screwed."

"An understatement," Paul said.

"Get going on it. You're getting this promotion."

Audra moved to Paul, removed the silver clip, shook her hair free, and put her arms around his neck. Her lips were almost touching his. Her breath, warm and still cognac sweet, disquieted him. She slowly ran her tongue over his lips. "Bedtime, darling. Let me show you how much I appreciate the success you're going to bring us."

THURSDAY

"Hi, Dad," Erik Shannon said.

"Hi ya doin', Champ," responded Brent to his twelve-year-old son. "Understand yesterday was huge on the soccer field."

"Was cool, Dad. We won, but they were tough."

"How'd you do?"

"Okay, I guess. Yeah, okay."

"Okay? Reliable sources told me you nailed the winning goal."

"I did," said a beaming Erik. "Dad, you gonna be there Saturday?"

"Wouldn't miss it."

From the laundry room, Annette asked, "That a promise I heard?"

"A promise," Brent said.

"Thanks, Dad," Erik said as ten-year-old Tawney appeared in the kitchen doorway.

"Good morning, Daddy," she said in the most refined voice a ten-year-old could muster.

"Hi, Miss Pris," Brent said. "How 'bout a kiss for your Daddy?"

"But of course, Daddy," she said climbing onto his lap and throwing her arms around him. She gave him a loud kiss on the cheek. "How was that?"

"Umm, wonderful. Now, hop down 'cause Daddy's got to go to work."

"My kisses would be much better if Mommy let me wear lipstick, you know," said Tawney, jumping off his lap.

"Girls can't wear lipstick till they're thirty years old," Brent said smiling.

"Don't forget Saturday, Dad," said Erik. "Big game. Hornets are undefeated."

"I won't."

Annette stuck her head out of the laundry room. "And don't forget our talk last night, Mr. Shannon. I meant every word of it."

"I won't, and I know you did," said Brent kissing her lightly on the lips.

"What was the talk about?" asked Tawney.

"About how you can't wear lipstick till you're thirty years old," said Brent going to the garage.

The last twenty-four hours gave new meaning to fiasco, he thought backing the Audi down the driveway. Marlene leaving with Kruger hugging the inside rail for her job. Twenty-four hours ago he would have thought that Kruger as a boss, although not something to relish, would be workable. Now, according to Patricia if Kruger got Marlene's job, ole Brent was in the unemployment line. The only way to secure his corporate future was to get Marlene's job himself. That option created just one little problem. If he took the job, his marriage was headed south and his wife was headed north. Annette hadn't said that, but she meant that. Talking to Marlene was top priority and the sooner the better. He punched the number four speed dial on his cell phone. On the second ring, Marlene answered.

"Hi, Marlene. I'm heading in. Can we get together?"

"Sure. Paul's with me but things'll be wrapped up soon. Come right in."

"Thanks." Brent flipped the phone shut. Wonder what part of him they were discussing. God, he was elevating paranoia to cosmic heights.

Marlene not saying a word to him about this move had his shorts in a bundle. Bolivar was probably right though. Ben had instructed her to keep her mouth shut. But, it had done a number on his head. Then Bolivar put the full court press on him to go for the job. Complete with the leaning over, get intoxicated by me, tactic.

As he turned the Audi onto Westinghouse Boulevard, his mind cascaded into the past. Brent grew up on the outskirts of Janesville, Wisconsin. His father still lived in the same house and went to the same blue collar job every day.

After high school, Brent went to the University of Wisconsin in Madison. He graduated in five years with a degree in business administration and a 3.6 GPA. In Madison, he'd had an active social life that revolved around bartending at the Nitty Gritty. Along with being his social center, the job paid a substantial portion of his living and education expenses. He had neither the time, money, or desires to involve himself in the upscale climate of the Greek social scene. Social snobbery and caste systems were repugnant to him which was how he had perceived that campus sub-culture.

He had been true to his social philosophy until his fourth year. One night he had been introduced to a sorority girl who was the most dazzling creature he had ever seen, and she immediately captured his heart. Over the next four months, they saw each other constantly and fell madly in love. Oh, no. Back off, he commanded himself. He had worked hard to cleanse those memories from his mind.

Then Annette had come into his life. A smile spread across his face as he remembered meeting her. It had been in the University of St. Thomas' evening MBA program. They enjoyed each others' company immediately and began spending as much time as possible together.

Annette came from a middle class family in Albert Lea, Minnesota, a small agricultural community two hours south of Minneapolis. Her family had opened their hearts to him. Slowly, over eighteen months, he succumbed to falling in love, and they had been married.

Crossing Steele Creek Road, he pulled himself back to the present. Thank God for Patricia. He was glad she was on his side. The other division directors would avoid eye contact, hide behind the nearest rock and keep their ear to the ground to hear which way the buffalo were running. He couldn't blame them. Smile at the wrong person during this cock fight and you could be flat out of luck. Corporate jockeying. What a productivity drain.

Ben Voorhees had to be handling this himself. Marlene might have input. Probably, a lot. But ultimately it would be Ben's call, and he would make it. Marlene and Just For You's results had elevated Ben to hero status with the Board of Directors. He wasn't about to see the division slide down the profit hill.

Brent pulled into the Just For You parking lot and looked for a space. No reserved parking spaces with Marlene Wolff captaining the ship. If Kruger got the top job, there would be a canopied walkway from his reserved space to the office. It would be the closest space, too. Screw handicapped folks and the employee of the month.

Brent used the employee entrance and headed to his office. Barely in the marketing department area, Ashley Weedon his bright, precocious administrative assistant intercepted him.

"Is it true?" she asked while keeping up with his pace. "Marlene's leaving?"

"That's it, Ash. She's history."

Brent went into his office with Ashley close on his heels. "What's going on today, Ash?" he said dropping his briefcase in a side chair.

"Staff meeting this morning. And don't forget, got about two days to get the seasonal promo plan to Atlanta."

"Yeah, I know. How's Neal coming on his part?"

"Don't know. You're getting her job, right?"

"What?"

"Marlene's job. You're getting her job, aren't you?"

"Nothing's decided yet. Remind everyone about the staff meeting. Have to see Marlene."

"My bet's on you, boss."

"Don't bet the rent money."

Brent said good morning to Neal Stuart and Dina Minsky as he passed their offices. Neal was the Advertising Manager, and Dina the Merchandise Manager. Both reported to Brent.

Walking across the atrium lobby of Just For You's general office, Brent considered how to approach Marlene. He knew it wouldn't be terribly bright to jump her case about not confiding in him. After that weighty thought, his mind became a void. So he decided to play it by ear, which he always thought to be a very flexible strategy. It worked really well with Annette last night.

As Brent approached Marlene's office, he saw Marlene and Paul Kruger come through the office door. They finished their conversation smiling and after a cheerful goodbye, Paul walked toward Brent.

"She's in a great mood," he said walking past Brent.

"Hi, Brent," said Marlene. "Come on in. Want some coffee?"

"Thanks. Need a fix."

Marlene turned to her admin assistant. "Terry, mind getting a couple of coffees?"

"Coming up."

"Have a seat," Marlene said. "Leave the door open till the coffee gets here."

Brent walked to the far end of her office. He sat at the circular conference table with his back to the office's picture windows. Brent watched Marlene standing behind her desk arranging papers. What a striking woman, Brent thought. Tall at five-ten or so, she had very little body fat for a woman. Lean but proportioned and well coordinated. He would bet she had some serious swimming in her background. Brent knew her to be fifty-three. She had beautiful, short, auburn hair and friendly green eyes that could be piercing if it suited her purpose.

“So what’s on marketing man’s mind today?” said Marlene walking to the table and sitting down across from him.

“First, I wanted–” He was interrupted by Terry bringing in the coffee.

“Thanks, Terry,” said Marlene. “Shut the door, please.”

Marlene smiled. “Want to try again?”

“First, congratulations. Ben picked the right person. You’re going to light up Atlanta.”

“Thanks, Brent. Ben took me by surprise. I wasn’t looking for anything. Could’ve stayed here the rest of my career. So, what else is happening?”

“Having a staff meeting this morning. Seasonal sales promo should be ready to look at next week.”

“Good. If things go right, the new GM will sit in.”

“Corporate wants it this week, but there’s more work till I’m satisfied it’ll do what we want. Doing the corporate two-step to hold them off.”

“Let me know if you need help. But, you should be able to handle Tom Carthage.”

“There’ll be no problem. It’s a lot easier to seek forgiveness than permission from Tom,” Brent said. Tom Carthage was Richmont’s vice president of marketing and Brent’s first boss with the company.

“Okay. Glad we’re wrapping that up. Need to beat the hell outta last year. Anything else?”

“Yeah, any idea when your replacement will be announced?”

“I’m not certain. Ben mentioned about a week, didn’t he?”

“Think he did. Was a shock, you know. When you’re part of a great team, you want it to go on forever.”

"But the team'll still be great. A new GM won't change that."

"Any idea who?" said Brent.

"I don't. It's Ben Voorhees' decision. All he asked for were my thoughts."

"Can understand that. Division's been a real feather in his cap."

Marlene leaned toward him. "You look worried. What's the matter?"

Brent knew what thin ice felt like, and he was on it. "Not worried exactly. Just concerned about the team changing."

"A new GM doesn't mean the team's changing."

"Maybe. But you know team dynamics better than I do," Brent said. "Everything plays off the leader."

"That's right. And Ben Voorhees isn't putting someone in here that'll destroy our culture."

"Know Ben wouldn't intentionally do that," Brent replied. At least, he wasn't on thin ice anymore, he was in the water. What the hell. Go for it. "Marlene, am I well-thought-of in the company?"

"Of course. You've done an outstanding job in the division and corporate marketing certainly has no problems. Tom Carthage thinks the sun rises and sets on you."

Brent could feel her becoming exasperated with this conversation and concluded he better get out while he was still somewhat intact. "Well, that's good to know. Thanks," said Brent as he started to stand.

"Whoa. Not so fast, marketing man. Keep your seat. These questions? So I'm leaving. Though I'd like to think so, the world—as Just For You knows it—won't crash and burn with my departure. You're one of the most self-confident humans I've ever worked with. Makes you good in your line of work. When it's crunch time, Shannon steps up. But this conversation isn't like you. If I didn't know better, I'd say you were worried about your survival."

"You never know, do you?"

Marlene's hands tightened and gripped the table. "Dammit, Brent. Are you hallucinating? No corporate assassin has you in the crosshairs, and you're not somebody's straw man. You've been a major contributor to this division's success and can continue to be, regardless of who is GM. What the devil's gotten into you?"

"Don't mean to be overly concerned, but the change was fast."

"Most are."

"I know. Aw hell, Marlene, I just wanted to know if I have a good credibility base in the company. Just in case."

Her green eyes bored a hole through Brent. "Just in case of what?"

She was making him very uncomfortable. "In case the new GM and I don't work together as well as you and I have."

"Let's you and me have a quick lesson in organizational reality," said Marlene. "You've a good credibility base. A base built through me. And like it or not, it'll continue to be built, damaged, or destroyed through the next GM."

She relaxed somewhat. "Come on, Brent. You know the score. Essentially, a GM's own corporate destiny is in the hands of others. The GM needs to have faith and feel comfortable with those people. That dynamic's never changing. And chemistry. It's illusive as a leprechaun but it's either there or not. For those reasons, the company will never take the staffing prerogative away from a GM. Especially, direct reports. You know that. When I leave it's no longer my call. This is the real world. The one we live in. It's not a world to obsess over but you've got to work within its parameters. Keep producing results and your success will be assured. Now is there anything else? Cause I've got a conference call in fifteen minutes."

Results assure success. That's not quite the pitch she gave him a couple of years ago in the understanding corporate politics lesson, Brent thought. He got up to leave. "No, nothing else. Thanks for your time and congratulations again."

"You're welcome. And thanks for the congrats."

As Brent started to open the office door, Marlene said, "Hey, marketing man."

Brent turned to see her at her desk looking at papers. Without looking up, she said, "If you're at all interested, I put your hat in the ring for my job. But you're not the only one in there."

"Thanks for your confidence in me."

"No thanks necessary. You've earned it. Now go back to work and quit feeling sorry for yourself. Doesn't become you. Surprise me with your best promo effort ever. That's how to move forward. Not looking for villains."

Brent nodded to the top of her head and closed the door. Now, wasn't that just precious? All he succeeded in doing was to remove all doubt that he was a certifiable idiot. Sure as hell, if he looked up, he would see the buzzards circling. After that meeting, Brent bet Marlene was thrilled that she threw his hat in the ring. Annette had nothing to worry about.

Brent walked back into his office calling for Ashley. She bounded in.

"The other two are in the conference room awaiting the master, oh great one," she said.

Brent shook his head and picked up the leather folder from his desk. "Okay, Ash. Let's do it."

Brent, with Ashley in tow, walked down the hall to the marketing conference room. Neal Stuart and Dina Minsky were already seated with coffee and papers in front of them.

"Okay, folks," said Brent. "Let's go over the seasonal promo plan. Dina, the merchandise run down."

"The selection is coming along fine. We've a fair assortment with adequate depth. Distribution says they'll have additional shipments out this weekend. Majority of the stuff they've got for us is sleepwear. Not going to rival Victoria's Secret in the lingerie classifications."

"That's a problem," said Neal. "Both our mailer and newspaper layouts feature lingerie. All we're waiting for is to drop in photos, descriptions and price points."

"Now, that is a problem," said Brent. "How, pray tell, did that happen?"

"Neal, I told you what the merchandise mix was looking like," said Dina.

"Not, no lingerie," countered Neal.

"No, not no," Dina bristled. "But not a heavy mix or size assortment. Nothing even you could interpret as a candidate for feature."

"Hold on," said Brent. "Nothing's gone to print." Looking at Neal, he asked, "Has it?"

"No, of course not," said Neal. "But we're close. Just waiting for Dina's people."

"Close doesn't count," said Brent. "Dina, got any other inter-company lingerie opportunities?"

"Yeah, catalog division's got some stuff they'll send us."

"Don't sound so excited," said Brent.

"Wait'll you see it," replied Dina. "It's crap. The only women that'll buy the stuff are those who don't want to get laid. Plus, the size assortment starts at small and A-cup then gets smaller. Not a good deal unless Tinker Bell shops us a lot. No wonder they want to unload it. Tried to get some of those half-size bras the company developed. Atlanta told me to take a hike. Said the department stores would be very unhappy campers."

"They would," Brent said. "We've got to make some decisions here, folks. Atlanta's bugging Ashley for the completed plan. I cleared it with Marlene to put them off until the middle of next week, but that's it. No plan by then and they'll eat us for lunch. And by they, I'm including Marlene."

"Speaking of Marlene," said Neal. "When they going to announce the new GM?"

"Don't know," said Brent. "But it doesn't have any bearing on the seasonal promo plan, does it?"

"Hey, there's no question who's going to get her job," said Dina looking at Brent. "You are. Who else?"

"Paul Kruger's a big time candidate," said Neal. "In fact, smart money's on him."

"Say that ain't so," Ashley piped in. "That would be way south of horrible."

"Okay, back to the seasonal promo," said Brent. "Neal, how about in-store signage?"

"I'm working on the boards now," said Neal. "The theme's, 'This Season Everything's Just For You.'"

Dina looked over at Neal. "Hold it, Neal. You don't drop that bomb shell and walk away. No way. Why's smart money on Kruger? Guy ought to wear a condom for a hat. If you're mentally challenged today, that means he's a prick."

"People over in finance don't have much use for him," said Ashley. She laughed. "They really do call him Paul the Prick."

"Wait a minute," said Neal. "Kruger's a bright guy. Hell of a finance guy. He'd run a tight ship but worse things could happen." He looked over at Brent and quickly added, "Brent, don't mean you wouldn't be a great GM. Just think Paul would be good, too."

"Good back track, Neal," Dina snickered.

"Probably several people being considered," said Brent.

"Nope. Word on the streets, it's you and Kruger," said Neal. "One thing for sure. Kruger's GM, he leaves advertising alone."

"Forget it, Einstein," said Dina. "Kruger leaves nothing alone. But Neal, I'm fascinated why you're so delighted Kruger's the frontrunner. At least, that's the impression I get."

"Not true," said Neal. "Just reporting what I've heard. Thought Brent should know."

Dina rolled her eyes. "Right."

"People, people," said Brent. "We've got to get to this promo plan. The deadline—"

The door opened behind Brent, and one of the merchandise coordinators stuck her head in the room. "Sorry to interrupt, Mr. Shannon. Got a call from Mr. Kruger. Told me it's important he talk to you immediately."

He couldn't even keep control of his own meetings, Brent thought. "Thanks. Be right there.

"Okay. We're off point anyway. Dina, have a final promo list to me by Friday afternoon. Neal, have the boards and layouts ready for review next Monday morning. Don't miss that deadline. And Neal, for god sakes, you and Dina go over available merchandise. Stuff that's really going to be in the stores. Plus, call public relations in Atlanta to see if we can get some puff pieces in the markets we're running newspaper. And Dina, stop those merchandise coordinators from calling me Mr. Shannon. I keep looking over my shoulder for some old guy."

Brent went back to his office and punched the blinking light. "Yeah, Paul."
"Brent, I'm sorry to drag you away, but there's a meeting at two o'clock this afternoon in Marlene's office. Terry Thomas will be here. He wants to visit about the upcoming change. You remember Terry from the capital expenditure requests. Not a big deal, but Marlene wants you to sit in. She asked me to call you."

Terry Thomas was Richmont's Executive Vice President for Administration. "Okay, Paul. What do I need to prepare?"

"Nothing that I know of. As I said, no big deal."

Brent was glad about no prep. He had enough on his platter. "Okay. See you then."

Dina stuck her head in his door. "Watch out for Neal. He's trouble, Brent." She walked away without waiting for his reply.

Well now, another woman predicting the apocalypse. Why go to church? The authors of the Book of Revelation were among him. The lake of fire waited.

Patricia Bolivar sat tapping a pencil on her desktop. She wore a fitted, maroon, turtle-neck sweater with a black wool-blend skirt. Her clothing was always conservative but well tailored to accent the attractiveness of her thirty-three-year-old figure.

The events of the last twenty-four hours were overwhelming. She had been shocked when Ben Voorhees made the announcement of Marlene's promotion. Then shock had turned to anticipation. Brent Shannon would be the top candidate to replace her. A perfect situation. She would have the opportunity to work much closer with him. She felt herself to be Brent's confidant. This would allow her to help him as an integral part of her job. In the cab to Hartsfield, she had realized her euphoria had been premature. The sledgehammer of reality hit her.

Paul Kruger had to be the leading candidate. As she contemplated what a disaster his leadership would be, her spirits plummeted. She had long maintained that no one was more unsuited for corporate leadership than Paul Kruger. He was technically brilliant but wholly narcissistic. The division would not be fit for human occupancy.

The flight home had been even worse. She was thrilled to sit with Brent and have an opportunity to strategize. He crushed her with his proclamation that he did not want the job, and he would not take it if it was offered. What a tragic development. She had lain awake most of the night trying to develop an argument that would dissuade him from that course of action. Brent had told her it would screw up his marriage. The hell it would, she thought. His marriage was already screwed up with his wife smothering him and his talents. What a self-absorbed vixen. Patricia's best argument would be Brent's certain fate if Kruger got the job. But Brent had no idea how much Kruger loathed him. There were times when Brent could be so focused on his own job that it resulted in him being blind to the world around him.

Patricia's thoughts were interrupted by Nadia Swenson walking through her office door. Nadia was Just For You's director of store operations.

"So, what's the scoop, HR?" said Nadia.

"Hi, Nadia. I assure you, I know no more than anyone else."

"Not possible. Come on, give it up girl."

"You can bet your pay check on it."

"Tell you this," said Nadia. "It's between Shannon and Kruger."

"Someone from Atlanta could be under consideration."

"Not if Wolff has anything to say about it," countered Nadia. "One of her fair-haired boys will get the nod. Take it from the only woman in the good-ole-boy system. No offense, but you're staff. That's tolerated. But an operational job. Let Swenson be the token chick but keep her under control. And can you believe it? The system's run by a female who broke through the ceiling. Any help for those of us still hitting our heads? Not on your life. She didn't even put me up as a token. Good riddance to her."

Patricia was taken aback by the venom in Nadia's voice. She had no idea how the woman felt. "How do you know you're not a candidate?"

Nadia laughed. "Don't put that bull shit past me, Bolivar. It's between Shannon and Kruger. End of report. Quite a decision, too. Differences between the two aren't subtle. Kruger's a lot savvier and has a ton of contacts. He'd grow the division faster than Shannon. But his best quality is he'd stay out of the stores' business."

"Never heard of Paul Kruger staying out of anything affecting his career. What do you think of his management style?"

"Don't care about his management style. Told you his most important quality. He'll stay away from the stores. Ever seen him on a store visit? Get him past register procedures and daily cash worksheets; he knows less about how we run stores than a picker in distribution. No. He'd leave the stores to me. I'm traveling most of the time; I don't give a rat's behind about his management style. I'll leave that worry to you office homesteaders."

"How about Brent?"

"Shannon? That's easy. Thinks he knows everybody's job better than they do. Nicer boss to be around but a pain. Into your business all the time. Doesn't have Kruger's network, either. Naw. Kruger's the lead dog, but bet they're having a time deciding."

"So you think Kruger's the best choice?"

"Don't put words in my mouth, Patricia. Just expressed my opinion. Division's in good hands with either one. I'm just a bipartisan observer." Nadia pointed at Patricia. "Dammit. Don't make me anything else. I'm not on either side of this political mud wrestling contest."

"I wasn't trying to imply anything like that." This woman could aggravate you, Patricia thought.

"Don't. And another thing. If I were you, girl, I'd put distance between you and this struggle. You're real attached to Shannon and everybody sees it. You keep that profile, Kruger gets the nod and you'll find yourself logging on to monster.com and updating your resume real quick."

Patricia became livid by her accusation. She bolted out of her chair and pointed her finger at Nadia. "Not true, Nadia, and you know it. I resent that characterization of my relationship with Brent Shannon."

Nadia got up, walked to the door and turned to Patricia. "Resent it all you want. But fact is, everybody thinks it. In the real world, sweetie pie, that makes it so."

Nadia waved her arm at Patricia and continued. "So my advice to you is, watch it. If you're getting any, Shannon's going to be the most expensive roll in the hay you've ever enjoyed."

Patricia literally ran around her desk and stopped four inches from Nadia's face. "Well, *girl*, you pass that around this office and I'll kick your scrawny butt silly. Now get out of my office."

"Up yours, sweetie," Nadia said as she sulked off.

Patricia sat back down. That woman was the most unrefined, crude human she had ever been associated with, business or otherwise. Nadia couldn't be reflecting the opinion of others regarding Brent and her. They were close business associates but nothing more. She remembered their first meeting. She had been immediately drawn to him. In fact, she had found nothing about him she didn't like. He had a wonderful personality and the most self-assured man she had ever met. In most cases, self-assuredness in men turned her off. It usually manifested itself in some macho, pants down, yardsticks out, mentality. Not Brent. Thoroughly captivating, he buoyed her when she was around him. This resulted in a close business relationship but anything more was ludicrous. They usually came down on the same side of issues because they thought alike. Their relationship was strictly business and she intended it to stay that way.

Patricia's thoughts slipped back to last night's telephone conversation with Leslie Cook. Leslie had been her roommate at Bucknell University in Lewistown, Pennsylvania, where Patricia had earned an undergraduate degree in political science with a minor in economics. As roommates, Patricia and Leslie shared in each other's dreams and secrets. After graduation, Patricia was accepted into the Masters of Business Administration program at the University of Georgia. Leslie took a job with an advertising firm in Pittsburgh. They had stayed closest friends.

Last night Patricia had been so upset she'd called Leslie and gotten her out of bed to discuss the dilemma. Leslie had asked if there was something Patricia hadn't told her. She said that the urgency in Patricia's voice sounded much more than just business. More personal.

Patricia had dismissed that. She'd told Leslie it had everything to do with the running of the division. The telephone ringing brought her back to the present.

"Hi, Patricia. Todd Beamon here."

Todd was the corporate Compensation Manager. He reported directly to Stan Ascutney, Richmont's Vice President of Human Resources.

"Oh. Hi, Todd. How's Atlanta today?"

"Fine. Just fine. Doing a survey for Stan. Need to know if there're any perks or incentives for your division directors that aren't on the computer."

"No," replied Patricia. "Why the survey?"

"It's a companywide thing. Think the board wants it."

"If I called the other division HR directors, would they know about this survey?"

"Patricia, don't press."

"It's about the soon-to-be-open GM job in this division, isn't it?"

"I told you not to press. You gave me what I needed. Thanks."

"Don't you think of hanging up on me, Todd Beamon," Patricia retorted. "I've done some things for you above and beyond. What's going on?"

"Look. All I know is Stan asked for a complete compensation workup on both

Shannon and Kruger. Nothing sinister."

"How about Atlanta? Anyone there under consideration?"

"No one I know of. Think Shannon and Kruger are the candidate list."

"Who's your bet?"

"I'm only the comp guy. But when I reviewed the tentative packages with Voorhees and Ascutney, Ben had been more concerned with Kruger's deal. Almost perfunctory with Shannon's. I'd say that puts the odds on Kruger."

"Kruger's a foregone conclusion?" Patricia asked not certain she wanted to know the answer.

"Didn't say it's over. But Ben's always been more comfortable with number crunchers running divisions. Tell you this. Better not be hearing anything derogatory about Shannon or it *is* checkmate time. Now I've said a lot more than I should've."

Patricia realized she had just opened a great contact in Atlanta. Promotion decisions aren't finalized in the company without Beamon at the meeting. "Thanks for your insight, Todd. Appreciate it."

Todd was probably right about how Ben lined up Brent and Paul. However, Marlene could make an excellent case for Brent if she chose. He had been the driving force behind putting the top line in order so Just For You could make money. Also, there would not be any derogatory information in Brent's history.

This thing cannot consume me, she thought. She had a personal life, and that venue had a troubling issue as well.

She had been seeing Adam Jordan for over a year. Now he was looking for a commitment to something more. She did not know what to do. She was fond of Adam but how fond? Enough to go the next step?

She knew without question that he was the most accomplished lover she had ever shared a bed with and that was saying something. The lasting impact of her first intimate relationship at Bucknell had been a blossoming enjoyment of sexual activities. But only those that didn't come with long-term commitments. She became an excellent sex partner to those lucky enough to attract her. However, she was discrete, very selective, and even appeared distant in public settings.

As she sat at her desk contemplating her future with Adam, she was unsure of her true feelings. Her goal since Bucknell had been a rewarding career. She had avoided complicated, long-term relationships. She knew Adam made her go places sexually she had never been before. But was he the man with whom she wanted to grow old? They were going to have to talk seriously and she dreaded it. She felt they had a wonderful, casual relationship and she didn't want to lose that. But did she want more?

Brent looked in Patricia Bolivar's office and saw her staring into space. "Hey, can't be that bad," he said. "Come on. Let's have some lunch."

She looked up smiling. "Best idea all day." She picked up her purse and met him at the door briefly putting her hand on his arm. "You've got me, kind sir. Let's get out of here for a while."

On the way to Brent's car, he told her about the cat and dog fight that his staff meeting turned into. He warned her that a real firestorm was brewing over Marlene's departure and productivity could go down the drain. Patricia agreed with him. She recounted her conversation with Nadia Swenson.

After they got in the car, Brent said, "How about John's? Get some good ole country cooking cheap."

"I guess. Lord, you love that place."

"Hey, can't beat it. Try the side of black eyed peas or greens. Yum. What did Nadia have to say?"

"Playing it close to the vest. Doesn't want to be seen as taking sides."

"I see."

"She favors Kruger. Thinks he'll stay out of operations more than you." She laughed. "She obviously travels too much. Needs to be around the office to see him in action."

"That's interesting. She has to know Kruger's got little use for her. Incidentally, I ran into Lloyd Blackburn on the way to your office." Lloyd was Just For You's distribution director. "Almost got down on his knees and begged me to get the job. Said he'd never get a decent night's sleep with Paul. Guy would hang over him like a starved vulture."

"Seeing the effects of this? Hard not to take sides," she replied.

"Bible Ben screwed this up big time," he said. One of Brent's hands thumped the top of the steering wheel in annoyance. "Can't imagine Marlene wouldn't throw a fit. It's tearing the place up. Nobody likes change. Insecurity can go off the charts in the best managed cases. Atlanta outdid themselves. Spring a leadership change but only tell half the story. People aren't stupid. Majority think Kruger's lapped the field and he scares the hell out of most of them. I'm supposed to be the white knight. A role I can't fill. What a stupid stunt. There's going to be some long-lasting ramifications."

"Agreed," said Patricia. "They should have made both announcements simultaneously. Can't understand why Stan Ascutney didn't make sure that happened."

Brent pulled into John's parking lot. "Believe me, Patricia, there's enough complicity to go around on this screw up. Organizational cannibalism's gonna reign before it's over."

"There might've been leaks in Atlanta about Marlene that forced Ben's hand on the announcement even though they hadn't settled on the replacement," she said.

"Maybe so. But the results are destructive. Damn destructive."

"It's politics. Better get proficient playing them. Brent, for goodness sakes, you can't be so narrowly focused on your piece of the action that, to use your metaphor, you miss the cannibals."

Walking across the parking lot, she said, "General manager Brent better accept politics as the real world."

In the restaurant, they were seated at a window booth and ordered.

"Patricia, I'd like you to listen closely. Got to make something perfectly clear to you. I appreciate your faith in me. Means a great deal. I know you feel I'm the best person to be Just For You's general manager. I respect you as a businessperson and it's a magnificent compliment. Nonetheless, I've got to reiterate my comments on the plane. I'm not a candidate for Marlene's job. I've had a hellish eight years putting my marriage back together and I'm not going to jeopardize it."

"Brent, I appreciate your feelings. I assure you the respect is reciprocal. Know I'm treading on your personal life but this is very important to lots of people. There're literally thousands of general managers running our size businesses who're happily married. Please help me understand why your marriage is so much more fragile."

Brent saw she had become distraught. Her eyes welled with tears. "Patricia. Don't get frantic about this."

Patricia leaned toward him with gripping eyes. "Don't get frantic. Don't get frantic. Are you blind? Our division's about to be turned over to a barracuda who doesn't care about anyone but himself. He's a brilliant financial mind and that should be his contribution to the corporation. He should never be responsible for others' well-being. He's a menace. He's not a builder. He's a destroyer. Unless you stand up to this challenge, he'll be given responsibility for the sixteen hundred people in our division. And you tell me not to be frantic." She sat back in the booth, face crimson, eyes moist.

Brent sat for a moment and said nothing while Patricia composed herself. "Look, I understand how you feel. But I can't be the white knight. Annette's not a good second-chance giver. Last night I discussed the whole situation with her. She was as—"

"Did you ask her about taking the job?"

"Let me finish."

"Sorry."

"She was as determined as I've ever seen her. Didn't have to tell her about vying for the job. She anticipated it. Was told in no uncertain terms that I'd made a promise that she was holding me to. That was that. End of discussion. Now, I could get this job. But neither Annette nor my kids would be around to share in it. Annette has her faults just like anyone. Being pig-headed at times is one of them. But I love her deeply and I love my kids. I'm not threatening those relationships."

"Brent, the job's going to be demanding at first. That's fact. Voorhees won't trust you with the numbers because you don't have a financial background. But, it won't be terribly long till you've passed his numbers litmus test. After that the time commitment won't be much different from what you have now. Maybe some increased travel. If you delegate as you do now it'll be more than manageable."

"No way Annette can or will relate to that argument. She's going on her experience with me and I don't have a ton of credibility. I took a job once that consumed me. It cost me dearly. I'm not making the same mistake again."

"Do you think it would help if I invited Annette to lunch? I'm pretty good at discussing business versus personal issues."

Brent could visualize that lunch, and the picture was ugly. "Thanks. Appreciate the offer but think I'd better handle Annette."

"Help me out," said Patricia. "Are you telling me you're going to be satisfied not competing for any top jobs for the rest of your career? That's not realistic for the Brent Shannon I know."

"Don't mean that. Just have to gain Annette's trust. Takes time."

"Oh, I forgot. It's only been eight years," Patricia said with a sufficient measure of sarcasm to illicit a stern look from Brent. "Sorry. Forgive me for that."

"Patricia, what I need your help on is how to bury the hatchet with Paul."

"You can't."

"For god's sake, Patricia. I've always been able to strike effective business relationships. Paul and I should be able to establish one."

"Paul Kruger is an ambitious scoundrel who always covers his backside. It won't happen. If you discuss it with him, it'll be taken as a sign of weakness. Look, Brent. You can't roll over and concede. Okay, I might have selfish motives. I don't want to work for the man. But it's more than about me. Remember your encounter with Lloyd Blackburn."

"I'm not conceding anything. I can't take the job. Rephrase that. Won't take the job. Feel like I'm getting real redundant here."

"Okay. Talk to the guy if you want. But it's a waste of time and seals your fate." Patricia got up and walked out of the restaurant.

Guess splitting the check wasn't in the cards, Brent thought. He paid and walked out to the car.

"It's really a waste of time," Patricia said getting into the car.

Brent realized that this would become a rerun of the restaurant conversation if he didn't change the subject. "Hey, since we're heavy into personal lives today, how're things going with Adam?"

"That's a whole other story. Think it's coming to a crisis. Adam wants more out of the relationship than I'm prepared to give right now."

Brent had met Adam at the company's Christmas dinner. "Well, he seemed to be a stand-up guy when I met him."

"Yeah, well you're not the only one to get burned in the past. Do you know what's going to happen to this division if Kruger's running it and you leave? A division you put a lot of effort building."

This woman sounded like his mother-in-law, Brent calculated. Ground you to cornmeal when she decided something and you didn't go along with it. "Be hectic for a while but everything'll work out. And I don't plan on leaving."

"Brent Shannon, you can aggravate me like no other man I've known. I'll never say I told you so but you'd better start your resume update. Your last company was supportive. There'll be no help here. You're competition. When Kruger gets finished you'll find your butt scuttled with no references. He'll make sure Richmont never comes looking for you. And there won't be a thing I can do about it."

When they parked at the general office Patricia got out and walked to the office ahead of him. She did not acknowledge that he was behind her. How did the Mormons of earlier days do it? He felt like he had two wives. One on each shoulder kicking the hell out of him.

He used the front entrance. As he walked across the atrium, he glanced down the hallway toward the finance department. He saw Paul Kruger and Neal Stuart in a serious conversation. Hmm. Probably getting Kruger's input on in-store signage for the promo. There was no question. This place was driving him nuts.

After Erik and Tawney left for school, Annette climbed into her running outfit and did seven miles. She used to be a marathon runner. In fact, she found running to be her best therapeutic activity. During her first two years at St. Olaf College in Northfield, Minnesota, she had been afflicted with debilitating headaches. A physician prescribed running as therapy. It worked and she was hooked.

Running was her thinking time. She could not believe this was happening. No, she really could. Brent was an extremely talented businessperson. Opportunities were bound to come up. The dilemma was that Brent became hopelessly consumed by his work. He had proven that he could not turn off work enough to have a quality family life. He would not get the opportunity to do it again. At least not with his current wife and kids.

Annette slowed to a walk and cooled down during the last block to the house. She always felt so invigorated after running. She smiled remembering those first years of their marriage when she and Brent would make love after her run. Her body quivered with excitement thinking about it. She loved it so. Well, they hadn't gotten back to those days but they could. And certainly no job would get in the way.

She hopped in the shower to rinse off. She was meeting Megan at Raintree Country Club for tennis in forty minutes. Brent had done well keeping his priorities straight in Atlanta. However, that had been more a function of his boss being a recently divorced workaholic. Brent couldn't get consumed. It certainly had been no conscious effort on his part. Tom Carthage would not let him. There had not been enough work to consume them both.

She dressed, went to the garage and backed the Jeep Cherokee out of the driveway. Driving down Park Road, her mind returned to Brent. Intimacy between them had been rampant in Atlanta but it had waned somewhat since coming to Charlotte. Brent had taken this job with the challenge of turning the division around. An excellent leader, Marlene Wolff gave everyone an opportunity to contribute. Annette could see what she called creeping consumption in the last year.

She had struggled about reconciling with Brent. After agreeing to it, she had tried to make a family for him. She had put her career on hold and committed herself to their happiness. The old rural Minnesota family ethic. For her effort, she had gotten a self-absorbed husband whose commitment to his family was an afterthought.

Only the pleading of her father and Brent's sister Cory, had persuaded her to try and make a go of it. Brent had made a solemn promise before they left Minnesota that the family would always come first, and she was holding him to it. She had options. She had kept current in the legal profession if only on a part-time basis. Also, she certainly had personal options.

It was a vigorous doubles match with Annette and her best friend Megan Randle opposing their chief tournament rivals at Raintree. After the match, Annette and Megan showered, dressed, and Megan followed Annette to 131 Main for lunch.

After being seated and given menus, Megan said, "Really ferocious today, partner. Out to embarrass them?"

"Oh, I was taking my frustration out on Phyllis and Jamie."

"Frustrated about?"

"Brent came home last night from Atlanta. His boss got promoted. Brent's probably one of the people in line for her job."

"God, Annette. That's great. What're his chances?"

"He's not taking the job."

"What do you mean?"

"Just what I said. Brent and I were separated in Minnesota. I never gave you the details. He became consumed with his career. All he could see was partner on his business cards. Meanwhile, little wifey, me, gave up her career and stayed home with the newer members of the family. Finally, I'd had enough and left. I agreed to try reconciliation. Brent got the job with Richmont and here we are. He made a promise family would come first and he's not going into a job that facilitates, no demands, he become consumed again."

"You feel it'd happen again?" said Megan. "Sounds as if you think it's a foregone conclusion."

"You bet it would. I know Brent and he can't help himself. He gets involved, he gets consumed."

"Annette, I'm surprised you don't think he's learned anything from the last experience."

"Once a workaholic, always a workaholic."

"I don't think that's necessarily true. Has he taken himself out of the running?"

"He met with Marlene this morning and he'd better have. He knows the deal he made. He'd better live up to it."

"You sound like you'd break up the marriage over this."

"I would. I'm not going through that living hell again."

"Annette, you're convicting Brent without as much as a serious discussion that has more than one option. How can people prove they're trustworthy if you don't trust them? You see the box you're putting him in? People who love one another can surely come up with some guidelines agreeable to both. You do love Brent, don't you?"

Annette leaned back folding her arms across her chest. "Of course, I love him. What a thing to say."

"Then it's beyond me why you're putting Brent in an either-or situation. You're setting up a win-lose that, in all probability, will become a lose-lose."

"That's not the case," Annette retorted. "Brent wants a good family life, too."

"I'm certain he does, honey," said Megan. "But, does he want it at the expense of everything else in his life and you being the only one who can define what a good family life is?"

"You don't have to believe me. But if he takes the general manager job, he'll destroy a pretty good life."

"Annette, it almost sounds like you want him to go against your wishes. Sometimes that's the motivation behind either-or declarations."

Annette became furious. In a low voice, she said, "Whose friend are you? I think you're siding with my husband."

"That's silly. I'm not siding with anyone. Just don't want you to make a terrible mistake."

The check came. They split the bill, walked out to the parking lot and stopped at Megan's car.

"I'm torn," said Annette. "He hasn't said as much but I know Brent wants this job. But I can't go through it all over again. I want him to be happy but I need happiness, too."

Megan looked at her. "Remember all the sweat and tears I went through getting my shop off the ground? Can't imagine how I'd react if Mel said I couldn't have it anymore."

"You see Brent's point more than mine, don't you?"

Megan got into her car, started the engine and put the side window down. "Have to get back to the shop. Honey, I don't see one point over another. I love you lots, but this is a self-centeredness I've never seen in you." Megan blew Annette a kiss and drove away.

Brent walked in his office and closed the door. He did not have much time until the meeting with Marlene but he had to focus for a few minutes.

He titled the top page of a legal pad, "Survival Strategy." Appropriate, he thought. The way out of this quandary was through Kruger. Annette would not budge. Of that he could be certain. Over the course of his career, he could remember colleagues with whom he hadn't seen eye to eye nor had he cared for their personalities. Yet he'd been able to forge effective business relationships with them. Why would Paul Kruger be any different?

Patricia had been adamant that there was no hope with Kruger but that had to be ridiculous. Business relationships evolve due to self-interests. A relationship's objective was the facilitation of career ascension, monetary rewards, job security and job satisfaction for the participants. Or some combination of those. He had seen some selfless acts in business. Johnson and Johnson taking the horrible hit recalling every Tylenol pill on the shelves had been a great example. But he had seen few individuals who magnanimously acted with only their own interests at risk. There weren't many people who would fall on their spear for the benefit of a colleague.

He did not know a lot about Kruger but he did know that the guy was one ambitious businessman with a brilliant financial mind. If he got Marlene's job and hit it out of the park, he would be right up the totem pole behind her. Brent pondered what type of business relationship he could provide Kruger that played to that strategy. One that also assured his own survival and career progression.

He wrote, "Meet with Kruger," on his pad. He had to convince Paul that he was not his competition but his ally. If there was one thing he had learned over the years, it was that the fastest way to succeed was making his boss a hero. He had a major hand in making Marlene a hero. He could do the same for Paul. He had to get that across to him. What was the best way to deliver that message? He would tell Paul that his marriage was completely back together and posed no problem for work commitment. However, it precluded him from competing for Marlene's job. Said properly, it just might fly.

Brent jotted down, "Marketing Expertise." Paul was not well-versed in working the marketplace but he had seen Brent's results. The guy could throw him in the Dempsey Dumpster and take a chance on someone new. But that course of action had a downside risk and Paul Kruger was a risk-adverse person. He had to drive home the contributions he could make to a Paul Kruger team. He had been working on a skeleton two-year marketing plan using three different store-growth scenarios. It was still an "in-the-drawer" plan. He had not even shared it with Marlene. He would share the plan outline with Paul. His pitch would center on coupling his expertise in making sales happen and Paul's expertise in finance and acquiring capital to grow. The combination would be unbeatable. They would not have to sit around and slug beers together to become a great profit-generating team for Richmont. This could work. Paul Kruger might think Brent to be competition now but after they'd had a chance to visit, he would feel differently. There was a sane approach to this. This was not a personality-or- corporate-politics problem. It was a sales challenge. A type of challenge that Brent had successfully accomplished before in his career. He had to meet with Marlene today to tell her he couldn't be considered for her job. That would be a valuable hole card in the sales job with Kruger.

Brent's desk clock read one fifty-five. He grabbed his pad folder and headed to Marlene's office. He felt better than he had since the announcement. This could work. He could feel it.

"They're waiting for you," Marlene's assistant said. "Go on in."

"Hope I'm not late," he said walking through the door.

"No, right on time," Marlene said. "Brent, you know Terry Thomas."

"Certainly. Nice to see you, Terry."

"The same," Thomas replied.

Thomas looked at Paul and Brent. "This move's very exciting. I know you both hate to lose Marlene but we're delighted she'll be returning to Atlanta as a senior executive. Know this meeting's short notice but wanted to go over a couple of pending capital expenditure issues while Marlene was still in Charlotte."

"It will be smoother for the new GM if capital expenditure issues are resolved before I leave," Marlene said.

"As director of finance, I certainly appreciate that approach," said Paul.

"As you know, Terry heads up the capital expenditure committee. They've a few questions about our requests. He had time today so he came over to get answers directly from you," Marlene said.

Brent noticed Paul smile and nod in agreement. Why the hell did they have him involved in this, Brent thought.

"Paul," said Terry, "the committee has some questions regarding the payback period for the accounts payable software under consideration."

"Certainly, Terry," replied Paul. "I'll be happy to address that."

Paul removed spreadsheets from his briefcase and opened them in the center of the table. "The new software will dramatically decrease missed payment terms. We've simply gotten too large and aren't able to adequately handle the volume.

"If I can direct your attention to this column, you'll see a substantial cost-of-goods savings this year and an even greater payback as we bring more stores online in the out years.

"This plays into the second benefit. We can handle the three-year store and merchandise expansion plan with no increase in staffing. You can see the financial results of that benefit in the second column."

Terry studied the spreadsheet for a moment and asked, "Paul, how confident are you in these projections?"

"Very," answered Paul. "My people were very conservative when compiling them and I've verified everything personally."

"Good," said Terry. "Okay. These come true and the payback period is what?"

"Twenty-seven months."

"Excellent," replied Terry. He nodded at Marlene and said, "I certainly appreciate your thoroughness, Paul. Can't say I expected less. Your financial work's a model for the company."

Paul smiled. "Thanks, Terry. I just want the transition to go as smoothly as possible."

Brent sat and watched this pat-each-other-on-the-butt exchange and wondered why in the name of god he was sitting here.

"Well, that's one down," said Terry. "Brent, I need you to clarify a few things about the capital request for advertising's Macintosh Graphic Computer."

The old adage that ten percent never got the word was alive and well, Brent thought. "Terry, the major justification is increased control of advertising quality, increased flexibility and decreased turnaround time for quicker reaction to necessary changes."

"All that's fine, Brent," replied Terry. "But, the committee's having a difficult time squaring those justifications with the payback numbers submitted. Help me out on this."

"Terry, I'm sorry," said Brent. "I was unaware of the specific purpose of this meeting. I'll have to prepare a response to the issues."

Marlene started to say something but Paul got there first. "I'm sorry," he said. "But Brent, I told you about the meeting and mentioned capital expenditure review questions. I was sure you would pick up on it because the MAC capital expenditure was under review."

The coyote running off a cliff chasing the road runner ran through Brent's mind. He felt his pain. "I'm sorry, too," replied Brent along with a stern look at Paul. "Because I sure didn't hear you mention any expenditure reviews." Brent wondered if he would get fired if he punched the fucker's lights out.

"I admit I did assume," said Paul. "When I realized that, I called Neal Stuart just to make certain everything was prepared for Terry's review. I would've called you, Brent, but you had left the building."

Marlene being furious would be a serious understatement. "This is an annoying setback," she said in a very measured tone. "Paul might have been more specific but Brent; you must have realized Terry wasn't over here just to pass the time of day."

"Well, nothing can be done at this point," said Terry. "Brent, you'll have to send clarifying numbers to Atlanta tomorrow. Make certain they're to my attention."

Terry looked sharply at Brent. "You know this puts the MAC project on hold."

"Terry, I'll get on it right away," said Brent.

"If you need to run some numbers by me, I'll be available anytime," said Paul. "Brent, get with Neal. After discussing it with him, I never gave it another thought because I know you have good communication with your people."

Get screwed, Brent thought but didn't say.

"Okay," said Marlene. "Brent, that's all for now. I'll see you tomorrow morning with the revised figures. Nine sharp. Paul, please stay. There's one more issue we need to discuss."

Brent nodded, thanked Terry and Marlene for their patience and walked out, closing the office door as he went.

After Brent shut the door, Paul said, "I'm terribly sorry about this misunderstanding. Terry, I take full responsibility for the answers about the MAC request not being available."

"Nonsense, Paul," Terry Thomas replied. "Sounds to me like Brent was preoccupied or something. What you told him just didn't register."

"I agree," Marlene said. "Brent isn't himself lately."

"Could it be because of the upcoming change here," Terry said.

Marlene looked at Paul. "Oh, I don't think so."

"Absolutely not," Paul said. "Brent's too much of a pro. But maybe things aren't going well at home again."

"No, that's not an issue," Marlene said.

Terry looked at Marlene then back to Paul. "What do you mean by again?"

"No, Terry. Marlene's right. That's probably not an issue at all," said Paul.

"Does the man have a shaky marriage or not?" said Terry.

Paul saw Marlene becoming more distressed by the second. "Probably not," he said. He would have to play this card very carefully.

"There was a separation. I think about eight years ago or so. I heard part of their reconciliation was that he leave his job. In fact, I believe that's when he came to Richmont. The primary stipulation by his wife was his family would always come before work. I could be wrong but I think that was it. I was only thinking we've had a busy quarter. He may be getting some pressure from home. But Terry, Brent Shannon's a consummate professional. I'm probably way off base."

"Now, that's a very interesting situation, isn't it," said Terry.

Before Marlene could respond about Brent, Paul said, "You had something for me, Marlene. What can I do for you?"

"Oh yes," said Marlene. "I need a current reading on the store manager incentive pool, year-to-date versus plan."

"Sure. No problem at all. I'll have it for you by the end of today. Anything else?"

"No, that'll do it. Thanks."

"Terry, good to see you. Have a good flight home."

"Thanks, Paul. And thanks for the thoroughness of your answers to my questions."
"You're quite welcome," said Paul as he left, closing the door behind him.

Paul walked back to his department recognizing that the meeting had altogether exceeded his expectations. Thomas talked to Ben Voorhees every day. Shannon's screw up and the marriage issue would get top billing. Voorhees heard about Shannon's family problems when Marlene brought him over to Charlotte. She probably said they had gone away or, at the least, downplayed them if she was backing Shannon for her job. What a two-fer this turned out to be. It kicked the hell out of Shannon's fitness for the job while taking a bite out of Marlene's credibility with Bible Ben. He hated to do that to her because she had been very good to him. But careers had to be secured.

No way could he be seen as the bad guy in this. Marlene would even have to agree. Except she had been quite upset by the marriage problem conversation. She also had to be questioning where Paul got so much detail about it. Good old Wilson. Her degree of distress pointed to her backing Shannon. It would be most prudent to move ahead under that assumption.

As he passed Kelly Martin's work area, he said, "Come in my office." Kelly Martin was his senior financial analyst.

He was just sitting at his desk when Kelly came through the door. "Yes, Paul," she said.

"Get me a spreadsheet on the store manager incentive pool, year-to-date versus plan. I need it by district, by store, in about an hour and a half."

"Paul, I'm swamped with plan revisions."

"I didn't ask for your project list. Have it to me in an hour and a half," Paul said. Kelly turned and left without a word.

Paul had two calls to make. The first was to Evan Roth.

"Roth here."

"Hi, Evan. How's the Atlanta scene?"

"Oh, Paul, nice to hear from you. Things are fine here. How's it feel to be a brand new GM?"

"Don't know about that. My money's on Brent Shannon."

"Oh no, Paul. Was talking to Stan Ascutney about an hour ago. Think you have a marked advantage over Shannon. However, I must tell you I've heard good things about him."

Paul knew that Ascutney, along with being the HR Vice President, was Evan's closest friend in the company. "The guy's really good at his job and would be a terrific GM," replied Paul. "Someone I'd be honored to work for as long as his personal life's in order."

"I'm somewhat aware of Shannon's past marital problems but Stan said that was old news. Everything's fine."

"Evan, they probably are."

"Well, is the assumption that his marital problems are history a good one or are you holding something back?"

"No, I'm holding nothing back, Evan. But you're putting me in an awkward position."

"May be. But, you've a responsibility to this company. If you're aware of something that might negatively impact the performance of a division GM, it's your obligation to share it. Shannon gets that job and can't handle it, it's a disaster."

"Shannon's acting very tense right now but if his wife said no go, that would be that. Shannon's a pro. He'd withdraw his name. Of course, she could say yes then renege when the going got tough. But that's just speculation and not fair."

"Then help me out," responded Evan. "If that's the case, what's the awkward position you're in? You're talking in circles. I don't think you're being straight with me. It's upsetting."

Paul smiled. He'd hooked Evan. Now be careful and reel him in. "I'm not trying to talk in circles."

"The hell you're not. There's an issue out there you're not sharing."

"Evan, okay. It's not Brent's family situation that's got me concerned. It's the relationship between Shannon and Bolivar."

"What relationship?"

"This is absolutely unsubstantiated but there're growing undertones among the employees that they're an item."

"Help an old man out. Does that mean they're having an affair?"

"Yes."

"Well, what do you think?"

"Hadn't given it much thought to tell the truth. Blew it off as office gossip. Recently, though, I've been paying more attention. They spend a good deal of time together. Frequent, long lunches. She looks at him in a very fond way."

"So you think they are?"

"I'm not totally convinced."

"I'm not sure how to handle this," said Evan. "You said anything to anyone?"

"No."

"Would strongly advise you don't. Ben Voorhees would go nuts under any circumstances. But if Shannon was the GM and this turned out to be true, the damn roof'd blow off. No, I'm not sure how to handle this but you stay out of it," said Evan.

"Oh, Evan. There's one person I talked to about this but only one. Neal Stuart. The advertising manager who works for Shannon. I mentioned the ugly rumors going around about Brent and Patricia and asked if he could help me quell them. I got concerned when he lent credence to them."
"Is Stuart reliable?"

"Solid as a rock."

"Okay, Paul. I may be back to you but probably not. I'm probably going to have to talk to Stuart. You sure he's reliable?"

"Absolutely."

"For your own good, stay out of this fray," said Evan. Paul heard the click of the phone disconnection.

Now, that couldn't have gone better. Evan will be hot on the trail. He will also handle it like a pint jar of nitroglycerin. Paul hated to dupe his mentor. No, not really. He needed Evan Roth to help him make this career leap. After that, his usefulness would diminish greatly. Paul would always look out for Roth. It would be the least he could do for the help Roth had given him.

His hallway encounter with Neal Stuart at noon had been illuminating. He had no idea how much the guy hated Shannon's guts. What a fortuitous situation. It made Stuart quite venal. Paul knew that Stuart had been angry when Marlene brought Brent into the division. Stuart thought the job should have been his. Yes, Stuart would make the perfect trigger man for the affair segment of Shannon's downfall. He would have to be well-coached, which could be taken care of tomorrow.

Paul loosened his tie. He sat back in his chair with his feet on the desk. This had been an extraordinarily successful day. With a smile, he picked up the phone to make his second call. The one that was going to be much more enjoyable than the first.

Brent went back to his office, shut the door, sat at his desk and put his head in his hands. He could not believe it. What in the name of god had he ever done to Kruger? Yeah, they'd had some disagreements but good grief. Disagreements always happened when a bunch of energetic people tried to get things done. The guy had absolutely screwed him.

First Annette stuck it to him or at least had every intention of doing so. She walked around like Chicken Little ranting and raving that if he got Marlene's job the sky would fall. There had been no reasoning with her. Aw, hell. That suddenly became less critical.

Want some critical, he thought, rubbing his face with his hands. Kruger. The jerk. Damn, though, he had to hand it to him. Kruger got him big time. How do you fight an ambush like that? Do some whimper act that Kruger's been a bad boy? Don't think so.

So furious that he could hardly contain himself Brent stood up and walked to the window just to move. It substituted for throwing something against the wall. Like maybe Kruger. He looked out of the window. All he needed now would be Bolivar walking through the door spouting that she had told him so. Hell though, she was the only one who had the faintest concept of the political landscape. However, she was on a one-option crusade that would not help him a bit. Why was she so loyal to him? He bet she thought, or knew, she would go in Kruger's trash heap right along with him.

He continued looking out of the window while hitting the sill with his fist harder than he should. That no account jerk, Kruger. Even if Brent was in hyper-drive for Marlene's job, after that little episode in her office, they wouldn't promote him to be the janitor. He needed some unbiased, third-party advice. He went to his desk and dialed George Barnes' office. He asked the receptionist for George.

"Hey, business honcho," George Barnes said. "What's up?"

"I need a drink bad, man. And I need it with you."

"Hmm, okay. I can make Village Bistro in about forty-five minutes. That soon enough?"

"See you there." Brent hung up the phone. George Barnes was a dentist with an excellent practice in southeast Charlotte. He was also Brent's golf partner and best friend.

Brent closed down his computer, gave a few last-minute instructions to Ashley and headed to his car. He used the side entrance, praying he wouldn't run into Patricia or Marlene. He needed to get out of the office with no encounters.

He got to the Audi uninterrupted and headed up Westinghouse Boulevard. He got angrier by the minute. He had to watch his speed. He didn't want to hit some poor biker who, in all likelihood, wasn't Paul Kruger's political consultant. If he did want the job, he now knew that the decision-maker on his side was Marlene. Until today's meeting, of course. Kruger had set him up to not only look like an idiot but embarrass Marlene in the process. He had to hand it to the guy. They didn't teach a class in peer destruction in MBA programs. Kruger mastered it all on his own.

He remembered Patricia offering to talk with Annette. If that happened, he wanted a video. God, Patricia's heart was in the right place but she had no idea that Annette thought he had a trophy case of Patricia's thongs. Video, hell. He could sell tickets. He parked, went inside the Village Bistro and found George already sucking up his usual Manhattan on the rocks.

As Brent sat down, George said, "Business honcho, you look like hell. Profits gone south?"

Brent ordered a Wild Turkey on the rocks and proceeded to tell George why he looked like hell. He started with the announcement and went through Annette's unexpected reaction. Brent's drink came. He finished it with two rapid trips to his lips and ordered another.

"Slow down, my man," said George, "or you're going to be sleeping here and never finish the story."

Brent told him about Patricia Bolivar's reaction and pleading. He emphasized that she was the only one who had the correct lay of the land. He finished by telling every detail of the tank job in Marlene's office.

"Okay, fine," said George. "Now tell me what you want. Not Annette, not Patricia, you."

Brent began a rambling reply and George cut him off.

"Brent, answer my question."

"I want my marriage and if I don't get the job my career is screwed. So I want the job too. That's probably as honest as I've been in the last thirty hours or so."

"So tell me why this job and your marriage have to be mutually exclusive? Annette's always impressed me as a logical person. Good grief. She's a competent attorney."

"It's a very emotional issue for her. I'll tell you, buddy, I took, screw up, to a higher level in Minneapolis."

"Brent gotta ask this. Was there another guy in her life while you two were separated? Maybe she's using this deal as an excuse to head back north."

"Absolutely not. Was with her parents. No, George, she thinks I'll go down the same path. She's convinced of it. She sees workaholism as analogous to alcoholism."

"Not the case," said George. "But perception is truth. So what assurances could you give her that you've learned from previous mistakes and this would be different? It seems like this has to be negotiation not persuasion."

"You tell me what card I have to play except my word."

"Hell of a point. So let's forget Annette for now. I know Marlene's a smart woman. She comes to me for her teeth, doesn't she?"

Brent gave him a don't-get-off-the-subject look and George said, "Sorry, back to the issue. Marlene knows this afternoon wasn't like you. She may even think you got set up. Let her get over being upset and go see her in the morning. You owe her some numbers anyway, right?"

"Yeah. I've got to burn some serious midnight oil to get those done."

"Good. So go in with flawless numbers and apologize. Take the hit. Then, my man, you have to emphatically tell her you want her job. And you can handle it. She's got to know you're back in the saddle. If she's backing you to the

Atlanta crowd she needs ammunition."

"Can do that."

"Another thing. Don't you think she knows Kruger's a certified jerk?"

"She's insightful. She may. But Voorhees is just infatuated with bean counters."

"That's off the table," replied George. "We're concentrating on controllable things. That's not one of them. Give Marlene ammunition. Let her fight that battle."

"Okay. Good point."

"Now the dicey part," said George. "There anything in the woodpile Kruger can hit you with out of left field?"

"Nothing I can think of."

"Buddy, I'm your friend and you got to level with me. You're not fuckin' any of the help?"

"Honest to god, no. I might be dumb but I'm not stupid."

"Good," replied George. "Got to watch your backside real close till this thing's decided. Got to play the game, buddy. Kruger's not screwing around. He wants your ass for some reason and he ain't pulling any punches."

"Having a tough time figuring out how to handle Patricia Bolivar in this whole mess," said Brent. "Annette sees her as competition. She almost hyperventilates when her name comes up."

"I can see that," said George. "Saw Patricia at one of your parties. She's knockdown gorgeous. Let me ask you this. Turn it around. Think Patricia sees Annette as competition?"

"For what?"

"Naw, you didn't just say that," said George. "For you, you dumb shit."

"No, that's ridiculous."

"Just keep it in the back of your mind, ole buddy. Now, one more time. None of the help have felt your magnetic self?"

"One more time. No."

"Excellent. So the core problem to this affair, just a figure of speech, is Annette," said George. "The other bases are covered. Marlene backs you and will clean up this afternoon's mess. If you don't have her backing, we might as well have another drink and talk golf because the fat lady's on stage. Kruger's got nothing else to dig up. Right?"

"Right."

"Just keep your eye on the guy. And Brent, use Patricia for what she's offering. She can be a lot more nosey than you can. She's your scout so nothing blindsides you."

George drained his glass. "Got to get out of here or I'm going to be staying at Extended Stay America. So your mission, my friend, is to convince Annette you're sincere and things'll be different this time. Admit to her that you want the job. Lay out how and why this won't be a repeat of Minneapolis. I can't help you with that, buddy."

They walked out to their cars and Brent said, "Thanks, George. I really appreciate the ear."

George patted him on the back and as he walked away, waved over his shoulder. "Keep me in the loop, big guy. A dentist's life is a boring one. That's why I got friends like you."

Brent shook his head and got in his car for the drive home to Annette and god-knows-what reception.

He drove down Pineville-Matthews Road thinking about nothing in particular and everything in general. This was a foreign state of affairs to him. During twenty years in business, there had been disagreements with colleagues. Some intense. On occasions, hard feelings had remained over time. However, most knew conflict came with the territory and worked through it.

Was this a case of Paul Kruger's blind ambition? Brent could not answer that question. But he knew his experiences contained nothing to help him anticipate or combat a covert attack on his reputation such as the one carried out by Paul Kruger today. Why would someone do that to a business colleague? Enough of this. The SOB did it. Brent realized this would be the fight of his business life.

How was he going to reason with Annette? She seemed open to nothing. During their darkest days in Minneapolis, he never saw her like this.

Brent stared at the darkening clouds and lightning in the distance while the first drops of rain fell on his windshield. Appropriate weather, he thought. Driving through the early evening rainstorm, Brent recalled his transformation prompted by Annette leaving. His marriage was a precious gift. The day they were married had been wonderful. He was desperately in love. However, he had been too self-centered to consider that his marriage would have a significant impact on his work and vice versa. He had yet to learn the fundamental truth that in every yes, there is a no. Time is a finite commodity and must be allocated across the entire spectrum of one's life. But learn it he had.

His insensitivity to another's needs had shamed him. His calloused concept that balancing marriage and work would be analogous to balancing an MBA program with his day job deepened his shame. He knew Annette wanted something out of the marriage but certainly nothing that would impact his career. His quest for executive excellence and success was paramount. She knew how important it was to him. Of course, she would be willing to sacrifice. What a dumb schlepp he had been. It had been all about his needs. She was to be the follower.

It had taken him a long time to come to grips with his self-absorption. The shock to his psyche had been piercing when he came face to face with himself. But face himself, he had.

He agreed to her demand about family first because he recognized that his enlightenment resulted in a new Brent Shannon.

However, the new Brent still had career aspirations. He wanted to run a business. The opportunity to do so was staring him in the face. He and Annette had a relationship that they had worked hard at repairing. Yet had it been repaired? Or did it survive because it had not been tested? He had changed the fundamental way he viewed living. But he realized that Annette had never acknowledged the change. In her mind, he had never been under circumstances that created a proper audition. Now came audition time, yet she would not give him the opportunity to perform.

One of Annette's most adamant contentions was that she had given up her career to raise the children. She saw that as the major change in their marriage. She never considered him as changing. He simply started to do the right thing. How could he convince her that he had changed in a most basic way and being GM of Just For You would not destroy their marriage? He did not have a clue as he turned into the driveway and hit the garage door opener on the sun visor. The flexible, play-it-by-ear strategy had worked so well with her last night, why not try it again? Practice makes perfect. Into the lioness' den. The one with very sharp teeth.

Brent closed the garage door and walked into the kitchen. He found Annette working up one of her famous salads. The one Brent thought barely qualified as an appetizer.

He walked over and gave her a kiss. "Hi, honey."

She turned, put her arms around his neck and gave him a kiss that intimated the evening might have a hell of an ending. "Hi, darling."

"That was nice," he said. "To what do I owe that greeting?"

She put the salad bowl on the counter. "The kids are eating at Mitchell's. I thought we could have a leisurely, light dinner to celebrate the end of your work trauma." She gently stroked his cheek. "Maybe a little wine, in fact."

Brent looked through the door to the dining room. The table was set for two complete with flickering candles. “What work trauma? You mean Marlene’s promotion and the brouhaha over her replacement?”

“Yes, darling. How did your meeting with Marlene go?”

“Terrible,” Brent said. He spent five minutes recounting the disaster with Terry Thomas, Marlene and Kruger. Concluding, he said, “Got to hand it to Kruger. The SOB didn’t read Machiavelli for nothing.”

Opening a bottle of wine at the kitchen counter, Annette said, “You certain Kruger intentionally did this or is this another supposition on your part?”

Brent answered to the back of her head as she took the wine to the dining room. “Hell, yeah, I’m sure. Even you’ve said what a political animal the guy is.”

“Come on, let’s eat,” she said. “Bring the salad.”

Annette sat down and while Brent was serving salad, said, “Brent, he’d be stupid to do something like that. He needs a good working relationship with you.”

Brent looked past Annette out the dining room window. He was about to lose it, but he needed to get his message across without raising emotions. It would be vital to keep this discussion on an even keel. “Honey, you’re missing Kruger’s goal. He doesn’t want to work with me. Wants me on the street.” He bit his tongue realizing his comment had come out a bit condescending.

She didn’t miss the tone. “Don’t patronize me, Brent Shannon. It does nothing for the quality of this discussion. I believe the primary point is you’ve become paranoid. You’re seeing imaginary villains. And that gold digger, Patricia Bolivar, is the facilitator. She is so self-serving.”

Brent almost blurted out that Patricia was the only friend he had in this dilemma but he thought better of it. “Annette, I know what I know. And I know a set up when I see one. I was set up.”

“All right. You’ve never gotten an argument from me that Kruger’s an opportunistic drip. Probably unethical as well. Let's say you're right. Kruger set you up. The miserable jerk did it to get himself promoted, not you fired. You said yourself that you were his competition and he knows it."

"You're right, up to a point. He doesn't get the job, everything's moot. But he's attacking my competence. He's setting the table for after his promotion."

"That's unadulterated paranoia. Brent, I've never seen your self-assuredness so fragile. What's happening to you?"

Brent could hardly contain his emotions. He felt his throat go dry and his stomach knot. "Without trying to be melodramatic, my dear, I'm being attacked by this fanatic. Can't you see my career, and incidentally, our long-term financial security, being threatened? Lot hangs in the balance."

"That's melodramatic. The man's going to want you for your competence. You're a hell of a marketer." Annette smiled. "You've said so yourself. Many times."

"Doesn't need my competence. Can hire that. Look, honey. This isn't some government job," Brent said. He saw from the narrowing of her eyes that his comment would have been best left unsaid. "I mean, in the private sector it's easier to change bodies. GM has to feel comfortable with the people who work with him. Company supports that concept. For some reason, Kruger doesn't feel comfortable with me. Voila', a change'll be made. I've a pretty good rep in the company. He's got to set it up carefully. That's what's going on."

Brent saw his wife on the launch pad ready to ignite. This would not be a pretty site.

"You listen to me, Brent Shannon. I may've only had government jobs but I'm no idiot. And I don't appreciate being treated like one. In fact, the only idiocy in this discussion is you're idiotic paranoia."

"Annette. Let's not fight. I need your support."
"You're right," replied Annette with what Brent thought was a wicked little smile. "Why are we fighting? You haven't even mentioned the important meet-

ing. How did Marlene take it when you told her you had to take yourself out of the running?"

Brent knew she was not going to be pleased with his response. "Didn't meet with her about that. She had been so upset in the first meeting I thought better of it."

"Probably a smart move. It can be done in the morning."

"Yeah, It can. Honey, have a question for you."

"Yes."

"What's happened in the last eight years to cause you to distrust me so much? Don't you think I've learned to keep my priorities straight?"

"Brent," she said, "On what basis should I trust you?"

Brent saw red. He had never been this angry with her. Brent's temper was a weakness. One that he had learned to keep under control. However, Annette had approached the limit. "That's unfair, Annette. I've done everything I said I would when we reconciled."

"I know what you've done. And I appreciate it. But look at us since we've come to Richmont. In Atlanta, you couldn't be a workaholic. Tom Carthage had just come off his divorce. There wasn't enough work to make you both workaholics and he had seniority. When we first came here things were fine but your work hours have been creeping up with more shop talk at home, especially on weekends. You're telling me I should trust you to take a job with increased travel and pressure. Don't see where you justify I'd be secure doing that."

"You telling me I can't ever consider upward moves?"

"I know you think I'm being unfair. But you've never appreciated how hurt I was. I can't, no I won't, go through that again. And it was hard for me to leave Minnesota."

"So that's a no?"

"Brent, I didn't say no, exactly."

"I've tried to understand, Annette," he said. "I think I do understand. But I feel trapped. How can I gain your trust if you put all these "yeah but that time doesn't count" on me? I'm sorry, honey. This takes a leap of faith on your part. Think I've proven myself worthy of that leap."

"Now please wait a minute," she said, her eyes narrowed, "lest we forget I gave up a promising career even if it was a government job. I did that for the good of the family and don't you tell me there's any difference. This is your turn." Brent knew it was time to tiptoe through the tulips. She was right at the precipice of maximum burn. "I never thought of your career as any different or less important than mine. I know you enjoy the law. You subordinated your desires for the good of the family and I love you for it."

"No, not quite right, Brent," she said. "I didn't subordinate anything. I made a choice. The self-centered idea that you can have it all always amazes me. I had to choose whether to be a fulltime, the-kids-come-first mom or a career person whose kids come first as long as the job doesn't that day. I made a concerted decision to be a fulltime mom."

"Okay. You comparing your choice to mine with the GM position?"

"Of course. Follow my logic, please. I made that choice because I knew, I very well knew, I wouldn't be able to maintain the proper priorities in my life as a career woman who was a mom when the job allowed it. At least, as I saw the priorities. I made my choice because of my priorities. As I see it, it's no different with you."

Brent was starting to wear down. The woman had that effect on him. "I know I performed horribly in Minneapolis. But in all our talks before getting back together, we never discussed nor did you ever intimate you would never trust me in more responsible positions."

"Darling, I know how unfair you think I'm being," she said. "Right now, I'm just not ready to take that leap of faith."

"What can I do to help? What can I do or say to help you step out?"

"Nothing, Brent. It's going to take time. And the time isn't now."

"Well, regrettably the time for my chance at a GM position is now. This is a defining point in my career. I've worked hard to get to this point. I know some of my work commitment in Minneapolis caused you undue pain. I'm terribly sorry for that. I've dedicated the last eight years to regaining your trust. To reinvent myself as a husband and father. What have I gotten for those eight years? A wife I adore that neither trusts nor believes me."

"Oh no, Brent. I know you're being very truthful. That you believe what you feel to be true. What you believe you can do. You've proven in the past though that you're not capable of keeping your priorities in order when the demands of your job increase past a certain level."

"There've got to be some guidelines or checkpoints we can set up to keep us on course," he said.

"None I think you could adhere too," she said. "We shouldn't argue about this anymore. I do know one thing. Brent Shannon is an honorable man. He made an agreement, accepted by his wife, based on his word."

Annette got up from the table. "I know he's a man who'll honor that agreement." She pushed the chair under the table and left the room.

He heard her footsteps on the stairs. After looking at her uneaten salad and half empty wine glass, he put his elbows on the table, head in his hands and moaned, "What a crowning end to the evening."

Paul had finished his second call some time ago. As always, it exhilarated him. He had gotten some valuable information. Ben Voorhees favored him over Brent Shannon. It had been a bit disconcerting to learn that Marlene endorsed Shannon but the meeting today would put a dent in that.

He looked out of his office window and saw rain clouds forming in the southwest. Time to call it a day. He logged off his computer and threw some spreadsheets in his briefcase. What a marvelous day it had been. The only way it could have been better would have been if Marlene and Terry Thomas found Shannon and Bolivar horizontal on Shannon's office sofa.

Paul crossed the parking lot with a walk that bespoke power and confidence. He could picture the prize being his. He felt betrayed by Marlene's stance. He thought she considered him her right hand. Shannon put numbers on the top line but Paul cut the expense fat out of the division when Marlene brought him over to this disaster. If not for Paul's superior financial expertise and cost management, Shannon would not have had the chance to shine. But Marlene's disloyalty was a fact he would have to live with and suppress his disdain. On the fast track to CEO, Marlene had to remain a staunch ally. After the division's performance rose for two or three years under his leadership, she would realize the mistake she had made recommending Shannon and be in his debt. Of course, Shannon would be long gone by then. The more he thought about it, her current stance might well be fortuitous for his future. As the blue Jaguar pulled out onto Westinghouse Boulevard, Paul thought how advantageous it was to have Wilson. In so many ways. Currently, it was like having an invisible presence at the highest level in Atlanta.

Neal Stuart could be very useful in tying this thing up. Paul would have to talk to Stuart. The man would have to be on his game if Evan Roth called him. Stuart was mentally slow. Just above imbecile level, Paul decided. Yet that had its advantages. Although there was the risk that he could make a serious mistake, his mentality made him quite easy to manipulate. Paul guessed he had to take the good with the bad. Of course, Stuart would have to be quickly replaced. He could not be on Paul's team.

The meeting with Thomas could not have gone better. Marlene, normally a composed person, had been furious with Shannon. The inability to hide her emotions ranked as her greatest weakness. Her face had been an open book. He did not get out of it totally clean but he accomplished his objective. Shannon looked like a deer caught in the headlights. The man had nowhere to go and just took the hit head-on. Paul had to credit the guy. He took it with dignity. The meeting changed the rules though. The gloves were off and now Shannon would watch every move. He could not forget that Shannon was super bright. However, Shannon could not fight him alone and he had a minimal network. His only ally was Patricia Bolivar, a lightweight.

He would have to be covert with Neal Stuart. He could not afford to have him compromised.

Yes, Shannon would crash and burn. When it came down to Voorhees versus Marlene, if Bible Ben had ammunition, there would be no doubt who won. As the Jaguar crawled along the freeway, Patricia Bolivar crossed his mind. She would find out how he dealt with disloyalty.

This coordinated attack on Shannon would establish the rationale to fire the pig. Shannon was just like the vermin he grew up with on those army posts. He fancied himself such a hot shot. He had the same personality. The same swagger. Paul hated the word swagger. It almost made him throw up. Paul could not stand being around him. It brought back memories of earlier days and the suffering under his father's roof.

Although painful, his mind would not shut down as it retreated to those earlier years. His father had been a non-commissioned officer in the army. His family had been stationed at Fort Benning, Georgia, when his father went to Vietnam for the second time. Paul and his mother moved off post into Columbus, Georgia. At ten years old, this had been his first real association with non-military family kids and his mother had fostered those friendships as much as possible. He found himself attracted to the more stable, gentle environment of civilian society.

His father returned from Vietnam as a highly decorated first sergeant. They moved to Fort Bragg, North Carolina, and Paul attended the school on post. He had a terrible time finding a social niche. He had nothing in common with the military kids and his standoffishness caused his schoolmates to consider him a snob. They made him pay. More than once, he returned home from school bloodied. His father had been disgusted with his son's weakness and he marched Paul to a Tai Kwon Do master in town. His instructions were to make his son a man. After some time, Paul took to this ancient Oriental training of mind and body. He had vowed to gain the power to dispose of problem people. Tai Kwon Do provided him the confidence and discipline to stand up for himself.

Paul's mind returned to the present. He mentally ached every time he recalled those hateful years. That sub-human Shannon was a composite of those people of his youth who had tried to destroy him. But Paul's day had come. He would destroy Shannon. Literally destroy the scum. The days had gone when men like Shannon kept him from what was rightfully his.

Paul walked into the house and out to the deck where Audra waited.

"My, you seem happy," she said as she gave him a perfunctory kiss on the cheek.

"How'd your day go?" Paul asked.

"Never mind my day. How about yours?"

He reviewed the details of the meeting in Marlene's office. "Thomas was affronted Shannon wasn't prepared. He's egotistical. Not getting the numbers wasn't the issue. It was impertinence by a lesser person. He was puffed up like a blow fish. You can bet ole Bible Ben will hear about it in emphatic language."

Audra went over to the bar for another drink. "Fine and good. But not a deal breaker. A drink?"

"Dewar, please. Might not be but the next meeting could."

Audra walked over and handed Paul his drink. "Go on."

"Managed to get Shannon's marital problems out on the table. Marlene tried to deflect it but couldn't do it. Thomas jumped all over it. He was cool but you could see him making lots of mental notes."

"An adequate start. But how's it reinforced? One pass's not enough. Got to go for the kill. No reinforcement and Shannon's back won't break. Wolff'll go to her deathbed denying it's an issue."

"I have a way to make that happen."

"Make sure you do."

Paul smiled. "Had a talk with Evan Roth. Even played down the marital thing. Acted like it was probably nothing. I led and Roth followed right into the possible affair."

Audra laughed. "You're getting as diabolical as me. Give me the details, cause this, my sweet, is the poison pill."

She walked up to Paul and kissed him on the lips. "Hope for you yet, Paul. With an affair over his head, Shannon's ruined. No fucking chance for recovery. Marlene's got no choice. Has to withdraw her support or face the certainty of losing Bible Ben's confidence. She likes Shannon but not a career's worth. Not only do you get the job but Voorhees takes care of Shannon for you. And hot-pants Bolivar goes with him. Damn, hate that little whore."

"I set up Neal Stuart to do my talking with Roth," said Paul.

"Think Stuart's reliable? Impresses me as an idiot."

"You've no idea how much he hates Shannon. He's perfect. Got to school him to get the right words out of his mouth. And come out so Roth never figures I put them there. Course, I don't know if Roth will talk to him."

"Better put them there fast," she said. "Cause Roth'll talk to him. Bet on it. No way Roth goes to Bible Ben unless he's got his ass covered. He'll know it's an atom bomb. But he thinks of himself as your mentor. He'll figure if he's covered and if he has any confidence the affair accusation's correct, you're in and Shannon's screwed. You know Roth. Justify fucking Shannon by saying he's looking out for the company.

"A good day. But you've got to keep working our plans. This promotion's not an option. You'll be the next GM of the retail division. Means getting what's rightfully mine. Plus, remember what my father thought of me marrying the son of an army enlisted man."

"You don't have to continually remind me of that, Audra," responded Paul.

"Oh yes I do. Thought my father would disown me when I defied him and married you. Hadn't been for mother, don't know where we'd have been married. I've given you all my strength and support, Paul. This promotion's how you repay me. No executive husband and I'll damn well be screwed out of my rightful inheritance by my ass-kissing brother. Help you any way I can, but it better happen."

"Don't worry, baby," he said putting his arms around her. "Good as done."

She pulled away from him. "Good. Let's go to the club for dinner."

"Great idea."

Walking out, Paul knew he had all the cards he needed. The final support piece walked alongside him. He did not think there was a more ruthless human on earth than Audra. God, she could help him go all the way to the top and she had the motivation to do it. He smiled the smile of certain victory.

FRIDAY

Brent's Audi worked its way down Park Road. A tribute to German technology and engineering, the automobile was an example of fine tuned excellence. The same could not be said of its driver. Brent was a wreck. Annette's abrupt departure from last night's discussion had been done with an air of finality that unnerved him. Her viewpoint held no flexibility. In fact, if he read last night's episode correctly, her position had hardened. Tired, feeling like hell, he knew this would be a critical day.

He had been up until three o'clock working on the MAC capital request. Terry Thomas had been correct. The write-up and justification had been sloppy and Thomas had every right to throw them back in his face. Brent had let Neal Stuart's unsatisfactory work slide by him. Busy when Neal handed the request off to him, Brent had thought it would be a slam dunk and signed it. Bad assumptions always create bad outcomes. Why couldn't he quite grasp that truth? Well, it was corrected.

He could not construct a worse situation for himself with a year-long sabbatical to work it up. What had he ever done to deserve this? Yesterday's ambush had been brutal and vindictive. Brent could not imagine why a target was on his forehead. His career could be headed for the toilet with the fat lady reaching for the flush handle.

After consuming a four-ninety-nine breakfast at The Kopper Kettle, Brent headed to the office. It had been about the time his Audi passed under I-77 that he answered the core question. "Dammit, I'm going for the job. It's not like I've got a hell of a lot of options," he announced to the windshield with determination.

Great to have that settled but how would he pull it off, he thought. For openers, he had to avoid Kruger. God knows what the guy had planned for act two. Brent had nothing in the woodpile that the Machiavellian disciple could dig up. The challenge would be avoiding self-destruction. He would throw himself on his spear with Marlene. Just as he and George had talked. He had a nine o'clock with her and after yesterday, he had to get the air cleared. Any fears she might have developed about continuing to support him had to be allayed.

Annette? He shook his head. She was another story. How does one argue with illogic? He adored her but her attitude bewildered him. It appeared that she had put him in an untenable position and dared him to defy her. Brent could not remember any time in their relationship when she had acted in such a manner. Even in their darkest Minneapolis days, she had been a logical thinker. For a considerable amount of time she would have nothing to do with him. She had been angry and hurt. Yet when they talked, even if it got emotional, she searched for a reasoned, win-win approach. This was a dramatic departure. It became win-lose, period. Deal with it. It seemed she had no appreciation that they could both lose. Or maybe she could not lose. No. That was asinine conjecture.

Brent walked into his office, gave Ashley the "not now" sign and called Marlene who said to come right over. He walked by Neal Stuart's office and stuck his head in the door.

"Neal. Going to see Marlene. When I get back, let's visit."

"Got to leave soon."

"Not till we've talked. Not optional." Brent didn't wait for a reply.

He picked up some coffee on the way. When he got to Marlene's office, Terry indicated to go in. He walked through the door and said, "Good morning."

Marlene nodded to him. She motioned to shut the door and take a seat at the conference table. She sat across from him looking about as friendly as the grim reaper after a particularly bad day. "Let's hear the new numbers," she said.

"Two problems with the request. First, the new equipment's necessary to execute the three-year store expansion plan, the broader merchandise mix featuring more non-Richmont SKU's and heavier use of local newspaper advertising. The equipment will allow us to accomplish those plans while realizing significant payroll savings. We'll require no additional staff over the three-year time horizon. There were payroll savings included in the numbers but at a lower wage level than should've been used."

"How come?"

Her tone sounded like she knew the answer to her own question. Brent looked her directly in the eye. "Missed it in my final review."

"Go on."

"Retail division is covered under the master maintenance contract through corporate. Our numbers included a separate maintenance contract. That cost was significant and unnecessary.

"How come?"

"Missed it," he said. He did not mention that he had been busy and relied on an advertising manager who was dumb as a box of rocks to put the finishing touches on it. Brent had signed it without review. He better re-evaluate who was dumb as a box of rocks.

Marlene studied the figures a few minutes while Brent felt skewered and about to be hauled over the barbeque pit. "Looks better now. Okay. I'll take it from here," she said.

"Could I have a few minutes?" Brent asked.

"Morning schedule's brutal. Can't it wait?"

"Promise I'll be brief."

"Okay. Clock's on."

"I take full responsibility for this request falling through the cracks. That's bad enough. But I embarrassed you and regret that. Want to apologize."

"I was embarrassed, Brent. A lot. More than that, you've any idea how befuddled and incompetent you looked? Quite an exhibition. Almost training video quality on how not to be an executive."

"Marlene, I understand. I'm sorry. There's not much I can do about it now."

"No. Not much. Look. Paul was vague with you. He doesn't like you a hell of a lot. He's cool about it, but you don't have to be a shrink to catch it. I've got to admit there've been times when I've considered locking you two up in a conference room, feeding you pizzas under the door and not letting you out until there was a mutually satisfactory working arrangement hatched. Or only one guy was left standing."

"Honest to god, Marlene. What have I ever done to the man?" He was getting angry and could not keep it out of his voice. "Never screwed him in business and guarantee I never made a pass at his wife. She'd chew me up and spit me out like spoiled meat."

"Know what, marketing man? You're fun to be around even if you've the political savvy of my potted palm. It's because you're here, Brent. You're competition. You're a forceful, results-oriented guy. You've stepped on Paul's toes several times, in what he considered an embarrassing way. That doesn't sit well with self-absorbed, ambitious people. They tend to take themselves way too seriously."

"Just trying to get the job done," said Brent. He was starting to get a little protective of himself.

"Don't get defensive with me, Brent. You need this talking to and you'd better listen. If you don't think your long-term career depends on it, you're wrong."

He congratulated himself for hiding his feelings so well. "Sorry. Just seems every time I turn around I'm stepping in a bucket of manure."

"You are. Because you're not looking. You've got to be politically aware or you're never going to realize your potential. We've had this talk before. The idea that I'll let my work speak for itself is the biggest bunch of garbage ever concocted by people who don't have a clue what working in an organization's all about. Business organizations are political. They run on relationships built on mutual interests. That's a fundamental truth. Quit fighting it. You're losing. Being able to maneuver around the politics of getting things done and getting to where you want to go is part of your work.

"Think about this. Paul told you about a meeting in my office with Terry Thomas. Think you had been included because Thomas couldn't resist spending an hour with Brent Shannon? Maybe for spiritual value. Ever occur to you to call me and say, oh by the way, you need anything specific from me at the meeting?

"Paul Kruger was playing his game and you fell right into it. And he played it because he knew you could be had. His probability for success was on top of the scale."

Brent shook his head and looked out the window. "I can be a brick at times, can't I?"

"Pretty good self-appraisal."

"Sure agreed quickly enough."

"As long as we're having a good ole shakedown cruise, marketing man, what the devil's wrong with you the last couple of days? Spent more time picking up the ball than throwing it."

"Shock of you leaving," he said. "We really had this thing humming. A selfish reaction. Really want to congratulate you again. No one deserves it more."

"Don't patronize me, Brent. It really sets me off." She was doing the piercing eye contact thing complete with slight smile. That usually meant, here comes the zinger. "You're too much of a pro. Let's cut to the chase. You want my job?"

Well, all right now folks. Fish or cut bait time. Brent had reached the point of no return. If he said no, Marlene would withdraw his name from consideration and the cannibals cometh. If he said yes, would it be a decision that was a testimony to his self-centeredness because it could result in the end of his marriage? He didn't think so. His task would be to allay Annette's fears, not give in to her irrationality. This was what is known as a defining moment.

"Yes, I do. I'd be honored to run the division."

"You've quite a method of selling yourself. Now, I've a basic issue. Your marriage able to survive this job? No hedging, Brent. Yes or no."

"Yes," Brent said. "Annette will be fine with it." One way or the other, he thought. "Take some adjustment but I can structure my time to meet the responsibilities of both sides of my life."

"You delegate well. It's a strength of yours. And you're as quick with the numbers as anyone I've worked with that didn't have a financial background. Your marketing expertise gives you the vision needed to grow the division. Businesses don't operate to a profit. They grow in the marketplace. You've got a unique capability to visualize and respond to our market."

"I appreciate your assessment."

"Rest assured, I'm not placating you. We're about to share some information. If Ben Voorhees hears about our discussion, we'll be opening a taco stand together. And you can bet your last dollar you'll be on pots and pans. Understand?"

"Think I've got the thrust of it."

"I've recommended to Ben that you replace me as GM of the division."

"Thanks for your support. I'm delighted."

"Don't be. The good news ends there. You're going out of your way to make both of us look like idiots. A sterling job of subverting my efforts."

"Would seem the case," replied Brent.

"Paul Kruger's the other candidate," said Marlene. "I came to the conclusion that Paul shouldn't be GM. Brilliant business person and will be a highly successful financial executive. But not a leader. I believe you'd bring a unique skill set to the job and the company's interests would be better served."

Brent nodded. He had never had this type of discussion with his boss and did not quite know how to react. He thought the best response would be to shut up.

"Now keep your wits about you," she said. "Go back to doing your job the way I know you can. And stay away from political traps. Can you do that, marketing man?"

"Yes."

"Quick soul searching. Any skeletons in your closet I should know about?"

"No. None."

"Wonderful. Let's see if I can patch up yesterday."

Brent got up to leave. "Thanks for your trust."

As he got to the door, Marlene said, "This is the first time in my business career I've shared information against instructions from my boss. I intend it to be the last. My act of sharing should indicate how critical I consider this. Now that you understand that, understand this. Any of this conversation's repeated inside or outside the company, have your office cleaned out. Anything about that you don't understand?"

"Crystal," said Brent.

Brent returned to his office knowing that he had just received the most elegant ass-chewing of his life and he was exhilarated by it. As bad as Brent had screwed up, Marlene still supported him. The only way he could repay her would be to make the retail division an even bigger star in Richmont's galaxy. She had sure put it all on the table for him.

He passed Neal Stuart's door and motioned for Neal to come to his office.

Neal walked through the door. "Really don't have time, Brent. Late already."

"You've as much time as we need. I revised the MAC expenditure request last night because of some critical errors." Brent recapped them.

"Wasn't aware of any master maintenance agreement. How was I supposed to know that?"

"How about calling Atlanta and asking."

"We're all busy. Didn't have a lot of time."

"Did you check with HR about wage levels?"

"Didn't have to. Know the wage levels. Okay. I was busy and missed a few items. But you had the chance to review everything."

"Yes," said Brent. "I dropped the ball, too. But with your experience, I expected higher quality, completed work. Wasn't dealing with a marketing intern."

Ashley stuck her head in the office. "Brent, Marlene's on the phone for you. Doesn't sound optional."

"Okay," he said. He turned to Neal. "That's all, Neal. But this sloppy, sophomoric work isn't to happen again." Neal mumbled something unintelligible and left the office.

"Yes, Marlene," he said picking up the phone.

"Name Theodore Faulkton mean anything to you?"

Brent felt his stomach fall to just below his knees. "Yes."

"You, my compatriot, have skeletons you don't even know about."

"Marlene, I knew Theodore Faulkton's daughter at the University of Wisconsin."

"Well, Mr. Saturday Night, she must've really taken a shine to you. Her father's about to become the newest member of Richmont's board. He spent last evening with Ben Voorhees. Small talk, let's get to know each other better, thing. Ben mentioned he had a mover and shaker from Wisconsin being considered for a big promotion. Faulkton asked who it was. Ben told him and got a verbal dissertation on what a mistake it would be to promote Brent Shannon to any responsible position. So you might've just innocently known his daughter. But get your butt down here cause I can't wait to hear the rest of this story."

Brent walked to Marlene's office with his head spinning. Theodore Faulkton on Richmont's board. What's next?

Brent's mind pictured Jennifer Faulkton for the first time in years. She had been the most beautiful woman he had ever laid eyes on and he bet she was still a ten. It was like yesterday. They met at Effien House over beers and the attraction had been immediate. She had been a junior, a sorority girl, and not in Brent's social circle.

From Milwaukee, she was fourth generation in one of Wisconsin's elite families. Her father had turned a sleepy, family business into one of the largest and most profitable retail companies in the upper Midwest.

Over the next two months, their attraction turned to a passionate love affair. One weekday Jennifer's mother came to Madison and Jennifer asked him to join them for lunch at The Edgewater.

Jennifer went home the next weekend and came back to Madison devastated. Her family told her they wanted her to break off seeing Brent. Her parents felt Brent could never provide for Jennifer as she deserved. Also, he did not have the upbringing to travel in the Faulkton family's social circles.

Brent and Jennifer decided the only way to make things right would be for Brent to go see her father. Brent tried to talk with him and explain that he was working hard to get a good education. He had a good work ethic and would do very well. Faulkton told him that regardless of how hard he worked there was nothing he could do about his family background.

Brent's famous temper exploded and he called Faulkton some seriously vile names. Worse, he grabbed Faulkton by the shirt.

Faulkton had him thrown out. Brent never forgot his last words. "If you want to do well, young man, stay away from me." It was one of the few times in his life Brent was frightened of another human being.

Jennifer came back to Madison but avoided Brent. Several of her friends told him she never wanted to see him again. Brent had been devastated.

Now Faulkton was on Richmont's board. He was one hell of a businessman and Brent could certainly see Ben Voorhees pursuing him. Brent walked into Marlene's office.

She motioned him to the conference table. "Wanna camp out here? Why's Theodore Faulkton so enamored with you?" Her half-smile wasn't from humor. "Take the time you need."

Brent gave Marlene a detailed summary of his short relationship with the Faulktons of Milwaukee. When finished, Brent said, "It was a long time ago, Marlene."

"May be true. But Ben thinks this guy walks on water. Been trying to get him on the board for three years."

"He'll be an asset. No doubt about it. But, this was twenty-some years ago, Marlene. I was a young kid in love. The guy was a total jerk to me and I lost my temper."

"Brent. Your temper's his point. He's not going to count years and neither is Ben. He can—"

"But that's ludicrous, not to mention unfair."

"Don't believe I mentioned fair? What's fair? Tell you what's fair. How the person with the power defines it. Think Faulkton's dispassionate about you? He appears to have a long memory, high forgiveness threshold. Folks of his station tend to have a narrow range of what they consider acceptable behavior toward themselves. Whether or not their own actions incite that behavior. Poor judgment, loss of control. That's what he pitched to Ben. Guarantee he didn't finish his oration with, 'but it was twenty-some years ago.'

"I know it's a long-held grudge but it's held nonetheless. I cannot interject myself between Ben and a board member. I'll do what I can to neutralize this. You're the best person for the job, and this hasn't changed my mind. But we could have a deal breaker. Straw that broke the camel's back. Etcetera, etcetera."

"Understand," said Brent. "But how could Voorhees take this into consideration? It's ancient history."

Marlene leaned so far over the table Brent thought she was going to lay on it. "There're two things you need to understand, my friend. Listen for once. Ben's got to get along with the man. He's an outside board member who's going to sit on some sensitive committees. Compensation for one. More seriously, perceptions formed from these incidents tend to aggregate. First the Terry Thomas meeting. Then criticized by a highly-respected new board member.

"I'll do what I can, Brent. But all bets are off. Now, one more time, any other skeletons I should know about?"

"Didn't know about this one but nothing I'm aware of."

"Fine. Do your job, keep your head down and don't get ambushed again. Now get out of here."

Brent decided that a dismissal such as that required no response. He left.

He went to Patricia Bolivar's office, leaned through the door and said, "Got a few minutes?"

"Sure. Come on in."

Brent admired Patricia's office. The decor was professional, yet feminine.

"You win," he said. It wasn't until he was walking through the HR department that he realized he had neglected to tell her of his decision to go for Marlene's job.

She smiled. "I love to win. Was it the lottery?"

"I told Marlene I wanted her job."

She got up from her chair with her eyes fixed on him, walked around the desk, shook his hand and put her left hand on his elbow. "I'm very glad. To say my prayers have been answered would be a bit fraudulent but I've willed you to change your mind." She sat down in an arm chair and unconsciously rubbed a figurine on the table between two arm chairs in her office. "What changed your mind?"

Brent sat in the other chair and said, "It was on the way in today. Recounting the whole mess, it dawned on me I was trapped. Only had one way to turn. Kruger made a categorical statement yesterday. He wants to dice me up like an onion. It's no win with Annette. Her attitude's not a onetime thing. Next time her status quo is upset, she'll give me the same inflexible ultimatum. Capitulate now, I'll be a hostage to her irrational demands and forfeit my career aspirations. Don't believe it's fair for her to ask that."

"I know that was very hard to say. I'm honored you felt close enough to me to share it."

"Patricia, I'm embarrassed to entangle you in my family turmoil. But you're my only friend here. Certainly the only person I trust. Don't know what I'd do without you." He wasn't sure, but he thought he saw her blush. Not something he had seen before.

"Don't worry about that, Brent. I only hope I can help. I respect you a great deal and know you'll be a tremendous leader."

"Believe me, you've been a big help already."

"So. Where do we stand now?"

Brent stood and paced her office while recounting the Faulkton incident. His pace quickened and he became more agitated with every sentence. Finally, he sat back down. "Everywhere I turn, I get screwed."

"Brent, settle down."

"Pray tell, what's to settle down about? Didn't want her job in the first place. Still wouldn't if Kruger wasn't out to waste me."

"Brent, are you being true to yourself? Can you honestly tell me you wouldn't enjoy the challenge of the division GM job?"

"I don't want the job!" He looked down at the floor. Who's kidding who, he thought. "No. That's a lie. Of course, I want it. It's what I've worked for."

"Then you should have an opportunity to compete for it. You're a courageous man, Brent Shannon. It'll be a privilege to work for you."

"Not for me. With me."

"With you."

"Don't crack out the champagne yet," he said. "Don't even put it on ice. Kruger's got me on a spit with an apple in my mouth. What could he possibly have against me? Acting like a man possessed. One, who hates my guts."

"Kruger's not comfortable around people as strong as himself. Look at his staff. Name me one of his direct reports in finance or accounting that has a strong personality."

"Never thought of it. You might be right."

"Look at them. Of course I'm right."

"That meeting set up still has me shaking my head," Brent said. "Good lord. Masterful assassination."

"It was," she said. "What's scarier, he didn't do it because he felt trapped. That maneuver was a laid-back, icing-on-the-cake shot. He thinks he's got you hanging on with one finger. Think what he'd do if he felt threatened."

"Yeah, well Kruger I can watch. And avoid," said Brent. "But Faulkton is unreal. I mean, go figure. How can a guy hold a grudge that long? It's not like I ran away with his daughter, got her pregnant and deserted her. Point of fact, she did a great job of having other people tell me to sit on a sharp fence post and spin." Brent looked down at the floor and put his head in his hands. "Yes ma'am, I'm skewered. Right through the heart or more painful parts of my anatomy."

"No, you're not," Patricia said. Brent felt her hand squeezing and then rubbing his arm. "What happened was a long time ago."

Brent lifted his head and moved his arm. Her touch made him feel too comforted. "Faulkton is the newest outside board member. Ben doesn't want him to think the company makes poor people decisions."

"You can't give in to Kruger because of Faulkton. I agree. Faulkton was bad luck. But, I don't think he controls your destiny. What did Marlene say?"

"Honest, I think. All bets are off. Her hands are tied. Can't get between Bible Ben and a member of the board."

"We can't do anything about Faulkton's interference," said Patricia. "That's in Marlene's court. We're going to have to ride it out. To continue worrying about it is counterproductive."

"You're right. But one more strike and I'm out. Who knows what Kruger has cooked up."

"He has an information pipeline into Atlanta," said Patricia. "Have no idea who it is. I know Roth and Kruger are tight. But Roth's too light to generate the kind of influence Kruger is able to."

"This is going to be won or lost in Atlanta, not Charlotte," said Brent.

"Right. We've got to get some ears there. I can lean on Todd Beamon. He gave me some insight this morning. There's not much he doesn't have an ear to."

"That's great. Think he'll help us?"

"Yeah, he'll help."

"Don't know what I'd do without you."

"I'm doing this for selfish reasons. Told you that before."

"All I know is that you're the best friend I have," said Brent.

"Who's in Atlanta to give you feedback and guidance?"

"I'll call Tom Carthage. As vice president, marketing, he doesn't get into corporate intrigue. But he's so self-effacing he might be able to get some information people don't realize they're giving him."

"Good contact. Brent, anything else that might give Kruger ammunition?"

"Not that I can think of, but hell, who'd of thought of Faulkton."

"Annette knows you're competing for the job, right?"

"Sort of."

"What's that supposed to mean?"

"Means I count innuendo as communication. She's pretty belligerent. Off the charts, you could say."

"So you told her but she doesn't know you told her." Patricia shook her head. "Leave it to men. You do realize that's a weak point."

"Don't see it that way. Eventually, I'll be able to reason with her."

"You're out of your mind. You can't be blasé and let what happens, happen. Kruger'll eat you for lunch. You've got to get into this game. And you'd better have Annette in it with you."

"Well, don't know what I can do about her attitude in the next few days," said Brent. "It'll take time but she'll be cool with it. Eventually."

"Problem is you don't have eventually," she said. "You've got to get to Marlene with any potential problems before they come up. She needs to be armed with answers before questions are asked. Companies don't make a habit of giving promotions to people with serious marital issues."

"See your point. But don't see how Kruger could use any of this before a decision is made."

"Please be quicker on the uptake about the world around you. Kruger has a terrific 'in' with Atlanta management. He plants a seed. Then at the going away bash this Saturday night when every Tom, Dick and Harry from Atlanta will be here, Bible Ben or one of the boys will have a nice talk with Annette."

"What Saturday night bash?"

Patricia laughed. "You're so nice and so out of it. Didn't bother to read your e-mails yesterday, did you?"

"No." He could feel his stomach heading south again.

"Bible Ben's throwing a Charlotte going-away party for Marlene tomorrow night. Just about everybody from Atlanta will be here. And everybody from Charlotte. Including spouses, I might add."

His neck was getting damp with perspiration while a nasty picture emerged in his mind. "Nobody told me about this."

"Sure they did. They e-mailed you. An e-mail invitation from Stan Ascutney. Actually, it wasn't an invitation. It was a command appearance announcement."

"Come on. Couldn't set up a bash for that number of people so fast," said Brent.

"Brent. They've probably known about Marlene's future for a couple of months. Think Ben got in the shower Wednesday and decided to promote her? And I'll bet she's out of here by the end of next week."

"I can't put Annette in the middle of those vultures."

"You've no choice. I can hear it now. 'Oh, sorry Ben. Couldn't bring my sweetie. Was scared she'd tell you the deal with Marlene's job sucked, and your company's shenanigans were destroying her marriage.' The sacrificial wife. Now there's a winning scenario.

"I don't know how you're going to orchestrate this but you'd better have Annette primed for Saturday night. They're going to be on her like a blanket if Kruger has anything to do with it and he will. And to exclude her would be worse."

Brent got up from the chair. "She'll do fine. She's always come through in the clutch."

"This is the true definition of clutch," Patricia said. "I'll get a hold of Todd Beamon and see what I can find."

"Thanks," he said walking out the door. He continued in a mumble, "Going-away party. Fuckin' great. What else? Annette, honey bunny, better get open-minded real fast."

Paul Kruger sat at his desk smiling. The morning had been a smashing success. The phone call from Evan Roth was still difficult to believe. Bible Ben got an earful from a new board member about the instability of Brent Shannon. What a marvelous development. Shannon was in total destruction mode. The activities after his promotion occupied Paul's mind. A party would be necessary. They would hold it at the country club with Audra handling all the arrangements. The attendees would be the directors and their direct reports. No need to go lower than that. No one from Atlanta. The gathering had to make the statement that he was in charge. Shannon and Bolivar must be gone by then. That would be no problem. Voorhees would take care of them. In fact, that could happen at the same time as his promotion.

Why not plan? The board member incident took it over the top. It was the perfect appetizer for a main course of marital strife and an illicit affair with a co-worker. Oh my god, Paul exclaimed to himself. Brent Shannon is doomed. Good riddance to the obnoxious scoundrel.

Neal Stuart flashed through his mind. He had to be tied down tight. Paul picked up the phone and dialed Stuart's extension who answered on the first ring.

"Hello, Neal. Paul Kruger. How're things going this morning?"

"Oh, Paul. Just fine. Can I help you with something?"

"I wanted to see if you're free for lunch today. There are a couple of issues I'd like your opinion on." Paul smiled. He could almost hear Stuart bubble over the phone.

"I'm free, Paul. Sure. Lunch would be super."

"I don't want to put you in an awkward position. But I've gotten some information from Brent that I'd just like you to verify. Not that I distrust Brent, just like another opinion."

"Be delighted to help any way I can."

"Very kind of you. Why don't we meet at the Harper's on Woodlawn? About twelve-fifteen."

"I'll be there."

"Oh, and Neal, let's keep this low key. I need your expertise but I certainly don't want to put you in a compromising position with your boss."

"Keep it completely to myself."

"Good. See you then." Paul hung up.

The day just kept getting better and better. That dimwit Stuart would be the *coup de grace*. Who would have ever thought that? He put in a call to Wilson Rachet's private line.

When Wilson answered, Paul said, "Hi. Things are going great here."

"Good," replied Wilson. "What else has to be done?"

"First, did you hear about this new board member's denunciation of Shannon to Ben Voorhees?"

"No, didn't hear about it. Was there. The guy, his name's Faulkton, came positively unglued at the mention of Shannon's name. Ole Ben almost fell off his chair."

"Wonderful," said Paul.

"Was a remarkable performance. Man delivered a cutting indictment. It was twenty-some-odd years ago and he made a brilliant argument. Faulkton is extremely bright. If you have an opportunity to meet him, don't take him lightly."

"I'll remember that. We can stick a fork in Shannon. He's done."

Wilson's voice turned firm. "No time to let up. Nothing left to chance. Nothing, Paul. Shannon's got to be thrown out of the company. Not just the division, the company. Happen to know Tom Carthage is going to retire the end of next quarter. I'm involved in sweetening his retirement. You don't want the answer to be that Shannon gets Carthage's job."

"God, no," said Paul. "That would be terrible. The hideous man would simply wait for something inconsequential and then pounce. He's that type."

"I know. Vital his business reputation be destroyed. Be negligent if you didn't fire him. Can be no position available for him in Richmont and we've got to make certain they never go looking for him. With him thoroughly out of the picture, your short and long-term future's assured."

"I understand, Wilson. That's the reason for my call. Have to get the marital issue in front of Voorhees. Can you help?"

"Has to be done correctly. No seams."

"Right. It can never be traced back to Charlotte."

"Let me think," said Wilson. He was silent for almost a minute. "I think we can get this accomplished quickly."

"How so?"

"Assume you want this planted before Saturday night."

"That's essential."

"Answer's here in my office," said Wilson. "It's Katie Lockhart. She knew Annette Shannon very well. When Annette was in Atlanta, she did part time legal work. Worked with Katie. Think they stay in touch."

"Don't see the angle."

"Here's my plan. I talk to Katie very informally. Be easy. She's doing research for me. I'll mention Marlene Wolff is being promoted and my understanding that Brent Shannon may be in line for her job. Ask her didn't I remember she had been friends with Annette Shannon? Hadn't they worked together?"

"Great. Say that you knew they'd had marital difficulties in the past. Good they were behind them because this would be a super promotion."

"Right. Say all jobs put a strain on a marriage. But since Brent has always had difficult assignments and excelled, they must have a strong marriage and gotten everything behind them."

"One flaw," said Paul. "What if she validates they've developed a strong marriage?"

Wilson laughed. "Ah, Paul. You don't know cautious Katie. That's why it's so fortuitous she's the target. No way is she going on record endorsing the marriage of someone getting a promotion in one of our firm's largest clients. Not going to take the chance of it coming back to bite her. Very politically astute, and I'm her ticket to partner. Nope. No way. She'll hedge and I can use what she says to ignite Ben Voorhees. Might even embellish it a bit."

"Masterful."

Wilson laughed. "I know. Listen. Better get to her right away. Even be worth a lunch. Got a meeting with Voorhees at two. Drop the bomb then. Real quick. What's the status of the affair?"

"In place." He briefed Wilson on Neal Stuart and the upcoming conversation with Evan Roth.

"Sounds good. But no phone calls. Get them together at the party. Can brief him all you want but to make certain it happens right, facilitate it."

"Good idea. I'll see if I can arrange it that way. Thanks for everything. Anxious to get to Atlanta to see you. Been too long."

"It has. But once this job is settled you'll be coming to Atlanta more frequently. Talk to you soon." Wilson hung up.

Annette never finished her "to do" list around the house. She was still seething over Brent's performance last night. He was such a one-dimensional human. God, it was work, work, work. The family was fine until a blip at work. Then forget it. She was still so angry she could cry. She thought she had better do something more constructive. She picked up the phone to call her brother. Tom Lind was Annette's older brother by four years who held a senior position with the 3M Company in St. Paul, Minnesota. She had three siblings, but Tom was the one whose opinion she respected the most. She always went to him with the big problems in her life. He had always been level headed, able to analyze complex problems and get to core issues. He answered the phone himself on the second ring.

"Hi, Tom. Have a few minutes?"

"My southern connection," Tom replied. "For my sexy sister, anything."

She cursed her eyes for starting to tear up. "I don't feel very sexy right now."

"What's wrong, Annette?"

"Oh Tom, it's happening again. Sorry if I cry but I'm so emotional about this."

"Honey. Got to tell me what it is if you want to talk about it."

"Brent wants to go on the fast track again. And the family be damned." She could not help breaking into a sob.

"Is that what Brent said to you or is that what you're thinking?"

"Didn't say it in so many words. But he knows the way I feel and he's still trying to get the job. Hasn't said that either but I could see by the look on his face last night. He's going for it."

"Brent must really feel this is important."

"God, Tom. Everything having to do with work is important to him."

"Annette, I think I can be objective, but you know I've never been a staunch supporter of Brent's. Always thought you could've had a more settled husband. That he was a taker more than giver. Nothing would ever totally satisfy him. Some people spend their earthly existence being restless, and Brent appeared to be one of them."

"I know," she said. "But, you're the only one I can talk to about this. Our reconciliation had one stringent rule. He had to keep his priorities straight. Family came first."

"Has he kept that rule?"

"Yes, mostly he has."

"When has he violated it?"

"He hasn't. Honored it to this point."

"Fine. What makes you convinced he'll not honor it if he takes this job? By the way, what's the job?"

"General manager of the division," she said.

"Okay. What's got you convinced he'll renege on his promise?"

"He will because he's done it before."

"But he's kept the non-violate agreement of your reconciliation."

"I'll admit that. But he put me through hell in Minneapolis and I'm terrified he'll do it again."

"I understand," said Tom. "So what's Brent's situation if he doesn't get the job?"

"Stay in his present job."

"Many times it's not that simple. Who's he in competition with? Who'll get the job if he doesn't?"

"It'll probably be Paul Kruger. The finance guy."

"How do Kruger and Brent get along?"

"Brent's talking about some ridiculous thing—that Paul Kruger has it in for him. If Kruger gets the job he'll get rid of Brent. It's just silly."

"Why do you think it's silly? Happens in business. In companies the size of mine, if it's a talented person, an internal company move might be the solution. In mid-sized companies like Richmont, that's not always possible or desired. Look, honey. There're cases where personality problems can't or won't be overcome. The myth if you're good at your job, that's what counts, is just that. A myth. At Brent's level, basic competence is more or less assumed. What you're left with is personality and social comfort. Commonly called chemistry. No, it's not silly."

"In this case, it is," Annette said. "Marlene, the current general manager, really likes Brent. She wouldn't let anything happen to him."

"But she's moving," said Tom. "She's out of Brent's loop."

"Don't think she's totally out. Plus Brent's being influenced by this co-worker, Patricia Bolivar. He likes her. Says he respects her opinion. But all she wants to do is get him in her bed."

"Think it best I not go there. But there's something that's disturbing in all this."

"There's plenty. What's your something?"

"You're not making sense. One of the things I've always respected about you is your logical mind. You always had the ability to concentrate on the relevant and dismiss the irrelevant. That's absent here."

"That's wrong, Tom. I know how things are in this."

"In the time we've been talking, you've made three points," he said. "You don't trust Brent to keep his word on priorities. In spite of the fact, he's kept his word since you reconciled. You've said that Brent is lying about the consequences of him not getting this job. And you've been emphatic about a co-worker wanting Brent sexually. In a tone that infers you feel he might not fight it."

Having a difficult time holding back her tears, Annette replied. "It's not as black and white as you make it."

"Maybe not, Annette. But something's missing here. You're not thinking straight. There's something hidden under the surface. What is it?"

"Nothing," she replied. "Just very emotional for me."

"The reconciliation was emotional and you thought through that very well," Tom said. "If how you feel now is how you felt eight years ago, you made a serious mistake reconciling. Or once again, is there something you aren't sharing with me?"

"I'm telling you everything. Just want Brent to do what he's agreed to."

"We've already covered that point, Annette. He has. I love you as much as a brother can love a sister but there's more to this story. If you don't wish to share it with me that's your prerogative. But your marriage can't survive based on how you view Brent. Take some time and reflect on it. If you really feel this way, then leave him. Do it as kindly and graciously as possible but leave.

"This web you're constructing seems to have the purpose of looking for or creating an excuse to justify some action you want to take. Or an attempt to extract punishment. Search your heart, Annette. Be sure there's not some subconscious motive driving your thinking."

This conversation was not going at all like Annette had played it in her mind. "That's ridiculous."

"May be. But think about it. Might you be punishing Brent because you gave up your career and now his seems on the verge of really taking off?"

Devastated, Annette replied. "That isn't it at all. How can you say that?"

"Because I love you," Tom said. "Not cutting you off but you need thinking time. Reflection. Some searching for what's driving you. Call back and we'll talk after you've thought about it more."

"Okay but I know I'm right. My marriage is about to be destroyed. Talk to you soon. Bye," said Annette. She hung up and began to sob.

After gaining control of her emotions and dressing, Annette grabbed her briefcase, got in her car and began the short drive to the church. She participated in a church program that gave pro bono legal counsel to persons who could not afford normal attorney fees.

In recalling her conversation with Tom, she could not believe he had taken Brent's side in this. She was not punishing Brent for his career. She had always been supportive. She had made the decision to stay home and raise the kids. That had not been a unilateral decision by Brent and forced upon her. That had been the most ridiculous statement of the conversation. Tom always had the pulse of important issues but he had really missed the points on this one. Turning into the church parking lot, she reviewed her reasoning. All she wanted was a good family life. She had an opportunity for that in Minnesota and she let it slip away. After moving to the southeast, away from family and friends, she certainly would not settle for anything less. Brent had made a promise to her, and he had to live up to it. Her life had been turned upside down. The result would not be misery.

There were normally two or three retired or not actively practicing attorneys on hand to provide legal services. Today, only Annette and retired Charlotte attorney Peter Ludlow were there.

After assisting two persons, the waiting room was empty. Annette and Peter got into a conversation that centered mostly on family.

Peter asked, "Annette, where does Brent work?"

"He's director of marketing for a retail chain called Just For You."

"That's part of Richmont Corporation in Atlanta, I believe."

"Yes, it is. You familiar with the company?"

"Have you ever met Ben Voorhees, Richmont's CEO?" Peter asked.

"I have."

"Ben and I were classmates at Wake Forest. Very close friends. Still are. Until I retired three years ago, I represented Richmont's interests in North Carolina."

Annette smiled. "Well, it's a small world, isn't it?"

"Your husband works for an excellent company. And he couldn't have better leadership than Ben Voorhees. He's an excellent businessman. More than that he's a fair, good man."

"Brent's been very happy at Richmont." Annette thought she would omit the current week's turmoil.

"Looks like there aren't a lot of legal issues tormenting the populace today," Peter said waving at the waiting area. "Guess I'll call it a day."

"Think I'll give it fifteen more minutes," said Annette. "Peter, wonderful meeting you. Hope we'll be paired up again."

"Annette, you're not only a very good attorney but a charming one as well. You know how to make an old man's day," he said reaching into his briefcase, pulling out a business card and handing it to her. "If I can ever be of assistance, please give me a call. Possibly my wife and I will run into you at church. I'd enjoy meeting your husband and children."

"We'll make a point of it. Be safe going home."

Annette watched Peter Ludlow walk through the waiting room. What a nice, gentle man, she thought. And a close friend of Ben Voorhees. Great they had been paired up today. What a stroke of luck. He had said that Ben Voorhees was a fair man and he had no reason to hedge the truth with her. It validated what she had thought all along. Ben Voorhees would not permit Kruger to sack Brent because of a personality difference. People who maintain close friendships over long periods of time do so because of like philosophies and values. Peter Ludlow was a living example of a compassionate, fair-minded person. Ben Voorhees would be the same. She could not wait to tell Brent about her afternoon.

Brent walked back toward his office knowing that one more negative would be the deathblow. What could be out there to screw him? Hell, how did he know? The Faulkton deal came out of thin air. He reminded himself to quit worrying about what he did not know and concentrate on what he did. Patricia had been right. The lightning rod was Annette and tomorrow night they would be cozying up to her. To characterize Annette as a strong-willed woman would be a gross understatement. If she got pressed by the Atlanta crowd and went in orbit, it would be all over but Kruger's coronation. He knew that. Kruger knew that. How could he convince Annette that he had the ability and desire to handle both the GM job and his responsibilities as a husband and father?

He needed help. Walking into his office, he concluded that he needed someone to help him develop an argument that would reach Annette's logic. Nothing he had thought of worked. He needed a fresh perspective. Megan Randle was Annette's best friend, which meant she had heard what a creep he was and would not want anything to do with him. However, she might have some insight into Annette's perspective. It had to be worth a shot. He picked up the phone and called Megan at her interior decorating shop. Maybe she would be free for lunch.

Megan answered the phone. "Hi, Megan. It's Brent Shannon."

"Hi, Brent. What can I do for you?"

"Wondering if you're free for lunch."

"Hmm," she said in a guarded tone. "What do you want to talk about, or is this strictly social? Which would be a first."

Brent was not feeling a great deal of warmth in the conversation thus far. "No, it's not social, Megan. Like to visit with you about an issue between Annette and myself." He was getting frantic. Time was running out. If this woman told him to buzz off, he had no idea where to turn.

"Brent, I'm surprised you called me." Her tone beyond icy. "Annette's my dearest friend and if you think I'll put myself between you two, you're mistaken."

Brent could feel the hair on the back of his neck standing up. This was turning out to be one of his better ideas. "Never ask you to do that Megan."

"Seen desperate men do worse."

Brent suddenly did not know if he wanted to have lunch with her or rip her throat out. Keep your temper Shannon, he told himself. "Look, Megan. Annette's reacting to something of importance in a manner I've never seen before. Having a terrible time understanding her thinking and behavior. Know you two are close. Thought you could provide me a perspective that would help me understand her thought process. Megan, I don't know where else to turn." Begging was not something he did well but he had run out of options.

In a more amicable tone, she said, "I'm aware of your job situation. If you're asking to use me as a sounding board, might be a help to Annette more than to you."

"Can we meet for lunch?"

"Yes. Have an appointment in Ballantyne at two. Meet at Firebirds in Stonecrest, oh, about thirty minutes?"

"I'll be there. Thanks, Megan."

"See you," she said and hung up.

Good grief. He had forgotten Megan's assertive style. He had to get control of himself. This lunch would not be a hearts and flowers session but it could be instructive.

Brent told Ashley he would be out of the office until at least one-thirty and left the building. He drove up Westinghouse reviewing Annette's stance. It was out of character for her. She must not trust him at all. If this was the way she thought now, where had her mind been eight years ago? It must have been difficult for her to reconcile with him. Her trust could not have lessened since they moved south. He had been the model life-balancing act.

Negotiating the ramp to I-485, his mind drifted to Jennifer Faulkton. Until Faulkton's intercession, he had not thought of her except the fact that Patricia Bolivar was strikingly similar to Jennifer.

He met Megan at the front entrance of Firebirds. They went in and the hostess sat them in a booth.

"Megan thanks for meeting me."

"It's fine. As long as you understand, I won't take sides or get in the middle of this. In fact, I might lose a good friend if Annette knew we had lunch. I would appreciate this staying between us."

"Certainly. Megan, I've never seen Annette this way. One of her intellectual strengths has always been seeing all sides and finding a win-win resolution."

"Talked with Annette at lunch yesterday after tennis. She's convinced you'll disregard the family if you get this job. Don't know the details of your separation. Don't want to. But you must've hurt her badly."

"I did. Consumed with my job. But the experience taught me that a one dimensional life was an empty one. Done everything in my power to keep my life in perspective since our reconciliation."

"Would it be the end of the world if you didn't get the promotion? It's not like you don't have a good job now."

"But I won't have," said Brent. He filled in the blanks. The ones that Annette failed to tell her.

Megan had a surprised look. "Annette neglected to tell me that. Certain that would be the case? It's pretty severe. Sure you're not overreacting or justifying the outcome you want?"

"I've thought it through and I've seen the actions of Kruger toward me. Actions to my face. God knows what's going on behind the scenes."

"Anything else going on between you and Annette? You're right. This is unlike her."

"Nothing I know of."

Megan leaned over the table toward him. "Tell me about Patricia Bolivar."

Taken back, Brent responded, "She's the human resources director at work. Why do you ask?"

"You aware Annette's convinced you and Patricia Bolivar are having an affair?"

"Ridiculous," Brent said. He could not believe he was being confronted about this.

"Patricia Bolivar and I have a close working relationship, period. In fact, she's been seeing the same guy for a year or so and I believe it's getting serious. Why would Annette ever think that?"

"You tell me."

"I can't."

"I'll give you a supposition that'll muddy the waters but it's the only one I've got. If there's a dynamic driving Annette in addition to the time commitment, it might be, as general manager, you would have an even closer relationship with Patricia Bolivar. One that would require the two of you to travel together and so on."

"I'm doomed. I'll lose my job if I don't get promoted. My wife won't support me because she's convinced it'll consume me. And while being consumed, I'll be in bed with the human resource director. The only solution is marital trust and I'm beginning to think she doesn't trust me to take out the trash. What in hell am I supposed to do?"

"Brent, I don't pretend to have a solution. But think your assessment is pretty much on target. Truth is no one can help you with Annette. You're on your own."

"Yeah, you're right."

"Please. This has to remain between us. But you needed to know how Annette felt about you and Patricia Bolivar."

"I've made some snide remarks about Patricia but nothing that would raise a flag we're having an affair. Unless Annette's paranoid about that, too."

Walking out, Megan said, "Knock off any references about Patricia Bolivar. I can tell you unequivocally Annette thinks you and Patricia are intimate."

Leaving the restaurant, Brent said, "Thanks for seeing me. Appreciate it, and it'll stay between us."

"Good. Let's make sure of that. Good luck. I'd hate to see your marriage end over this."

Brent watched her walk away as he got in his car.

Paul Kruger's Jaguar merged onto I-77 northbound. He knew Neal Stuart would have to be well coached. Wilson's idea of matching Neal and Roth at the party was a good one, but Paul could not completely control Roth's actions. Roth might think it would be imperative to get to Voorhees before they came to Charlotte. Paul had to prepare Stuart in anticipation of Evan calling him. If it happened at the party, Stuart would be all the better prepared. Besides, Paul could not hang on Stuart's arm all Saturday night.

Paul's mind played out the upcoming lunch scenario. Mentally slow made Stuart an excellent trigger man for the affair indictment. Adding how he hated Shannon's guts made him perfect. He would be more than willing to make a few assumptions in order to get Shannon.

Paul would have to stroke him. The excellent job he had been doing. How he had not been seen or appreciated because Shannon hid him. He would tell Stuart that whoever became GM, he would make certain they knew of his talents. That ought to put him in Paul's corner. Of course, the guy was a dim bulb. He would have to be replaced. But Paul would make certain he got a decent severance.

Pulling in Harper's parking lot, he saw Neal waiting outside. Why didn't the moron go in the place? There was no need to broadcast this meeting. Of course, no one would assume that Paul would be meeting with someone on Stuart's level but no sense taking chances.

Paul acknowledged Stuart and marched into the restaurant. There was a waiting list but some first-come-first-served tables available in the bar. Paul said he had a meeting at two and guided Neal into the bar area.

"Glad you had time to meet," said Paul.

"Delighted to help anyway I can. Lunch wasn't necessary but appreciated."

"My pleasure, Neal. You make a major contribution to our division's success. Time we got to know each other better."

"Thank you."

"So. What do you think of Marlene's promotion?"

"Shocked at first. But glad. She deserves it."

"Agreed," said Paul. "Whoever takes over will have a tough time matching her accomplishments."

"Don't think so because you're going to be the new GM. Got money on you in the office pool."

Paul feigned surprise although he knew about the pool ~ almost evenly split between him and Shannon. "Appreciate your confidence but don't think I'll get the nod. Be honored if I did, though.

"Neal, I recognize the contribution you've made to the marketing efforts of the division. And I assure you the new GM will know about them. That's my message today. Thought it better said outside the office."

"Thanks, Paul," said a beaming Stuart. "Didn't think anyone noticed my efforts. Your support means a lot."

This would be easier than he anticipated, Paul thought. "I've always thought it odd but Brent seems to get in the way of you shining and being recognized for the professional you are. Been a rift between the two of you?"

"Brent's very opinionated on how things should be done. Doesn't leave a lot of room for others' creativity. He's a stifling boss."

"A micro-manager. That's too bad. That type of management hurts everyone involved."

"You can say that again."

"It's too bad I'm probably not going to get the GM job because I'd see you having a much expanded role in management."

"Don't think Shannon's getting it, do you?"

"I think there's an excellent chance," said Paul. "But that would mean an automatic promotion for you, Neal. You should be excited."

"You kidding? No way Shannon's giving me the director job. Has his eye on an assistant marketing guy in Atlanta."

Paul thought that he and Brent could agree on one thing. The incompetence of this boob. "That would be a travesty of justice, Neal. After the loyal support you've given Brent. You certain?"

"Yeah. Overheard conversations."

"I'll guarantee if Brent's the new GM, I'll try my best to dissuade him from bringing someone else in."

"God that would be great. Thanks a lot. Can never repay you for befriending me."

Oh, yes you can, little man, Paul thought. "Of course, if Brent becomes GM, Patricia Bolivar would be the only person with a certain job. They seem to relate very well to each other."

"Yeah. I'm sure some's social. Real social."

Paul waved his hand in a dismissive manner. "I've heard those rumors for over a year. I don't think there's anything to them."

"Don't be sure of that. Seen them together at business social functions and they looked pretty friendly. Seen them at lunch and having drinks after work. Twice they didn't see me. They looked more than friendly."

"Are you being serious, Neal?"

"As a heart attack."

"It would be serious indeed if they were involved," said Paul. "Especially with Richmont's organizational culture. Mr. Voorhees is a very devout Christian and wouldn't tolerate it. I'm certainly not going anywhere with it. It's unsubstantiated and would look close to unethical if I brought it up given the current situation."

"You're the only one I've mentioned it to," said Neal. "I'm sure not planning on spreading it around."

"Excellent idea. But be careful. If you're asked by a company officer, you must tell what you know. You don't and it's found out later you had been aware of something, your job could be in the balance. We don't want that to happen. With this change in GM's, your job might become much more rewarding."

"Damn. Don't want to get screwed because of Shannon."

"You don't have to be. If someone in authority asks you about Brent and Patricia's relationship, just say you've seen instances where they appeared to be more intimate than appropriate. You've made no accusation but cleared yourself. I'm sorry, Neal, but I've got to run." He paid for lunch with cash. No expensing this rendezvous.

Walking to their cars, Neal said, "Thanks for helping me, Paul. Don't think anyone would ask me about Brent and Patricia, do you?"

"I really don't know. Rumor's been going around for a year that I know of. If something comes up during Atlanta's decision about Marlene's replacement, they'll check it out. You're the senior person reporting to Brent. If it were me, I'd pick your name out."

Paul could see the color drain from Stuart's face. He had to fight back a laugh. "But don't worry. Just go back to doing your typically superb work. If someone calls, handle it as we discussed. Everything'll work out fine."

Neal shook Paul's hand. "Thanks again. Really appreciate it."

"No thanks are necessary, old boy. Keep doing your fine work. Now I must go," said Paul getting in his car.

Driving back to the office, Paul assessed Stuart as more of a fool than he originally thought. At least two slices short of a full loaf. Shannon must have made a commitment to Stuart's church to keep the guy employed. He wouldn't last a week in his department or the division after Paul's promotion. However, he would be perfect for Evan's call. It would be the fatal thrust. Shannon's reputation would collapse. There would be justice for all the hurt he had endured at the hands of vermin like Shannon. He could not wait to tell his mother. She would be so proud.

Brent drove back to the office in dismay. What an absolute goat screw. Annette had gone kuku for coco puffs, as the kids would say. Megan had been a strike out. A nice woman but couldn't help. She had given him the affair heads-up. That twist of fate would have occurred to him about as much as Faulkton coming out of the early morning mist to stomp the crap out of him.

Brent walked in the front entrance where he saw Patricia just ahead of him. He caught up to her and asked if she had a couple of minutes to come back to his office. A yes got him to lead the way.

In Brent's office, they sat in the two arm chairs in front of his desk. Brent knew he had to be careful how he approached this subject. Patricia was his one ally. He could not afford to have her bail on him.

"Patricia, know anyone in Atlanta who's heavy into the grapevine?"

"I'd mentioned Todd Beamon before."

"Not the official grapevine. The, 'did you hear about this,' kind."

"Todd's good with that kind, too. His wife Marilyn used to work for the company and had been the acknowledged gossip queen. She's raising kids fulltime now but really stays in contact. If you're talking dirt, she probably knows it. And Todd has a passion for it. If she knows, he knows. What's the topic?"

"This's difficult for me to bring up with you."

"What's wrong?"

"My wife's convinced you and I are having an affair."

"You've got to be freakin' kidding me," Patricia responded as her face turned crimson. "This is starting to really upset me."

"What?"

"This's the second time this week I've had this thrown in my face."

Brent could see she was either close to tears or to killing somebody. "Second time?" he said. "The other?"

She recounted her conversation on Thursday with Nadia Swenson.

"I don't believe everyone feels that way," said Brent. "But I can see Nadia making a comment like that."

"This is terrible, Brent. People are going out of their way to ruin our reputations."

Brent saw tears welling up in her eyes and he felt helpless. His stomach almost revolted. He went to his desk, got a box of tissues and handed it to her.

"Patricia, no one's reputation's been lost yet. But you have to talk to Beamon to see if anything's circling around the Atlanta rumor mill. And rest assured. Annette might think it but she's not stupid enough to mention it to anyone but Megan."

Patricia looked at him and was visibly shaking. "First, your wife or not, she's out of bounds. Second, she could make an issue about it at the party Saturday night."

"Annette's assertive. But she's not spiteful."

"Brent, I never meant to hurt you. Just considered you a very close business associate. Kinda business soulmate. Nothing else."

Brent wanted to comfort her but he knew if he touched her, she would break down in tears and throw her arms around him. That would only exacerbate the problem and, with his luck, Marlene would pick that moment to walk in.

"I know that. But Nadia's correct about one thing," Brent said. "Perception's truth. Please get on the phone and discreetly see if anything's out there to put a stake in our hearts."

"I'll start making inquiries right now," she said.

"You close enough to Beamon's wife to call her? Might keep things out of the loop."

"Let me think. No, don't think there's anything in the past to prevent me from doing that."

"We have to be proactive. If Kruger's going to launch something, we have to get to Marlene before he does it."

Patricia stood up, took one more tissue and went to the door. "I'll get right on it as soon as I reconstruct my face in the ladies room."

"We'll get through this," Brent said. He thought that brought a little smile as she left his office. At least, he could be glad he gave her something to smile about.

After running several errands, Annette was driving home. Although still distraught, she saw a glimmer of hope. The conversation with her brother had been horrible. He never even tried to see her point.

The discussion with Peter Ludlow had been the opposite. She could give her husband an in with the CEO of Richmont. She could become Brent's partner. Tom angered her but he knew business. If Brent's fear was legitimate, with Peter Ludlow and Ben Voorhees' friendship, his job would be secure.

She felt marvelous and had to discuss her new-found hope with someone. She called Megan and said she was dropping by the shop.

When she arrived they went to the back room and sat down with tall glasses of iced tea.

"I had a long talk with my brother Tom this morning," Annette said. "He convinced me that Brent might have a point about losing his job."

"I think he does, too," said Megan. "Glad you recognized it. Talked to Mel and he said Brent had a reason to be concerned."

"Sorry you felt compelled to discuss this with your husband."

"Good lord, Annette. He's not putting an ad in the Observer about it. I'm concerned and needed some input."

"Well, I've got the answer to the 'losing his job' problem."

"I'm all ears."

"Met a gentleman at the church's legal assistance project. Name's Peter Ludlow. He's a close friend of Ben Voorhees, the CEO of Richmont."

"Interesting."

"Sure is," said Annette. "I can use Peter Ludlow as an in with Ben Voorhees so Kruger can't do anything to Brent."

"You're not serious," said Megan.

"Dead serious."

"Consider this. I have two shops and hire a new manager for one. New manager has some plausible reasons why she doesn't think the assistant can carry the load. She wants to replace her. You meet the assistant's spouse and he asks you to intervene with me. Of course, you don't know any of the particulars. Would you intervene? And if you were so stupid as to do so, would I listen to you or have any future respect for you?"

"That's a flawed analogy," said Annette. "Wouldn't be that way at all."

"It's not flawed and you aren't thinking straight."

"No. I'm the only one thinking straight. It's my life and I'm not going down the same path with Brent again."

"What's wrong with this picture?" said Megan. "You're driving me nuts. The poor man's been true to his word for eight years. That's a long time. Know guys who wouldn't keep that commitment for a week. You know, I think Brent's a hell of a guy. You oughta thank your stars you've got him. I know women who'd kill for a man like him."

Annette felt herself losing control. This was her best friend talking. "That's sweet. But he's never been tested. All it takes is one time. Just add some pressure or responsibility to get those juices of his flowing. And may I remind you, not just one set of juices."

"What are you talking about?" said Megan. "Is the real problem you're afraid he'll have a love affair with Bolivar if he gets the GM job?"

"Not future tense. Think he's having an affair with her now."

"You have proof?"

"No."

"Listen. You think your husband's going to discount his family if he gets this job. Although for eight years, by your own admission, he's put the family first. He's also having an affair but you've no proof. You're bonkers. There's more to this."

"No, there isn't. And my thinking's fine. I'm sick of people saying I'm not thinking right."

"Well, honey, everybody can't be wrong."

"Okay. Okay. Let's assume Brent's having an affair," continued Megan. "Is that the core problem? You think the GM job will make it easier for him to be with the woman?"

"Never thought of that," said Annette. "But it makes a good reason why he should stay put or maybe lose his job."

"What fallacious thinking. If you think Brent's having an affair, confront him with it. Otherwise, drop it. Or are you afraid what the answer might be?"

"That's silly."

"Why's that silly? Easy for you to jump in Brent's face over the work commitment. Why not the affair?"

"This discussion's ridiculous," said Annette. "Wanted your opinion how to best use the Peter Ludlow contact."

"Can't. It's that simple."

"I have to go," Annette said. "Kids'll be getting home."

"We're best friends, Annette," said Megan. "But this story's bigger than you've shared with me."

"Not so," said Annette. She kissed Megan on the cheek and walked out of the shop.

Why is the entire world crazy except for me, she thought as she got in her car?

Brent was sitting at his desk scanning the merchandise list from the catalog division when his phone rang.

"Brent Shannon."

"Brent, Terry from Ms. Wolff's office. She'd like to see you in the main conference room."

"What have I done now?"

"She didn't elaborate."

"Okay. Thanks, Terry." What now, he thought. One more kick in the ass would be terminal.

Brent headed for the main conference room. On the way, he stuck his head in Dina's office door. "Tell catalog what they can do with that merchandise they offered to send us. But do it nicely, Dina. They might have something decent down the road."

"Okay, boss," she replied. "Terrible, wasn't it?"

"You're assessment's too kind," he said.

He walked in the conference room to find Marlene alone. "Terry called. Wanted to see me?"

"Yes. And don't look so worried. No skeleton fell out of your closet."

"New twist for the day, isn't it."

"Sit down. I've been thinking about our earlier conversation. Need some blanks filled in about you and Annette."

The tone in her voice was concerning. What could she be missing? "How can I help? Told you Annette would be fine with it."

"You just said *would*. That gets me concerned. You used *will* in our first conversation and would now. Why's it would and will instead of is? You telling me Annette is okay with the increased commitments and time away from Charlotte? Or you telling me you've got convincing to do? Or you telling me she's fighting you? She's a strong-willed woman."

"Marlene, she's nervous about it. But I've proven over the past eight years I can keep my priorities straight."

"I know this is personal but it's important. How did you satisfy her your priorities would be kept straight? Knowing Annette, I'd think there'd be some pretty objective criteria required."

"We're in the process of doing that," said Brent. "But there'd be nothing that'd prevent me from giving the necessary commitment to the job."

"Brent, a GM job for a business of this size with its geographical dispersion can consume anyone. Needs never end. Always something, somewhere, that someone thinks is the most important thing in the world. Some you can plan. Some you can't. A significant number you can't."

"I understand that," said Brent. He became more uncomfortable with each passing moment.

"You understand it conceptually. But you've never lived it. People want a general management job because it puts them in control. Not so, I'm afraid. Reality is, your time's no longer your resource but the resource of others. Going to be times you'll have to call to say you can't make this or that. You telling me Annette's going to be able to handle that lifestyle without problems?"

"She's fine with it. Long as I do it when the business necessitates it, not use it as an excuse or make mountains out of molehills."

"Who'll determine necessity, you or Annette?"

"Marlene, you're hurting my feelings. Never thought you'd think it necessary to quiz me like this." Getting upset, Brent had to use every bit of his discipline to control himself.

"Maybe I'm out of line," responded Marlene. "But I'm not in the habit of breaking up marriages because of my business decisions. My marriage ended because I couldn't see mixing career and kids. It was something Frank and I should've discussed and didn't. Brushed it over. Neither one of us wanted to squarely face a core issue to a successful marriage."

"Never realized you were married."

"Because you were never so rude as to pry into my personal life as I'm doing to you. But it's a sensitive issue for me. Sensitive for the company, too. Ben Voorhees is aware of families and the conflict business responsibilities can bring to them. Some people snicker behind his back about being a Bible thumper. But they can be thankful he's the way he is. He's saved more than one career and family with his Christian ethic and compassion.

"As far as marriages are concerned, promotions to bigger jobs are almost analogous to having kids. Neither has been a high probability fix for a flawed marriage. The company's track record has been dismal when promoting a person to a bigger job who faces marital issues.

"Sorry for the third degree. But, I felt obligated to the company and you to discuss this if I continued to support you. My reputation is riding on this every bit as much as yours."

"Know that and won't let you down."

"All right. Let's make certain there's no miscommunication. You've just told me that Annette is comfortable and supports your candidacy one hundred percent. Is that correct?"

"Correct," replied Brent. Oh, what a web we weave, he thought. He was up to his hips in alligators. Why not venture deeper in the swamp.

"If I were to visit with Annette at the party tomorrow night, she would concur with this conversation we've just had?"

This woman is too bright, Brent thought. She had put him in a hole. First, Kruger's hole. Now, his mentor's hole. He'd had more defining moments in the last twenty-four hours than most people had in a lifetime. But he hoisted up his trusty hip boots and kept on trudging. What a masochist.

"Yes."

"Okay. You've got my support, marketing man. But no more screw-ups. And one more time. Everything's fine with Annette?"

Brent got up to leave. "No problem."

"Cool. Hang in there."

Brent left the conference room realizing that the last fifteen minutes left him with no control. He had put Annette in control, and she did not even know it. What would come of his life? He had painted himself into a very tight corner. The only person who could slay the cannibals at his door was his wife.

Back in his office, Brent realized this had been the first time he had ever hedged the truth with his boss. Hedged, hell, he lied to her. He wanted Marlene's job and his career at Richmont. But, he had put himself into an intolerable position. Wish there was somebody else to blame. Smart. Really smart. He needed his dentist again. He called George Barnes.

When George got on the phone, Brent said, "Need a drink."

"Okay. Can't stay long. We got tickets to see something I don't understand. But who gives a damn about me? My ability to absorb the arts has always been suspect. So. Meet you at Village Bistro in thirty minutes."

"Done."

Walking into Village Bistro, Brent saw George at the bar talking to Gary, one of the owners. Brent waved and he followed George to an outside table.

After getting their drinks, Brent recounted the day's activities.

"I'm supposed to help you, how?" said George. "Didn't get to first base with Annette, did you?"

"No."

"I concur she's on another planet but that's irrelevant. She's tuned you out, my friend. And this last little action with Marlene puts Annette in the driver's seat. Stroke of genius."

"Yeah, no doubt." George had really made him want to kick something.

"And let's clear up something. No such thing as hedging the truth. Either tell the truth or lie. Nothing in between. There're reasons to lie. Like not hurting other people's feelings over inconsequential things. This wasn't inconsequential. Can't believe you did that."

"What the hell was I supposed to do?" said Brent. "If I said anything else, Marlene would've withdrawn her support for me."

"Well, you'd better do the lovey, smootchy with Annette cause you've set it up for her to hold all the trump cards. She can fuck you big time now and I'm not talking about the feel-good kind. Good you have some time."

"There's something else."

"Oh lordy. Can't wait."

"There's a big going away bash for Marlene tomorrow night with spouses. Everybody, and I mean everybody, will be there."

"Brent, my man, you qualify for the Dumb-Shit-of-the-Week award. Just how're you planning on pulling this off?"

"Got to convince Annette to support me."

"I'm not the one to counsel anyone on marital relations being I'm on number three," said George. "But I'd level with Annette about your conversation with Marlene."

"How's that going to help?" asked Brent.

"Only thing you've got left in your bag is Annette's loyalty. They get to her on Saturday night and she doesn't back you, you're going to lose more than this promotion. Answer me this. How do smart guys like you get into these jams?"

"Really quite easily."

"Really screwed the pooch on this one, ole buddy."

"Thanks, friend. Your support nearly brings tears to my eyes."

"What? Want me to blow smoke? Should've told me."

"Got any words of wisdom about my talk with Annette?"

"Humble pie wouldn't hurt. Throw yourself on the mercy of the court," said George. "You've dug yourself a swell grave. Throw away the damn shovel and climb out the best way you can. Got to go pal. Good luck."

Brent watched George walk away, moved inside to the bar and ordered another Wild Turkey from Gary. His best friend now thought him to be a certified idiot. How could it get any better? Maybe he should tell the whole story to Gary. Naw. Nobody in their right mind would believe it.

Annette was in the kitchen cooking dinner. She could not go beef but did get pork chops. She came home determined to get Brent turned to her point of view. She had sent the kids to Mitchell's. She fibbed and told Doris that she and Brent had a special occasion to celebrate.

Earlier, she had showered and spent a great deal of time getting ready. Normally, they went out on Friday nights with the kids but she would tell him that the world had been so strained the past two days, an evening at home alone would be relaxing.

She had put on makeup with care. She knew Brent's definition of her physical beauty. Smokey, steel eye shadow highlighted her large crystal blue eyes. Just enough lip color to provide soft definition.

She had picked out her clothes with equal care. A v-neck stretch halter top with a faux wrap look. It had a side tie at the waist and a neck with sufficient exposure to be interesting. The side tie allowed the loose fit that Annette wanted. It was bare backed and made of silver rayon, metallic material with a string tie across the shoulders. Annette had completed her outfit with black satin pants that fit her like a second skin.

She set the dining room table as she had last night except she used a damask table cloth, sterling flatware, Lennox china and Waterford crystal water goblets and wines. She had looked in the wine cooler to make certain bottles of Geyser Peak Cabernet were available, Brent's favorite. Annette felt almost collegeish with her planning and she had to admit it really turned her on.

She had been unbending in her demands of Brent but not certain why. However, her life would be less than it should be if he took Marlene's job. Of that she felt certain. He had disappeared to the black hole of his work before and he would do it again. The kids would be an afterthought. He would leave her at home at a moment's notice and their sex life would be nonexistent. Brent thrived on making love with her assertive, sometimes aggressive, participation. But he would become preoccupied. Even if the desire arose, he would not be able to perform. It had happened in Minneapolis. In this whole screwy affair, she knew he had not thought of that consequence. Of how close they became when making love. Of the passion transformed to sexual ecstasy. Being transported, as one, to an intimate oasis sealed off from worldly concerns. The two of them physically and emotionally bonded together. Annette had decided she would show him that tonight. Aggressively take him to that world where they luxuriated in each others' closeness.

She heard Brent in the back hall. He came into the kitchen and said, "Thought we'd be going out with the kids tonight. Maybe that Chinese joint at Stonecrest."

"The last two days have been so stressful," she said smiling suggestively. "I thought a nice evening at home was in order. Arranged for the kids to stay at Doris and Pete's.

"Honey, sounds great to me."

Annette moved slowly to him, put her arms around his neck and kissed him lingeringly while caressing the back of his head with soft fingers. She could feel he expected the customary short and sweet but she continued the kiss and opened her mouth to accept him if he wanted. At the same time, she pressed the length of her body against him. He responded as she knew he would. She felt him growing as she began to pull away.

She looked into his eyes. Ones that told of his desire for her. "Can't we just have a nice evening alone?"

"Absolutely."

Annette went back to finishing dinner while Brent built himself a Wild Turkey on the rocks.

"Want a drink, honey?"

"No. Think wine for dinner will be fine. That daughter of ours is getting more precocious by the minute."

Brent laughed. "So what did she do now? She already acts like a ten-year-old Cameron Diaz."

"Just her whole being. She's a trip."

"Speaking of trip, traffic in this town's going from bad to awful."

"Yeah, I was at the legal advisors group today. Was a slow day, so I had time to go over to Southpark. What a mess that's become."

"Whole town's outgrowing itself. Oh, by the way, there's a going away party for Marlene tomorrow night. Hope we don't have anything planned. Not optional attendance. Sorry about the late notice but I missed it on my e-mail."

"We're free. Isn't that nice of the company? Be good to see everyone."

"Be great to see Erik's game tomorrow," he said.

"He's so looking forward to having you there." Annette wanted to stay away from anything controversial and it seemed Brent did, too. An excellent sign. They had a wonderful dinner with Annette beginning to feel dreamy and amorous. Wine had always been her most potent aphrodisiac.

"Darling, let's go in the den and have some cognac," she said. God, she needed him. It had been two weeks and she was hungry for him.

"Wonderful," he said. "First I'd like to tell you about tomorrow night."

"Sweetie. We have all day tomorrow to talk about it."

"Not without Tawney around."

Annette's instincts didn't like the heading this conversation seemed to be taking. But in order to get to step two, she knew they had to talk.

She kept her voice low and sensual. "Okay. It must be about work. What's going on?" She had a low voice for a woman and when she lowered it further it became a wonderful advantage in these scenes.

"I never mentioned a girl by the name of Jennifer Faulkton but I went with her for a while at Madison. College romance. Anyway, got crossways with her father. He said some derogatory things about my family and I lost my temper. He was steamed. Well, seems like he's got a long memory. He's the newest member of the Richmont board and lectured Ben Voorhees on how I shouldn't be given any responsible job. Did a hatchet job on me."

"Let me tell you something that'll make you feel better," Annette responded. "At the legal clinic, I met Peter Ludlow. Guess what? He's a personal friend of Ben Voorhees. Went to Wake Forest together and are still close friends. He said there wasn't a more fair or good man than Ben. No way is he going to hold something against you like that."

"Annette, Faulkton and Voorhees have a board relationship. It's not as easy as you would like to make it."

Annette came around the table and pulled a chair up to the table corner by Brent. "Darling, I think you're over blowing this."

She leaned on the table with one elbow and her other hand rubbed Brent's arm. She smiled to herself. Brent could not keep his eyes off her.

"Honey, I'd feel better if I got what's concerning me off my mind. Then I could completely relax with you."

"All right, Brent," she said fighting her sensual trance. "But let's at least do it over cognac." If he was as hot for her as she was for him, the conversation would be very short.

"Okay," he said. "Cognac's great." As he stood, Annette put her arms around his neck and kissed gently but with urgency. Her mouth opened. His tongue penetrated deeply. Her erotic feelings became frantic when his hand traveled down her back and found the satin mounds of her buttocks. He began to caress them with slow circular motions. She moaned softly and pressed firmly into him. He gently pulled away interrupting her bliss.

"Come on, honey," he said. "Let's talk a minute."

She could hardly open her eyes. Who's seducing who, she thought. "Go into the den," she said with a husky voice. "Make yourself comfortable, sweetheart. I'll get us cognac." She had to clear her head a bit. She could not remember a time in the last few years when she had been as overcome with desire for Brent. When he surrendered to her she would make him remember this night for a very long time. It would not be something he would want to lose.

She went to the bar, got out two Waterford brandy snifters and gave each a double pour of Remy Martin. Going to the den, she found Brent staring at her with eyes containing measures of somberness and sexual desire.

"Come on, sweetie," she said. "Sit over here on the sofa with me." Annette knew she had to get Brent relaxed and focused on her as his wife and lover. She knew he loved her and longed to make love with her. Long, slow, passionate love. That would be tonight. Brent does not want to lose his family, she thought. She would show him that intimacy with her was much more satisfying than with the Bolivar husband-stealing ogress.

Brent moved to the sofa and took the snifter. "That's quite a pour, Annette. You want us not to make it up the stairs?"

Annette smiled a slow smile. "It's a thought."

"Baby, we need to discuss something and we need to do it before the cognac," he said.

Annette could see him having a difficult time concentrating. Good. It mirrored her condition exactly. He probably wanted to tell her that it would be horrible to tell Marlene he didn't want her job and he would handle it tomorrow night. Why couldn't that wait until morning?

"Annette, honey, we need a serious discussion this weekend about what it would take to allay your fears about me being division GM."

She moved closer to him. "Sweetie, we've already discussed it and there's nothing to be done." She put her hand on the back of his neck and began to slowly massage it. "You'll have to take a pass on this promotion." She snuggled to him softly, kissed his ear and outlined it with her tongue. "Lover, there'll be other days and other promotions. Now can't this wait till morning?" She smoothly put his hand inside her halter making certain his fingertip felt her hardening nipple. She had become consumed with throbbing desire. Please, she thought. Don't talk. Make love to me.

Brent gently pulled away from her again. "Annette, we're going to have to discuss things because I told Marlene today that I wanted her job. I want to explain why. I know you have serious misgivings but I think we could develop guidelines that would put your mind at ease."

Annette's emotional universe traversed from erotic desire to revulsion and hostility in a millisecond. The trip had been much like the bends. She felt her stomach churn and develop a tremendous need to vomit but she had been able to choke it back. Her vision of Brent turned from lover to rotten, self-serving ingrate. Tears came to her eyes. Annette's entire existence became so filled with rage that she could hardly see.

Annette responded in a low, measured tone. "Why don't you repeat what you just said?"

"Had to give Marlene an answer. Told her I wanted her job. If you'll listen to me, think I can make you feel more comfortable and secure. We've gone through some challenging times before and made it."

Annette's body felt as if it were exploding. "All the challenging times were your making." She wanted to throw things. She had to get away from this career-crazed scoundrel who thought of no one but himself. The miserable, self-consumed fool. After all she had given up for him. Her career. Being near her family. The other chances she'd had for happiness.

"You unmitigated charlatan," she spat at him. "I'm going upstairs and you stay the hell away from me. Really don't give a damn where you sleep but it's not with me. You insufferable cad. Why don't you go over and maybe Bolivar will give you some." She hated for him to see her crying but she couldn't help it. He was sitting on the sofa in stunned silence. Good, she thought.

Annette got up so fast she spilled her snifter. She ran upstairs, slammed the bedroom door and locked it. Her tears were flowing freely as she stripped off her clothes and jumped nude under the covers. Tom had been right, she thought through her tears. Her husband's a taker. God, what a deceitful animal. Distraught as well as drunk, her mind allowed her to only think of the disintegration of her life.

Annette's heart finally stopped palpitating and she began to breathe normally. This allowed the alcohol to perform its magic. Her thoughts of Brent disappeared. Annette's hands freely roamed her body and found places of wonderful pleasures. She had done her best, she thought, as her mind and body began to enter the kingdom of self-induced escape. No one could see the world as it existed for her. Her last thought before giving herself to autoeroticism had been that she knew one person who would.

Paul drove into his cul de sac knowing the day had gone well. The emergence of Faulkton as a silent partner had been a gift from heaven if there was such a place. If, as the religious cults proclaimed, there was an Almighty, how were people like those he grew up with allowed to exist? Then he had been cursed with one in his business life. Well, that problem would soon be solved. Not by any Almighty but by Paul Kruger.

Faulkton was not a silent partner because he had not been silent. Paul had to laugh. If he did not despise Shannon so much, he would feel sorry for the swine. He pulled in the driveway reviewing the meeting with Stuart. It had gone well and he was anxious to cover the entire day with Audra.

In the house, he found her in the family room having a drink adorned in a bikini.

"Hi, babe," he said. "At the pool this afternoon?"

"Took a swim after tennis," she replied. Paul thought it best not to ask with whom.

"How'd your day go?"

Paul filled her in on the Faulkton blowup with Ben Voorhees.

"It's no better than that," she said. She walked to the wet bar and began to build another drink for herself. "What you like?"

Paul knew what this evening would bring. He could see it in her eyes. This would not be the evening to travel to scotch paradise. "I'll pass."

"Don't be silly. It's celebration time, sugar." She poured him a sizeable Dewar on the rocks.

Paul watched Audra at the bar. A very attractive woman, she had beautiful, well proportioned facial features. She had high cheekbones, a thin perfect nose set between expressive green eyes and full lips. Quite thin with small breasts and hips, she carried herself in a manner that exuded confidence and sexuality. Paul knew other men had experienced her eroticism since their marriage. In fact, all evidence pointed to at least one and possibly two current lovers. She had an insatiable appetite for variety, which did not bother Paul as long as discretion was the rule and he did not know the men. It came with the territory. He knew she had been a wanderer when they married. However, he had not married her for fidelity but for her social and political savvy and family name. She was old south and grew to adulthood traveling in social circles denied him because he had been sired by a barbarian. The influence of her family hadn't come to fruition yet but it would with time. This promotion would facilitate it.

Audra had been forthright. She had married him not for undying love and devotion but because she saw someone with the talent to be extraordinarily successful. He had been no fool. Also, he recognized another commanding reason had been an opportunity to torment her father. Paul always had to remind himself that her loyalty was fragile and inextricably tied to his success. Hell, he could deal with that. He did not need her to give his life meaning. He needed her to help him get to a position where his life would have meaning. After that, she could move on and he would gladly pipe her off the good ship Kruger.

He followed her with his gaze as she walked back to the sofa with the drinks. Her bikini had the top tied in the front. The bottom had ties on each hip. If both pieces had been put together, there would not be enough material to make a man's tie. Her walk and the look in her eyes told Paul her drinking had started much earlier in the day.

Audra sat down close to Paul with one arm over the back of the sofa and her knee touching his. "So. What else happened?"

"Had lunch with Neal Stuart. Got him primed for a call from Evan. God, he's half a loaf."

"Better talk to him again. Redundancy's a necessary waste of time when dealing with idiots. He in the office on Saturdays?"

"I don't know. But I'll talk to him again."

"Things go as planned, sugar, you'll be the GM by early next week. And everything's going to go as planned, isn't it?"

"Yes, babe. Everything's set."

"Glorious," she said. She moved closer to Paul. "We can mold the division into what we want. Want to be your partner, sugar." Her hand moved to rest on Paul's thigh. "Shannon and that bitch Bolivar will be gone. Voorhees will take care of that with the affair impropriety. Damn, he'll crucify them." She laughed in a witchlike shrill.

Paul never ceased to be astonished by Audra. How could she be so drunk and remain so lucid? He certainly didn't possess that quality.

"Hey. Finish your drink, guy," said Audra. "I want another and it's impolite not to keep up."

As soon as Paul drained his glass, she grabbed it and slowly moved to the bar to fix two more with her bikini bottom riding very low on her hips. She did nothing to adjust it. He knew what would end this night. Paul excused himself, went to the first floor master bedroom and got the container of blue diamond-shaped pills from his bedside table. He cut one in half and swallowed it with a splash of water. Returning to the den, he saw Audra sitting on the sofa with a smile and a whimsical look in her eyes.

"Come sit by me, sugar," she said. Sugar was her code name for wanting him to transport her to a state of rapture and exhilaration that only he could provide.

"After the promotion, you'll have to establish your authority. Should be no question who's boss and the culture's changed. Quite a change for them, sugar." She gently outlined his ear with her finger. Paul could smell her breath. Heavy with the sweet scent of Maker's Mark. "Think we should have the direct reports with spouses over for dinner," she continued. "I'll be able to help you determine their level of loyalty to us. Those who don't pass the test can find work elsewhere."

"Great idea, babe," he responded. Amazing, he thought. Planning with absolute lucidity while on her sixth or seventh drink. How could her small body consume that much bourbon and still function? Plus, drunk or sober she embodied the most nefarious soul he had ever known. A perfect mate.

Audra's hand slid to the back of his neck and she laid her head on his shoulder. Her other hand began to unbutton Paul's shirt. "Going to be wonderful to be in power, my love," she purred. "So proud of you and we've a perfect right to celebrate. Powerful men have always turned me on. I need some lovin' from my sugar."

His shirt undone, Audra leaned him forward with her hand at his neck and deftly pulled it off. She gave him gentle butterfly kisses on his neck, cheeks and forehead while unbuckling his belt. As she began to caress his manhood, his senses were filled with the aroma of perfume and sweet bourbon.

Paul kneeled at the sofa. With one hand on her arm and one in her hair, he pushed her tenderly to a position on her back. Her eyes were glazed and fixed on him. There was an almost serene look about her. He had always been struck with wonder that this completely Svengali human could take on a cherubic tranquility at times like these.

"Sugar, please do me," she sighed as Paul lightly traced the curves of her upper body. His lips touched her chin and then inched their way slowly down her neck to the soft skin between her breasts. Her arms stayed at her side, and her breathing turned to a soft rasp.

After thirty minutes of Paul carrying her to erotic bliss, Audra emitted a piercing scream and raised her hips off the sofa. Her breathing caught twice and she exploded in orgasm. After five spasms, Audra Kruger collapsed. Fully spent.

Oh no, my little sex slave, Paul thought. The night is young and it's repayment time. He gently lifted and moved her as far over on the sofa as the overstuffed back would allow. Nude, he laid down next to her with his head at her feet. Paul rubbed her inner thigh and buttock cheeks gently. She purred softly and turned toward his body. She knew her sexual role. Paul had placed himself perfectly and her warm, sweet mouth engulfed his hard manhood. Warmth flowed through Paul's body as Audra expertly ministered to his need. His mind escaped to a different place and a different lover. The one he longed for in his thoughts and dreams.

Brent Shannon watched, in disbelief, as Annette stormed out of the den. He heard her crying while rushing up the stairs. A door slammed. Their bedroom door, he assumed. He concluded that it would be locked and an attempt to enter, would place his long-term health in question.

Dinner went well, he thought. What a fiasco. Let's see. Yep, he thought. Tonight was the first time his pants stayed on when Annette wanted screwed. Another record. A memorable week with one day left.

His destiny had been handed to Annette. By him. To help the cause, he proceeded to alienate her to a degree never achieved in the past. Brilliant. When she stormed out, her face showed pure disgust. A hate-filled expression that he had not seen during the darkest days of their separation. Perhaps his directness had not been an appropriate tactic. But he had tried the oblique approach yesterday and she had picked up on nothing. It could be that he should have re-evaluated his timing when he saw her drunk as a skunk on Geyser Peak and hot as he'd ever seen her. Another splendid decision. Damn, she had a dynamite body and he adored making love to her.

He shook his mind to clear those thoughts. Not productive to dwell on things he seemed to be working hard to lose. If he had a roadmap to destruction with the route highlighted, could he have screwed this up any better? He didn't think so. Brent went to the wine cabinet and uncorked another bottle of Geyser Peak. Might as well get rip roaring drunk. Sometimes he came up with really creative stuff in that condition.

He went back to the den and slumped in a chair. This would be the first time in their marriage that Annette had not been willing to discuss an issue and work to find common ground.

Why so different now? Why this apparent one-hundred-eighty degree change? Brent had read the Mars, Venus thing when he started working for a woman but this was something else. Not a personality change because her other behavior had remained vintage Annette. This was a foreign approach to their marital relationship. She had always been lead dog in analyzing courses of action and she was doing that now. But for the first time, it became win-lose. Moreover, it was in a way that communicated that if Brent did not comply, lose would be acceptable to her. A first.

Geyser Peak lost its appeal. Brent went to cognac. Nothing like real fire water to sharpen the senses. He drifted back to the months of their separation. He had been distraught. He had driven to Sauk Center to spend a weekend with his sister Cory. Cory had married Tony Weiser and lived on a small dairy farm west of Madison. The visit had solidified his determination to reconcile with Annette because he had seen the dynamics of a good marriage. During that weekend, he had realized his work not to be the problem, rather his obsession with it.

He had been blind to the fact that although marriage produced dependence, it was shared dependence. By its nature, shared dependence demanded a healthy measure of independence by each party. His egocentrism had permitted him to conclude that his success would outweigh any needs of Annette. Cory had been his savior. She had helped him realize that he could have a fulfilling family life and a satisfying career. One did not preclude the other as long as one maintained proper perspective and priority.

Brent poured his third cognac. The stuff tasted better with each snifter. Maybe because it was older. He racked his brain but nowhere in their reconciliation discussions could he remember it being decided that Annette had the authority to unilaterally make decisions impacting his career. He loved Annette and the children desperately but he would have never agreed to that stipulation. Never. No, it had never been mentioned. Yet it was playing out that way.

Maybe she had another lover. A thought that caused him to tip the Remy Martin bottle toward his snifter again. He didn't think so. She loved the children too much. Of course, the children would go with her. She could almost out earn him now. But her morals would kick in, wouldn't they? "Don't know," he murmured to the bottom of the snifter. It could be someone else. It would not be out of the realm of possibility that she could be attracted to another man. Certainly enough around and Annette was easy on the eyes. Someone she considered stable and caring could be very appealing to her. Maybe he had a business in Charlotte with a local customer base. Never had to travel. Home for all the goody events. Okay. Who was the rotten, conniving son of a bitch? Brent poured another cognac and almost missed the snifter. Miserable character. If he thinks he's going to ruin my life, he's got another think coming. Another long draw on the Remy Martin crystallized his strategy. He would kill the guy. That would do it.

Brent laid his head back on the chair and stared at the ceiling. A very productive thinking session, he decided. So drunk he planned on killing some poor guy who played a couple of sets of tennis with Annette.

Something did not make sense in this scenario. A perfect time for Annette to find someone else would have been during their separation. What did she do? She ran home to her family and the safety of Albert Lea. Being the kind of man her father is, he would have personally lynched her if she had an affair while still being married.

Their marriage had been going well until this week. At least, he thought it had. He thought they were happy. Unless there could be something he didn't know. Something for which Annette needed an excuse and this issue gave it to her.

If he had another cognac, he would pass out. He poured one. Where else would he turn? His life in shambles and all control effectively gone. And it had been so good. As he stared at the ceiling, he thought about Cory. Could she help now? Possibly. Insightful and she knew Annette fairly well and would not pull any punches with him. He would call her tomorrow. She might add a measure of sanity. But she couldn't get inside Annette's head. Who could? How about Annette's brother, Tom? Had she talked to him? Tom had always been her family confidant. Brent had never gotten close to the guy. Tom always seemed cool toward him but not to the degree that he would facilitate a break up. Brent would leave that phone call as a last resort but he decided he would not hesitate if it became his last option.

Well, guess he would be sleeping down here tonight, Brent thought. These were the times he wished they had a dog. Although the way things were going, the dog would have bit the hell out of him and run upstairs with Annette.

Man's best friend. Fuck the dog. Didn't want the furry mammal anyway. Brent took his snifter and went over to the sofa. After draining the last drop of cognac, he turned the big screen television to TNT. He lay down and realized his condition required one foot on the floor. He had to get Annette to work with him. His eyes closed and he plunged into a fitful, alcohol-induced sleep.

After returning from a vigorous workout, Patricia Bolivar fixed a late snack of hot hoar d'oeuvres for Adam Jordan while the true love of her life, a white cat named Rutherford, freshened up on his pillow in the corner of the kitchen. Rutherford kept a watchful eye on the activities of his mistress. Something edible might just fall to the floor.

Tonight Patricia had a mission. She and Adam had been seeing each other for over a year. She enjoyed his company a great deal. In fact, this had been the longest period of time Patricia had seen one man. They enjoyed many of the same things including dining out, the triple-A Charlotte Knights baseball team and the theater. Also, they enjoyed their intimacy.

Adam had been making overtures of late that he would like their relationship to move to the next level. She wasn't sure how he defined next level other than cohabitating. Although she enjoyed Adam as a companion and lover, Patricia was not certain she was ready for that. Permanence in relationships with men had been something she avoided. Adam was the most fantastic lover she had ever experienced and her sexual appetite had always been high. She had to be certain that physical attraction would not cloud her thinking about long-term prospects.

She had never let any man get close to her. Patricia had spent her adult life searching for the right man and he had yet to materialize. Was Adam the one? After a year, she was not confident he was, which should probably tell her something.

Patricia's thoughts were interrupted by the doorbell. Way ahead of her, Rutherford scurried to the front hall. She opened the door to greet Adam. He encircled her with his arms and almost lifted her 5'8" frame off the floor.

"Hi, honey," he said. "Sorry I'm late. Flight out of New York was packed and late."

"I'm glad to see you. Week's been a train wreck." As he made himself comfortable, she briefly recapped the events from Wednesday in Atlanta through Friday afternoon.

Adam opened a bottle of Sterling Cab and poured two glasses.

"It's a shame. But if the worst happens, Shannon can get another job."

He brought over the two glasses of wine and sat on the sofa next to Patricia.

"Can't be solved tonight. Like some quality time with my girl."

Patricia took a swallow of her wine. Here goes, she thought.

"You're right. Let me ask. Last weekend you talked about us taking our relationship to the next level. What're you thinking?"

"We've been together for a year or so." After a swallow of wine he continued, "I care about you a great deal, sweetheart, and like to be with you more. Like us to share a place."

Exactly what she had been worried about, Patricia thought. If things did not work out, living together would complicate splitting up. She had never entertained the notion of living with someone.

"I really enjoy being with you. You know that. But not sure I'm ready to live together. Plus, neither place is big enough for two. We'd have to move."

Adam began to rub the back of her neck. "That's what I thought. New place would do us good. Not to mention Rutherford. What're you hesitant about, sweetheart? We've gotten closer each passing month."

The excitement of anticipation his gentle massaging of her neck began to cause within her concerned Patricia. She could not agree to something driven by physical feelings. She was an assertive, competent woman well into breaking the glass ceiling. What caused her self-discipline to crumble faced with the prospect of love-making with a man to whom she was physically attracted? She damned herself as she surrendered.

"Can't think of anyone I'd rather be with than you. But living together's a huge step, Adam. I just need time to be sure," she responded as her body grew feverish with desire.

Adam smiled slowly and put his hand where her skirt met the bareness of her thigh. "Know it's a big step but I'm ready to make a commitment to you, my darling."

Patricia felt hot waves sweep into her stomach. The pressure of the last three days disappeared into the moist world of physical pleasure. Adam gave her a peaceful respite from the current agonies of work. Patricia's body uncontrollably shuttered to the feel of his touch, warmth and affection for her.

"Seen you longer than any man. But do we have to decide this right now?"

"No, but wouldn't it be wonderful to be with each other every night?" His hand put pressure on her thigh as he moved it just under her skirt.

Patricia put her head on Adams shoulder and whispered, "You're so nice to me."

"Only want the best for you, sweet baby."

"Um, know that," she murmured as Adam turned her head to face him. His lips found hers.

A kiss that began gently became insistent as Adam's tongue slipped through her parted lips. Patricia lost all focus except for this exact moment and Adam Jordan. He kissed her ear and whispered, "Take your skirt off, kitten."

Patricia did as he asked. It left her dressed in a blouse, bra, and sheer thong. She kicked off her sandals as she sat down. Her mind had been transported to her dream world with his next deeper kiss. His tongue penetrated and filled her entire mouth. She turned on her hip, which allowed him to caress her buttocks. It drove her crazy with lust.

"Let's go upstairs, kitten," he said slowly helping her stand up.

Hardly aware of climbing the stairs, she floated in a warm space guided by Adam's hand on her buttocks. They stood at the side of her bed while he removed her blouse, bra and thong, leaving her nude. He laid her on the bed and her eyes ranged freely up and down his body as he slowly undressed. When nude, he lay down next to her and his hands and mouth escorted Patricia Bolivar to a land of rapture.

Lying on her side with Adam sleeping peacefully next to her, Patricia realized that, once again, she had been taken to the precipice and thrown into the abyss of ecstasy by Adam. Her body still quivered and the warmth still spread through her.

Her mother had told Patricia to save herself until marriage because her husband might not be able to match an earlier lover. Could that be the case now? Did she care enough for Adam to share her life and grow old with him? Or could she be afraid to lose him because of his ability to sexually satisfy her? Had she been imprisoned by her thirst for sensual pleasure? Had it become her Achilles heel to a full and satisfying life?

She realized that she enjoyed being with Adam but he did not fulfill her except sexually. It was not his fault. He was a kind and gentle man but something was missing. Something that made her feel empty. She could not define it. She just knew its absence.

Patricia began to cry. Would she ever find the illusive missing pieces to her happiness? Or would she be destined to go through life less than complete?

SATURDAY

TRUMPED

Brent loved the hand bell choir. Sitting with his family in the sanctuary's fifth row of pews, the hand bell choir performed to their right front. As he listened, Brent noticed the minister move toward the pulpit. Strange, he thought. Amazingly, upon reaching it, he began the sermon attempting to talk over the hand bell choir.

The minister kept talking in a louder voice. The hand bell choir increased their volume and the urgency of their bells to compensate. Suddenly, a tremendous thirst came over Brent. As demanding a physical need as he had ever experienced. It sent him into a panic. He had to get water.

His panic forced Brent's eyes open. The doorbell would come off the wall if whoever ringing the thing did not cease and desist.

Brent tried to get off the sofa but the hand he used to support himself slipped off the end of the cushion. His body hit the floor. His head already hurt and the journey to the floor caused the rest of his body to follow suit. And the door bell still rang.

Brent staggered to the front door. Looking at his watch, he couldn't see the face through the opaque haze in front of his eyes. His semi-comatose faculties told him his current condition had been defined throughout time as hung over. He had to get to the door so the bell would stop. Every time it ding donged some sadist put a knife in the back of his head.

He opened the door and found Doris Mitchell, Erik and Tawney impatiently waiting for him to respond to their summons. Where the hell could Annette be? Tawney seemed to be the culprit parked on the door bell.

"I'm here, Tawney," he said. "Quit with the doorbell."

"You're very slow, Daddy. And you look disheveled." She tapped her foot. A little Annette.

Who the hell taught the kid those words?

"I'm fine, Tawney."

"Sorry to disturb you, Brent," Doris Mitchell said. "Told Annette I'd drop the kids off early. We're going to the mountains."

"Fine, Doris. Thanks for letting them stay with you." Don't look at me like I'm drunk, lady. There's a big difference between drunk and hung over, his mind proclaimed. "Come on kids. Let Mrs. Mitchell get going. Thanks again, Doris."

"No trouble at all," she said with a quizzical look on her face. "Was the special occasion good?"

"The what?" he said and then remembered Annette's reason for the kids staying at the Mitchell's. "Oh yeah, it was incredible."

She smiled. "Looks like it."

Don't push it, lady, he thought.

"Thanks again, Doris," he said shutting the door.

Tawney looked up at Brent. "What's so special, Daddy?"

"Mommy and Daddy just had some important things to talk about."

"Was it about me? Was I bad?"

"No, Tawney. You weren't bad and it wasn't about you."

"Why'd you sleep downstairs," Erik hollered from the den. This incurred the wrath of the guy behind Brent who stuck the damn knife in the back of Brent's head again.

"Mommy got sleepy and went upstairs," Brent said. "I was watching a movie and just fell asleep."

Tawney asked, "Why'd you fall asleep instead of going up with Mommy?"

This conversation was doing nothing for his hang over.

"What you guys want for breakfast?"

"Pancakes," said Tawney.

"Yeah, pancakes," repeated Erik.

Where was Annette when he needed her?

"How about cereal?"

"No. Pancakes, Daddy," Tawney said. "Where's Mommy?"

"Don't know. Probably running."

"Why don't you know?"

His head was killing him.

"Okay, Miss Pris. One more question and no pancakes. Understand?"

"Well, sorry, daddy," Tawney pouted and sat at the breakfast room table.

"Erik," Brent called into the den. "Some help here. Sports Center'll wait. Set the table."

"Sure Dad," Erik said bounding into the kitchen.

Brent dumped the pancake stuff into a mixing bowl. He missed with a goodly amount, which produced a white cloud.

Erik asked, "Dad, anything wrong?"

"No. Why'd you ask?"

"Heard you and Mom arguing last couple nights."

"Weren't arguing. Something Mom and I have to decide. We were discussing it," said Brent.

"If you're discussing," said Tawney, "how come Mommy's crying?"

"Want more pancakes?" said Brent.

The back door slammed and Annette walked in the kitchen.

"Jeez, honey, was worried. Didn't know where you were," said Brent.

"Thought I'd get a morning run in. Glorious day."

"Want some breakfast?"

"We're discussing why you've been crying a lot," said Tawney.

"You kids finish up, go get showers and dress," said Annette.

Tawney asked, "Daddy really isn't going to forget us, is he?"

"What'd you say?" Brent said, looking at Tawney.

"You kids, up stairs right now," Annette interjected in her best no nonsense tone.

After Erik and Tawney left, Brent said, "Annette, what've you been saying to the kids?"

"Nothing, except you might be taking a job that would keep you away a lot."

"Now isn't that a warm thought for them."

"I'm going up to take a shower," said Annette.

"Can I come up to the bedroom and clean up?"

"Suit yourself," said Annette walking out of the kitchen.

Brent sat at the kitchen table contemplating when he had been cursed with a hangover this bad. His mind didn't go back that far. How much damn cognac had he drunk?

He poured another cup of coffee realizing he desperately loved Annette. Even her current selfishness had not dampened his desire for his wife. He had never wanted anyone else since the day they met. He wondered if Annette would say the same. For the first time in eight years, he could not be sure. Could she have someone else? Had she been building a case to leave him? The mere thought of her being with another man caused his stress level to soar. His intellect could not accommodate her being in another man's bed. Close to being suffocated with anxiety, for the first time in his life, he felt the emotional power of a male's defense and shielding of his mate.

Of course, being hung over didn't help. He had to calm down and get hold of himself. The clear and present danger to his career required sharp focus. If Annette was going to leave him, he was not certain he could do anything about it. But he needed her support at tonight's party. If she was about to embark on a new life, she had no right to leave his in shambles. If she was leaving, why would it matter if he had Marlene's job? She would be long gone. The only impact to her would be more child support.

Brent filled his coffee cup for the third time and went upstairs to dress. He found Annette putting on makeup in the bathroom.

"Sleep okay last night?" Brent asked.

"From what I see, a lot better than you."

"Guess I'm a bit ragged."

"A bit?"

"Okay, a lot. Can we calmly talk about something?"

"Calm as can be," she said.

"Know I'm being redundant but I've got to compete for this job. You think the point at issue is some macho creed of not letting Kruger go one up on me. I'm asking you to understand it's more serious than that. For some reason, Kruger's end game is the destruction of my reputation. I don't compete, my character will be shredded. You think I'm paranoid but I've sampled the wrath of Kruger's tactics. And the game's just started. I'll be ruined. Can't you understand my position?"

Brent was amazed he could say something lucid when so hung over.

"Only thing I understand is your practice of self-deception," said Annette. "But it doesn't matter."

Brent felt his heart sink. "What do you mean it doesn't matter?"

"Means just what I said, Mr. Shannon. We're at a marital impasse. You're unable to comprehend or cope with my fears. And husband, they're real fears. But you obviously don't care." Annette went into the bedroom.

"That's unfair," Brent retorted.

Okay, he thought. Enough of this poor little me line.

"I'm getting sick and tired of you telling me I don't care. If I didn't care, I wouldn't have worked for the past eight years to calm your fears. So knock off the 'I don't care' stuff. It's untrue and really starting to offend me."

His voice had gotten louder with each word out of his mouth. They say there's an ultra thin line between love and hate. It would not take much more of her attitude for him to cross that line.

"I'm not being unfair. And don't you dare talk to me like that. Don't you dare," she said putting on her jeans. "You never had an appreciation of how badly you hurt me."

"False," he said. "I realize what you went through. But can't understand your sheer lack of faith after all the years I've worked to regain your trust. And if you don't want to get talked to that way have some appreciation for my fears. Appreciation goes both ways."

"This discussion's going nowhere," she said. "I'm bored with it."

Brent asked, "Do you still love me?" The question just blurted out. He was sitting on the side of the bed dreading her answer. It was a question he thought he would never be motivated to ask.

"Never been in question."

"Your reaction to this has been dramatic and uncharacteristic, Annette. Put it another way. Do you want to leave me?"

"That would be a drastic solution. Don't think I've ever talked about leaving you."

"Haven't. But I'm starting to interpret your position as one in which you win or you're history. Am I way off base?"

"I cannot cope with your workaholism again."

"Senseless to go through the workaholism issue," said Brent. "I'm not debating a perceived future problem you can't begin to substantiate. But I've a hard time understanding that my reputation carries no importance to you. It's critical to my having a meaningful job."

"Not as critical as you make it. I have a back up," she said.

"What back up?"

"I'm licensed in North Carolina. I can go back to work and you can stay home with the kids. At least for a while."

"I've worked tenaciously to succeed at my work. You know that. Should I have to chuck it all now?"

"Why not? I chucked mine," Annette retorted in a tone laced with sarcasm and ice.

Temper about to erupt, Brent said, "That was voluntary, Annette. No one pressured you or issued veiled threats like I'm getting now. Wait a second. Is this what the whole thing is about? You want to go back to work."

"Don't be so self-centered," she said. "Not it at all. Just want a way out of this mess without losing my husband to Richmont Corporation."

Brent thought this to be the damndest twist so far. He would never have predicted it. He got canned and Annette went back to work. A fairy tale ending.

Well, he did not want to be the typical male chauvinistic pig. But feeding Tawney Ugal MaGoogles for lunch would not be his idea of a fun time. At least, not a steady diet of it. Suddenly, it dawned on him that Annette had provided a way out of this dilemma. Just not the way she envisioned it.

"Okay, honey," he said. "Think you're on to something."

"Thanks for little gifts."

"Make a deal with you," he said. "Sign it in blood."

"What deal?"

"We'll sit down and come up with a mutually agreeable definition of workaholic. Construct guidelines to prevent our definition from coming true. I'll take the GM job if it's offered. If I can't keep to our agreed guidelines, I'll step down from the job. If the company won't allow me to do that, I'll resign and stay home with the kids."

"You're not serious," said Annette.

"As hell. Deal would be win-win for you. Can't lose."

"I'll have to think about it."

"What's to think about? It's no risk."

"I said I'll have to think about it. Don't press me."

"Okay, no pressing," Brent said. "But I need your support at the party."

"That's your angle. You come up with this win-win to survive this party. Then tell me, on further review, no deal."

"Annette, I won't even dignify that accusation with a denial."

"I told you before," she said. "I'll tell anyone who asks I think it's wonderful you might have opportunities in the company and I support you for considering greater opportunities. But if I'm asked about that particular job, I'm not lying for you. I don't support you taking Marlene's job."

"You understand that response kills my chances," he said.

"I'll say it again, Brent. Listen closely. I am not lying for you. What about that statement do you not understand?"

"Think about my proposition," said Brent.

"I will. Don't expect an answer in ten minutes." Annette left the bedroom and Brent heard her footsteps on the stairs.

Something had to be terribly wrong. Any conversation that the Atlanta crowd had with her tonight would center on her feelings about him taking the GM job. Annette knew that. What she told him had been that she would not support him. Thus far, she had thrown every possible wrench into the engine. Brent wondered if she had a different agenda. One that she was unwilling to share.

Paul and Audra Kruger were eating breakfast on the deck off their kitchen. The evening storm gave birth to a beautiful morning. Lake Norman glistened in the early morning sun. A perfect weather day. Also, a perfect career day. By the stroke of midnight, Brent Shannon's whole world would turn into a pumpkin. Cinderella Shannon. Paul laughed to himself.

Eating an English muffin admiring the morning calm of the lake, Audra said matter of factly, "Last night was wonderful. You were such a beautiful lover."

Paul looked across the table as Audra's head buried itself in the newspaper. He continued to be astonished by the sexual switch in Audra's head. She had been a little sex kitten last night. Eager to be done and do. She fell asleep purring. This morning her comments had all the emotion of thanking him for going out for the paper. Other than she got serviced, it was as if nothing happened.

"Thanks honey," Paul said. "Was wonderful for me, too."

"Got to make certain you talk to Stuart again. Before this evening, Paul."

"Going to the office shortly. I'll take care of it. Going to get Evan on the phone, too. See if we can't have the talk at the party where I can monitor it."

"Either way, Stuart's got to be coached. He's the deathblow." She had just enough venom in her tone to make Paul uneasy.

"He will be."

"You know, having the meeting at the party is dangerous."

"How so?"

"If something prevents them from meeting, you've lost the opportunity to put the dagger in Shannon's heart."

"Point taken. We'll see how it falls out."

"No. Won't see how it falls out," Audra said. "Make it fall out our way. Want you to think about something and we'll talk this afternoon."

"What's that?"

"I might be the best person to get Annette Shannon in front of Voorhees at the party," she said. "Don't think she'd suspect anything. She'd be more relaxed when Ben questioned her."

"Great strategy. Let's discuss the details this afternoon. I'm heading to the office."

"When will you be home, Paul?"

"Don't know. But I'll call when I'm on my way."

"Please do."

Wonder what he would find if he didn't call, he thought. Maybe after all of this has been settled, he would try it. "See you this afternoon."

After negotiating the town streets, Paul merged onto the freeway and punched up

Wilson Rachet on his speed dial. In a few seconds, Wilson's deep voice said hello.

"Wilson, it's me."

"Morning. Everything well?"

"Excellent, if you've good news."

"I do. Had lunch with Katie Lockhart. Handled herself in predictable fashion."

"Great, I guess."

"Is great," said Wilson. "Said things were okay. But Annette's always had a trust issue with Brent. Her opinion, Annette's slow to forgive and never forgets. Thought she'd be uncomfortable with this type of job change."

Paul laughed. "Sounds like my kind of woman."

"Told her was talking with her because I always liked Brent and didn't want him hurt. Asked if I should talk to him. To make certain things were okay. That I was close to Ben Voorhees and knew the respect he had for Brent. Tell Brent that there'd be other opportunities if he couldn't to take this one. She thought it was a great idea."

"Think you got too close to the situation?" said Paul.

"No way. Told you I'm Katie's meal ticket to partner. Won't cross me. She's too ambitious."

"Okay," said Paul. He laughed. "Remind me to never get on your bad side."

"To this point, you haven't," Wilson said lightly.

"Did you get to Ben?"

"Yes, but not till five. He was concerned. Concerns were heightened because of his conversation with Terry Thomas. Shared their conversation with me."

"Did it work?"

"Perfection. Thomas told Ben that Shannon was preoccupied. It was affecting his work. Unprepared for a capital request meeting. Displayed incompetence."

"Zap," said Paul. "Strike one. More to follow."

"Ben said Shannon impressed him as a focused, intelligent, prepared manager who exhibited good judgment. Behavior with Thomas was out of character. Thought could be Marlene leaving. Or could be his marriage. Mentioned I should remember Shannon's past issues." Wilson laughed. "Led me right into the subject at hand. Told him, what a coincidence. Shannon came up at lunch with Katie Lockhart. Considering his concern, should know the substance of the conversation. Told him Katie's a friend of Annette Shannon. Did work together when the Shannons were in Atlanta. Told him Shannon may be so career driven he's in denial of his marital issues."

"Fantastic. Marvelous way to put it. Ole Bible Ben'll think he's the Good Shepherd doing God's work by not giving Shannon a job that'll destroy the important things in life. Great approach, Wilson."

"Yes, and even better, told Ben Katie said his actions over the past few years showed that Brent loved his wife. Told him that sometimes career ambitions can blind one to the meaningful aspects of life. Nothing to blame Brent over. Happens to a lot of ambitious, talented people."

"Oh, man. Wrapped the guy up and stuck a bow on his head."

"Wait, my man, there's more. Ben queried me why Marlene would support Brent. Must have knowledge about this. Touchy discussion turn. He was perplexed. Could see it on his face. In his tone. Told him she was most likely attracted to Brent's marketing expertise. But if the man's unstable or preoccupied with a shaky marriage, that expertise can be hired from the open market."

"Excellent."

"Touchy. Had to be careful. But it was the most exposed I'd seen Voorhees and had to capitalize. He needed an excuse. I planted one."

"Well done," said Paul. "Strike two."

"Ben wanted to know more. Told him I didn't know any more. Just my conversation with Katie. Told him he should query Brent himself. Or if he was really concerned, have Stan Ascutney visit with Brent's wife at the Charlotte party."

"Good thinking. I've got a way to get her in front of the Atlanta crowd," said Paul.

"Excellent. My talk with Ben ended telling him I knew how sensitive he was about families. That his strong Christian ethic was an inspiration to me. Produced a ten-minute sermon. Thought we were going to have to get down and pray."

"God, Wilson. Incredible. Don't know how to thank you."

"I'll think of something. How's the affair strategy going? That's what'll achieve critical mass."

"On course. I'm talking to Neal Stuart again this morning. He'll be primed and ready."

"Good," said Wilson. "Make sure you set it up for the party tonight."

"Only problem is if something screws up, we've lost the chance."

"Make sure nothing screws up."

"Calling Evan this morning to get it set," Paul said.

"Okay. Make sure there's no discussion of the marital deal unless Evan brings it up," Wilson said. "Then be careful. Can't be traced back to Charlotte or there're be questions you don't want asked and, even worse, can't answer."

"I'll be careful."

"If Evan says something, means Voorhees has talked to Ascutney. Only way Roth gets a whiff of it. Ben won't confide in Roth about a sensitive people issue."

"I'll be cautious. But if he brings it up, I'm probing him to see what Ascutney was told. Audra will get Shannon's wife in front of Voorhees tonight."

"Can you trust Ms. Blue Blood to help you?"

Paul laughed. "Oh, yes. She wants this as much as me. So she can stick it to her father."

"Okay, up to you. I personally don't see how you stand living in the same house with the witch."

"Wilson, calm down. This *is* my wife you're talking about."

"Okay. Okay. Have a productive day and get everything tied up at the party. Planning dinner when you come to Atlanta next week as new GM."

"That'll be nice," said Paul. "Talk to you soon." He disconnected.

Wilson had outdone himself. All he had to do was work with Audra to get the Shannon woman in front of Ben. He smiled thinking about what a sweet journey it would be to the Promised Land.

Brent finished dressing and went downstairs. The shower had helped clear his head. He found Annette in the laundry room.

"Running some errands and stopping by the office," he said. "See you at the sports complex."

Annette dropped the clothes basket she was carrying, looked at him with harsh eyes and said, "Oh, no you don't. You'll miss the game for sure. You can just stay with the family until after the game."

"Hear me," he said in a low, measured tone. "Running errands and stopping by the office. See you at the sports complex. I don't know all of your self-generated problems but I've had enough of your attitude. Get off my back and stay off it." Brent went to the garage without waiting for a reply. He hoped she wouldn't follow him. One more haughty remark by her would produce an ugly scene.

To her credit, she had enough sense to continue doing laundry. He backed the Audi out of the garage and headed to his first stop. On the way, he wanted to talk to his sister Cory and get her assessment of this debacle. If she shot holes in his point of view, his self-assurance would plummet past zero. Brent hit Cory's speed dial number, waited a few seconds and heard her answer the phone.

"Hi, Cory. It's little brother."

"Hi, little brother. How're things going?"

"Not worth a damn, if you want the truth."

"Uh-oh. What's the problem?"

Brent filled her in on what had happened.

"Brent, what's Annette's explanation why she feels like she does?"

"That's the problem. Either can't or won't say. Nothing. Just demands."

"Doesn't sound like her. And doesn't sound good."

"Wait till you hear her idea," said Brent. "She's my back up plan. I get fired, she goes to work. I'll be a house husband for a while. Told her she had the answer. I'll take the GM job. If I can't keep priorities, I'll resign and be a house husband."

"Tell me, Brent. Would you do that?"

"Told her I would cause not going to have to."

"Why agree to a scheme like that?"

"Cause it ends the issue and know I can do it."

"You can't."

"The hell I can't."

"Screw your head on. You're setting yourself up. You control no part of the deal. If Annette's terrified after this long, she's neurotic. Sees nothing but ghosts. If she has another agenda, she'll stack the deck. Can't win little brother. Shouldn't agree to that. Insane if you do. About to put her in complete control of your life. Puts you in jail."

"You're overstating."

"Hell, I am. Just for fun, what was her reaction to the deal?"

"Said she'd think about it."

"Think about what for christ's sake? Woman can't lose."

"Beats me."

"What're you doing if she says no?"

"Don't know," he said. "Sis, trying to keep hold of myself. But she's really irritating me. I mean really. Her attitude sucks. Almost bit her head off when I left this morning. Tell you one thing. Your brother's competing for this job. No changing that. But like her along for the ride."

"Well, you'd better think through your response to no," said Cory. "Cause that's what you'll get."

"How can she do that? It's a no brainer."

"Not so," she replied. "Cause she's got another agenda. Has to. This isn't woman's intuition talking. Whole thing's against the way she reacts to things."

"Right. That's what's driving me nuts."

Cory sighed. "Hard one coming. Think she's got someone else?"

"Don't think so. But she thinks I have."

"Say what?"

"Thinks I'm having an affair with Patricia Bolivar. The HR Director."

"Well, well," Cory said. "Little piece of info you neglected to tell me. Is she right?"

"Absolutely not."

"You get the promotion; do you work more with this woman?"

"Yeah."

"Annette could be gun shy about more exposure to a woman that threatens her. Know I would."

"Cory, I'm damned if I do, damned if I don't."

"Amigo," said Cory. "As my articulate husband would say, its balls on the table time."

"What the hell's that supposed to mean?"

"My opinion. Done what you can with Annette. She's going to do what's best for her. You can't influence that decision other than capitulate."

"Where's that put me?"

"Right here. Ask for her support at the party and let the chips fall where they fall. She castrates you, you've done all you can do."

"Swell visualization, Cory. But I've got a lot invested in this marriage. And I love Annette and the kids."

"Know it's tough sledding. But there's something you have to think about. Real hard."

"What?"

"Do you have a marriage? A life partner? A soul mate. Or have eight years towing her line created a self-absorbed, comfortable woman?"

"Nasty way to put it," said Brent.

"Sometimes we humans are nasty. You make the money to meet her lifestyle needs. Why should she risk leaving her comfort zone? She doesn't need another man to have a hidden agenda. One she can't share cause you'd rebel."

"That's a different angle."

"Better get your wits about you, little brother. This is a decision point in your relationship and your life."

"Hell, don't worry," he said. "I can handle life's decision points. Had six or seven so far this week."

"Know you've worked hard rebuilding your marriage. But if eight years got you this, its time you questioned the relationship."

"No idea how much I appreciate your input. I need an ear; can I lean on you again?"

"At your disposal. Take care, sweetie. Don't lose your balance. Bunches of stuff coming at you from all directions. Work your way through it carefully."

"Thanks again, Cory."

"One more thing," Cory said.

"Yeah."

"You're a risk-taking businessman. Very good at it. Glad you've developed a set of balls with Annette. You've appeased her at every turn. This is what appeasement gets you. Quit capitulating to her. Got a good start. Don't back off."

"Thanks, Sis. Talk to you soon."

Disconnecting, he thought about Cory's assessment. He never considered the comfort zone thing. There might be something to it. It sure beat the sleeping with another man scenario.

Cory had been right about making agreements with Annette. He had to be careful. He could box himself in.

After checking e-mails, Paul dialed Neal Stuart's extension expecting to get a voice mail message. He was surprised when Stuart answered.

"Hi, Neal. Paul Kruger here. How're you this morning? Everybody hard at work in the marketing department?"

"Morning, Paul. No one over here except me and Ashley Weedon."

If Ashley Weedon saw them meeting, they might as well do it in the front foyer of Shannon's house. "Neal, mind stepping over here? If you have time, like to follow up on yesterday."

"Plenty of time. Be there in five minutes."

"Thanks, Neal. See you shortly."

He liked that reaction from subordinates. Just a shame the guy had no brain. Paul worried about relying on this dimwit to put the dagger in Shannon's heart. But he had no choice. An immediate subordinate of Shannon would provide powerful circumstantial evidence. The loyalty of Shannon's people had to be impressed on Evan. It would make Stuart more credible.

Neal Stuart knocked on Paul's door. Paul waved him in and motioned to a chair in front of his desk.

"Neal, anyone talked to you about Brent and Patricia?"

"Haven't received any calls."

Paul feigned a sigh of relief. "That's good. I've been worried since we discussed the issue. Hate to see you in the middle of a political mess."

"Believe me, I'd hate that, too."

What a pea brain, Paul thought. Stuart turned ashen talking about it.

"I've heard some undertones from Atlanta. Don't want to alarm you, but wouldn't be surprised if you were questioned at the party tonight. Naturally, I wanted to give you a heads up."

Stuart combined his ashen complexion with a look of sheer panic.

"Don't get nervous," said Paul. "You can handle any question asked if you follow what we talked about. You remember our talk?"

"Yeah. Say I saw them a couple of times and their behavior wasn't appropriate for business associates. But what am I supposed to say if they want to know what wasn't appropriate?"

"Say they appeared too friendly. Too close. That's what you told me at lunch, isn't it?"

"Yeah. Exactly."

"Good. Look, Neal. You won't get the third degree. Just tell the truth. Too close and too friendly is how you observed Brent and Patricia."

"That's it, Paul. Precisely."

"You're a great asset to this division," said Paul. "I'm trying to protect you. Know you haven't had a great deal of interface with senior management. I don't want you to do or say something that stymies your career before it takes off."

"Thanks," said Neal. "Incidentally, jotted down some changes I want to make in marketing if something happens to Shannon because of his relationship with Bolivar."

A shame Stuart wasn't director timber. He had started to think like a political animal, Paul thought.

"We can go over them next week after this is settled."

"Fine. No way you're not the next GM. Going to be great to work for you."

"Yes, we should make a fine team. My wife Audra and I are looking forward to meeting your wife at the party this evening."

"Would be our pleasure," said a glowing Neal.

"Pleasure will be ours. See you tonight."

Amazing. The man elevated his stupidity with each encounter. He called Evan Roth who answered on the second ring.

"Hi, Evan. Looking forward to seeing you tonight."

"Hi Paul. Should be a nice affair. Anxious to see you. Rising star of Richmont. Not surprising. Saw your potential from the beginning."

"I wouldn't be anywhere without your guidance. Hope I can contribute to Brent Shannon's organization."

Evan Roth laughed. "Come on. You know the pendulum is swinging into your camp. Things I'm not at liberty to discuss. Just take my word for it."

"I don't know what you're talking about," said Paul. "But grateful for your continuing support."

"Paul, I need Neal Stuart's home number."

"Be glad to get it for you. But why don't you talk to him at the party tonight? Certain we can get some privacy."

"You might not realize the seriousness of this," Evan said. "There's anything to these allegations, Ben Voorhees must be informed soonest."

"I appreciate its serious nature. Thought a face to face conversation would be preferable to one over the telephone. Especially when the discussion concerns an issue affecting a competent man's career. With this company and possibly others."

"Point taken," said Evan. "Can you set up a talk?"

"I'm certain of it."

"Okay. Do it. It might be best. Ben could visit with Stuart if the need arises. Okay. See you tonight."

"Good. Anxious to catch up," said Paul.

Paul hung up the phone. This could not have worked out better. Stuart hated Shannon and would shave the truth. Roth wanted the truth shaved because he wanted Paul to get the job. Life kept getting more beautiful with each passing hour.

Patricia kissed Adam goodbye. She watched him drive away for his trip to Knoxville, Tennessee, to celebrate his parent's thirtieth wedding anniversary. The trip meant he would not be at Marlene's going away party which relieved Patricia. It would be a tense, uncertain evening. On the other hand, if she had a date, Annette Shannon might be reassured. Patricia could not believe the woman harbored the notion that she and Brent were having an affair.

She poured herself a cup of coffee reflecting that the affair lunacy had been only one facet of this tragedy. The events of the last three days were Shakespearean. She had no idea what was going to happen this evening but there would be futures affected by whatever transpired. Not the least of which, hers. She had to call Marilyn Beamon this morning to find out if any rumors were floating around about Brent and her. Marilyn would know. What a ridiculous turn of events. She really did not need more complications. It was unbelievable. She and Brent had never behaved in a manner that would cause someone to infer that they had an intimate relationship. She had always been fond of him but that was the extent of it. At least, that had been what she always told herself. She had never fantasized being with him in an intimate way. She enjoyed being around him but kept her distance. She had kept her distance because that was the type of relationship she wanted with him. Or had she kept her distance because she was scared what might happen if she got too close? God, the men in her life were driving her mad.

She had a rule that she never got involved with married men. Did the rule keep her at arm's length from Brent? Or did she know if she let her guard down she would break the rule? Was her hesitancy about Adam because of her lack of feelings for him or her intense, sub-conscious feelings for Brent Shannon?

She had hoped she could bring her personal life into focus. Instead, this work dilemma and her alliance with Brent added more uncertainty to an already confused state of affairs. On the other hand, could she see her life clearly? Would she like what she saw? Currently, confusion defined her life. A totally unacceptable condition. She had better get unconfused pretty fast.

Adam was sexually stimulating and a nice, kind man. But something seemed to be missing. What could it be? She did not know. Did Brent have it? How could she know if she had no idea what it was in the first place? It must be powerful. It was certainly doing a number on her mind.

Tears of frustration blurred her vision. Except for physical gratification, she had done so well keeping men at a distance. Could she be feeling the emotions of love but ill-equipped to recognize or deal with them? Damn it all, she lamented. The tears burnt her eyes. What a confusing morass her life had become.

She had to get control of herself. Today and this evening were critical. She fought back her tears, got another cup of coffee and dialed Leslie Cook's number. Leslie answered on the third ring with a rather sleepy hello.

"Get you up?"

"No, always talk like I got a mouth full of rice. Now that you pulled me from blissful sleep, what's up?"

"My life's in ruins. That's all."

"You sound serious. And you've been crying."

"Yes and yes."

"Going to tell me about it or am I supposed to guess?"

“One dilemma after another. Job predicament is working havoc with my whole life. Personal included.”

“Thought you and Adam were getting on famously. Longest you’ve stuck with one guy your entire life. Attraction must be strong.”

“I enjoy Adam. Something’s missing though.”

“That would be?”

“Les, that’s it. I’m not sure. No. I just don’t know.”

“Who’s the guy at work you talked about in the middle of the night?”

“Brent Shannon.”

“Falling for him?”

“He’s a wonderful business associate. Enjoy working with him.”

“That the extent of it?”

“Yes. Why’d you bring him up?”

“Because, dear heart, in the middle of the night I got the feeling it might be more than that,” Leslie said.

“I’m getting tired of people making insinuations about me and Brent,” said Patricia. The tone of her voice had turned defensive.

“Hello. You called me, remember?” said Leslie. “Just telling you the impression I had.”

“Sorry. Just tense. Associate of mine accused Brent and me of being inseparable.”

“Well. Have any feelings for him?”

“Don’t fantasize being in bed with him.”

“Emotional feelings have always escaped you,” said Leslie. “Ever since I’ve known you. Know why? You relegate all relationships to sex. Measure all men by their score on the 'pleasure to get screwed by' scale."

"I resent that. I enjoy Adam's company. You talked about how long I'd been seeing him."

"Yeah. What if he had a four-inch penis and the only thing he could do with his mouth was eat? Food that is."

Patricia had to laugh. "I love you BFF. You cut to the chase."

"Don't avoid my question. Have any feelings for this Shannon guy?"

"Crosses my mind once in a while."

"What the hell does that mean?"

"Sometimes think about it would be nice to do this or that with him," Patricia responded. She started to get nervous. Yet she knew better than to cut it off. Leslie would just call her back and scream into the message machine until Patricia talked to her.

"Hold onto your seat, sweetie pie," said Leslie. "Ever cross your mind that your emotional self longs to be with Shannon instead of Adam?"

"But I like being with Adam."

"Yeah, I like having a beer with my hair stylist," said Leslie. "Actually like to sleep with him once in a while. But liking and longing are two different universes of emotion."

Patricia felt tears coming again. Her lower lip quivered. Control yourself, she thought. "Les, you think I'm kidding myself?"

"You are."

"I have a hard time getting the man out of my mind. And Les, it's getting worse."

"So what's Shannon got that Adam doesn't?"

"I don't know. Just don't know. I'm going freaking nuts over this. But trying to hold my feelings in."

"Patricia, it's tough to hold in the look on your face or in your eyes. Your unconscious strategies for proximity. You don't think people pick up those cues? Let me provide the answer – yes they do."

"I don't do those."

"If you feel like you just told me, you're kidding yourself if you think you don't. The curse of us humans. Are you in love with this guy?"

"I can't be."

Leslie laughed. "That's like saying you can't be pregnant when the fuckin' rabbit dies. You know. Old pregnancy test."

"I know, Les. I know."

"I think you're being forced to come face to face with emotions you've avoided," said Leslie. "Realizing love is about sharing. Sharing your mind and time with another human. Not just getting laid. Although it's a great side benefit."

"Les. He's married."

"Well, well now. That brings up an interesting question. You working hard to help him get this job for the team or you think it'll break up his marriage?"

"That's an awful thing to say," Patricia retorted.

"Honey, you have to come to grips with your motives. They better be pure as the fresh driven snow. If not, you'll stand guilty of screwing up a lot of lives."

"I get more confused by the minute," said Patricia.

"Sit down and think this out. You're in love with a married man and have to deal with it as your morals dictate. You decide to go for it, you owe it to Adam to break it off with him. He wants more than you may be able to give him.

Have to allow him the opportunity to find what he's searching for. Keep me posted and hugs and kisses from Pittsburgh. Stay the course, girl."

Patricia hung up the silent phone with her head spinning. Leslie hung up with no warning. Patricia wondered if she had alienated her best friend.

Their conversation did nothing to bring her world into focus. The way things were going she would be in great shape for tonight. She had to introduce Ben Voorhees for a presentation to Marlene. At this rate, she might still be crying. Before the world ended, she had to make her second call. She got Beamon's home number from directory assistance. Marilyn answered the phone.

They traded small talk for a couple of minutes before Patricia said, "You know Marlene's coming back to Atlanta?"

"Yeah," Marilyn said. "Talk of the company. Understand that her replacement is between Paul Kruger and Brent Shannon. Hope its Shannon. Kruger's an insufferable bore and smart money says his wife's got a flying broom."

"Marilyn, have to ask a question. Heard anything on the grapevine about me and Brent Shannon being an item?"

"Why, Patricia, you vixen. He's a real hunk."

"We aren't. But have you heard anything? Even a rumor would kill Brent's chances for that promotion."

"Wow," said Marilyn. "Ole Bible Ben would cut off his penis and feed him to the sharks."

Very descriptive, thought Patricia. "Yes, he would."

"You may not remember," said Marilyn. "But you saved Todd's job when you stood up and quelled some awful accusations a few years back."

Patricia recalled the incident. It had been an unfortunate sequence of events.

"We owe you a great deal," Marilyn continued. "Let me see what I can find out. If rumors are floating, Todd or I will do what we can to stop them. If I find out quickly and there's something out there, Todd will let you know tonight in Charlotte."

"Thanks. You don't know how much this means to me."

"No thanks necessary," said Marilyn. "Talk to you soon." She hung up.

Brent stopped at Home Depot, Office Max and Barnes & Noble to complete his errands. He finished the last stop at twelve-thirty and drove to the Sports Complex for Erik's soccer game. When he located Annette her demeanor teetered between cold and frigid.

Waiting for the game to start he said, "Party tonight should be quite an affair. Bet the company goes all out for Marlene's departure."

"Probably right. Maybe they'll announce her replacement."

"Don't think so. This'll be her night."

"That's a shame. Why don't they just get this melodrama over with?"

"Be over with soon enough," he replied.

"Well. Hope you'll enjoy the power if you get it."

"It's not about power, Annette. It's about contribution and achievement. And in this case, survival," said Brent.

"Contribution? Please," she said.

"I don't know why that's a hard concept for you to grasp. Payoff is seeing something you've slaved over come to fruition. To see success. May need power to get things done. But it's only one means. Success and contribution are the ends."

"No lectures," she retorted. "You're boring me again."

It was a great soccer game that Erik's team won. The goalie on his team was phenomenal. They caught up with Erik and congratulated him.

"Brent," said Annette. "You run Erik home."

"Love to," he said. "But got more errands and have to stop by the office. See you at home."

"Fine," she said turning away. The kids followed her to the parking area.

Brent walked to his car. He needed to talk with Annette's brother, Tom Lind. He pulled out of the complex's parking lot punching Lind's number on his cell phone. Tom answered.

"Hi, Tom. Brent."

"Hello, Brent. To what do I owe this pleasure?"

This guy really doesn't like me a lot, Brent thought.

"Tom, could I talk to you about a sensitive subject between Annette and myself?"

"Concerning your possible promotion? If so, already discussed it with Annette."

"I see. What I want to discuss is Annette's attitude toward this."

"Not much to discuss. From my talk with her, she doesn't trust you."

"That's the crux of it. Problem is, since we came down here I haven't given her any reason to distrust me."

"I have a tough time accepting there's no reason," said Tom. "Known Annette her whole life. Always been a reasoned, logical thinker."

"I know. That's what's so perplexing."

"She being illogical or are you being self-serving?"

Brent started to get angry. Come to think of it, his and Tom's relationship was reciprocal. He didn't much like the son of a bitch.

"I'm not being self-serving. My god, man. Toed the line for eight years. That's got to count for something."

"Brent, you know you're not my favorite person. Felt you have always been far too career-oriented to provide Annette what she needed. I love her to death but she's a high maintenance person. Never saw you being able to meet those needs. I might not be the person for you to talk with about this."

"I've always known how you felt. I didn't call to make peace, Tom. Personally, I don't think either of our lives would be more fulfilled if we were buddies. Called to get your input because I love your sister and want to get past this thing."

"Fair enough," said Tom. "Where's your head at on this?"

"I adore my family. But this's a critical moment in our relationship. Think she's being unfair. Frankly, to accept her demands would set a dangerous precedent."

"Think she's being dishonest saying she's not ready to trust you?"

"No. Think she's being honest. Don't think she'll ever trust me."

"That what she told you?"

"No. But she can't tell me why she doesn't trust me except there hasn't been enough time. Ask when's enough time, can't or won't give me an answer."

"Have to admit it's strange behavior. Sure there's not something else driving her?"

"Don't know what it could be."

"Not sure I can help you anymore."

"What do you mean can't help anymore?" said Brent. "You know something you're not sharing? Come on, Tom. Good grief, I'm getting killed here."

"I'm hiding nothing," said Tom. Brent could tell Tom was getting upset.

Brent asked, "Think there's another man?"

Damn, he thought. Why does he keep asking that question when he isn't sure he wants the answer?

"Hasn't talked to me about anyone," said Tom. "But I'm not in Charlotte."

"Never given me any reason to suspect," said Brent. "Reaction to this is the only thing been outside her behavior pattern."

"I'm not comfortable talking about this."

"Hang on, sport. Think I'm lovin' it?"

"I have no reason to suspect anything," said Tom. "The only maybe might be, she could've met somebody while you two were separated."

"Tom. That's been eight years. Plus, she was so ticked off at me back then if she'd met someone, she wouldn't have touched me with somebody else's ten-foot pole. And living in Albert Lea, any hanky panky and your Dad would've put her in a stock on the town square."

Tom laughed. "Right about that. But she did some work here in St. Paul. There were times she stayed over. Met me sometimes for an early breakfast."

Brent's nerves awakened. Maybe he shouldn't have brought this bear out of hibernation.

"Naw, Tom. Have to go back to how angry she was. A viable alternative, she would've dumped me like a bad habit."

"Probably right. Even so, possible you're being compared to someone you don't know exists. She could be doing it subconsciously. Someone who has a job and priority orientation she agrees with. Admit, I'm as bewildered by her thinking as you are. Just got no answers. I'm holding nothing back, Brent. You and I have had our differences but I'd hate to see your marriage break up. You both have a lot invested and two great kids."

"Thanks," said Brent. "Hang on, Tom. Someone trying to get me." He hit the talk button and answered.

"Brent, its Marlene. You alone in the car?"

"Yes."

"Fine. Would you come by the office for a few minutes? Need to visit."

"Good, bad, or ugly?"

"Don't commit suicide," said Marlene. "But quickly as possible. Both got a party to go to and this girl needs to get ready."

"On the way."

Brent clicked back to Tom. "Sorry, boss calls."

"Know those calls," said Tom.

"Tom, appreciate your talking to me."

"No problem. Best of luck to you both. Hope things work out."

"So do I." Brent punched out.

What in the name of god could Marlene need him for now? One thing gets settled and something else slaps him in the face. The boys at The Alamo had nothing on him.

Brent drove down Westinghouse thinking about the conversation with Tom. It could be possible that Annette had another man in Minnesota. Why not. Everything else he had assumed about his life turned out to be an illusion. Why not the faithfulness of his wife. No, she could not have made it eight years. She wore her feelings on her sleeves. Wholly transparent. Her make-up did not possess the ability to conceal clandestine love affairs.

She could have a lover in Charlotte. But he could not afford to have his mind screwed up over it. There wasn't much he could do about it anyway.

What could Marlene want? They had the marital discussion. That should be a done deal. He hoped no idiot ran a Shannon, Bolivar affair rumor up the flagpole to see who saluted. That could not be it. Marlene would have told him to clean out his desk.

Brent parked, went in the side entrance and straight to Marlene's office. She waved him to the conference table.

"Had a call from Ben Voorhees," Marlene said. "Subject was your marriage and potential for difficulties. Seemed firm in his convictions. Brent, you being honest with me? My butt's way out there for you. No thank you's necessary. Just honesty."

"Marlene, I'm being honest. Annette's nervous. But she's in back of me," said Brent. Way back, he thought.

"That's good. Very good. By the way, I think Faulkton issue's dead. Ben had me talk to him. Wouldn't recommend him to head up your fan club. Got an earful. Guy can hold a grudge. Since he's had no exposure to you, twenty years is like last week. Think I convinced him you've become a talented marketing mind and a lot of maturity has taken place over twenty years. Wouldn't recommend you go to him for employment anytime soon though. Talked a little business. He's done quite a job with that department store chain."

"He's a business genius. Is he coming to your party?"

Marlene laughed. "You're safe, marketing man. Flew back to Milwaukee this morning. Go back to your marriage. One more time, want your assurance everything's all right."

"Everything's fine. Where would Voorhees get a different idea?"

"Don't know except he might have heard something from Terry Thomas."

"Terry Thomas? Why Terry Thomas?"

Brent noticed that Marlene looked a little sheepish. He decided this would be something he would not enjoy hearing.

"Brought up after you left the meeting on Thursday. In the context of a reason why you might be distracted and unfocused."

Brent asked, "Did Thomas say that?"

"No, Paul referenced it," she said. "Also said you were too much of a pro to let it bother you."

The slime-ball got me twice in one sitting, thought Brent. He's a clever little weasel.

"Everything's fine, Marlene," he said.

"Good. Cause I can guarantee the subjects' coming up tonight. With Annette," she said. "Ben's concerned and he'll not move till he's satisfied. You're just learning how thorough Ben Voorhees is before making a major people decision."

"Learning fast."

"But works to your advantage. Lot of CEOs would say they're more comfortable with Kruger's financial background. That would be that."

"They won't find anything from Annette other than what I've told you."

"Good. Now get out of here so I can get ready for my party."

"See you tonight," he said walking out the door.

He walked to his car thinking about the consequences if Annette would not support him tonight. He could visualize the look on Ben Voorhees face when Annette told him she thought the GM job sucked, would be a marriage killer and would not support her husband taking it. Yep, that would be quite a look. Of course, nothing compared to what his career would look like after Marlene got finished with him.

Annette drove the kids home whereupon both disappeared with friends. Her life had been turned upside down. Since coming to the south she had avoided thinking about life as it could have been. However, her mind would not allow those thoughts to be suppressed now and with them came memories of Charlie Radford. Her Charlie. Annette remembered those earlier days in the Twin Cities.

She remembered her constant frustration trying to get her career back on track. Due to Brent's travel schedule, she had almost complete responsibility for Erik. The situation had turned her work into a shambles. She had been counseled about her performance on more than one occasion.

One of her co-workers, Charlie Radford, an attorney six years her senior, had befriended her. As Brent became more obsessed with his work, Annette leaned on Charlie even more. She began complaining to him not only about work but her marriage as well. Charlie had been supportive, considerate and she became very attached to him. She remembered the exact week. Brent had been on the west coast for the entire week and she had taken Erik to her folks in Albert Lea so she could devote all of her energy to work. Charlie and she had gone out for a late dinner one evening. After drinks and a wonderful dinner, they found a most enjoyable end to the evening in Charlie's bed. It had been the most she felt cared for in a very long time.

That experience had turned into repeated encounters. With each one, Annette had become more emotionally tied to Charlie. He had been such a support anchor for her. She could not have coped without him.

On Brent's first anniversary with his firm, he had convinced Annette to take a ten-day Caribbean cruise vacation. Charlie had been distraught about her going but understood her position. To her horror, she had become pregnant with Tawney. She shivered as she remembered her total lack of discipline. She had considered an abortion but her religious upbringing would not allow her to do it.

She had taken a leave of absence after Tawney's birth. At the same time, Brent's travel schedule became intolerable. Charlie had been there for her and he had convinced her of the futility of her situation. He had been an invaluable resource in solidifying her decision to leave Brent.

After the separation, Annette had moved back to Albert Lea. Charlie had wanted her to stay near him in the Twin Cities but she had felt a strong need to be near her family. Nonetheless, she had spent a great deal of time with Charlie who had been completely open about his love for her. She could remember telling her family she was doing part-time legal work in the Twin Cities to explain her overnight trips. Annette had avoided a heavy commitment with Charlie because she had felt rebound romances to be fraught with danger. However, she had been very fond of him, emotionally and physically. She had known he could give her and the children the stable, caring life they had been lacking.

Then Brent had resigned from the consulting firm and taken a new job in Atlanta. Her decision to try reconciliation had been a late night conversation with her father. He had made a compelling argument that, after Brent's dramatic actions, she owed it to herself and the kids to try and work the relationship out.

The thought of leaving Charlie had been almost too much to bear. Charlie had been devastated. He had promised her that the reconciliation would never work out and he would be waiting when it did not.

As she dialed directory assistance, thoughts swarmed through her head. To allow him freedom, she had not talked to Charlie in over five years. Would he still be single? Would he recognize her voice? Would he want to talk to her? Would he still care about her? Had he meant that he would wait for her?

She dialed the number given her from directory assistance. Her body tingled as Charlie's deep, gentle voice came through the phone.

"You're talking to someone from your deep, dark past," Annette said.

"My god," said Charlie. "This the woman I'm still desperately in love with?"

Annette laughed lightly. "The same."

"You realize the Twin Cities have never been the same without you."

"I miss The Cities."

"That's easy to correct. Come back."

Annette laughed. "Not quite that easy."

"Annette, I've not heard from you in more than, what – five years. Now, you're on my telephone doorstep."

"Been committed to making my marriage work. Would have been unfair to everyone, including you, to continue communicating."

"You're talking to me now."

Annette lost her composure and began crying. "Oh, god, Charlie. It's all happening again. Just like before. Brent's going for a promotion that will take us right down the same path. The path where only you saved my sanity."

"So what's the issue?"

Annette told him about the events thus far. She concentrated on how egocentric and selfish Brent had become again.

"Can't do this again," she said.

"Hitting me pretty cold," said Charlie. "Ignored me for five years or so, sweetheart."

Annette did not know whether sweetheart was endearment or sarcasm.

"I didn't want to hurt you or anyone else."

"Might be wrong, Annette. But thought we talked about Brent's obsession eight years ago. He's not going to change."

"Promised he would. Up till now he has."

"That's laudable. What opportunity has he had to go back on his promise? Up till now?"

"None. Precisely my point."

"Brent can't understand that, can he?"

"Absolutely not."

"Why should he? In his mind, he's done a hell of a job and, I might add, made all the sacrifices," said Charlie.

"What're you talking about?"

"You haven't changed a thing. You went south as a stay-at-home mom. Is that what you are now or have you gone back to work?"

"No. I do some pro bono work though," she said.

"How have you changed in this relationship? What sacrifices have you made?"

"I've made sacrifices."

"Name me one."

"Coming down here. Lost you."

"That's sweet, darling," Charlie said. "Regrettably, he doesn't have a clue about me. Can't chalk that up on your side of the ledger. In his eyes, you've taken, not given. Except giving him another chance."

"That's silly, Charlie."

"It's not silly, Annette. Look at this from his perspective."

"Don't know what to do, Charlie."

"With Brent, nothing you can do. He's a career-oriented person whose career involves a good deal of time and travel. Requires away from home commitment. You've got to come to grips with that truth. Then accept it or not because fighting it's futile. You're probably coming off as a spoiled brat to Brent."

"Don't you dare talk to me like that, Charlie Radford," she exclaimed.

"Someone has to. Might as well be me. Doing it because I love you. You're making your life miserable, because you're hell bent on changing the unchangeable.

"Brent's a career motivated human. That's great. Those folks make the world go round. And they like making the world go round. When someone tells them to stop making the world go round they'll rebel, sooner or later.

"You've held on to the come-home-every-night Brent Shannon as long as you're going to. Has an opportunity to fly and fly he will. With you or without you. Got to decide if you're along for his ride. No one can make the decision for you. If you're not buying his ticket, get out of there. Quit making everyone's life unbearable, mine included. If you're buying, fine. Do so and knock off your whining.

"I loved you with all my heart. Still do. Want you in my life. But it's your decision not mine. Laid my cards on the table long time ago. Time for you to decide what you want out of life and go for it. I'll wait for your answer." Charlie hung up in her ear.

Charlie had answered one question for her. Brent's offer to be a house husband would never work out. She collapsed on the sofa while waves of tears and anguish flooded her body. Something had to be done that would change lives forever. Was it for better or worse? She had no idea.

He hated ties. The things never came out the right length. He either had it halfway up his shirt or down to his crotch.

As Brent tried one more time, he said to Annette, "You know, you're going to get talked to by the Atlanta people tonight."

"You've told me that," she said. "Redundancy isn't necessary. Will be nice to see some of the Atlanta folks."

Brent finished the tie and thought, screw it. This would have to do. He turned to Annette who was applying makeup at the vanity just inside the bathroom door adorned in one of those lift and separate bras and panty hose. She brought out carnal thoughts, he mused.

"Know I'm being redundant, Annette. Because I don't understand your thinking. One more time, what could I do to get you over the fear of me being consumed by my job?"

"Not the issue. Need you to demonstrate that you care as much about your family as your career. Like when you quit the consulting job."

"I have, Annette. Told you I'd be a house husband if I failed in my priorities as GM. What more do you want? Hell, it was halfway your idea."

"An unrealistic idea. Never work. You'd be miserable and make us all miserable. Don't want to see you miserable."

"That's the damn point, Annette. For the love of god. I'm willing to risk that to prove I can do this."

Annette walked over to her dress hanging on the door of her closet. "Don't want to see anyone miserable."

Brent started to have difficulty with his temper. It finally dawned on him that there would be no negotiating with her. For some reason beyond the scope of his knowledge, she had decided to draw a line in the sand. As if she had been waiting for this opportunity. What the devil could be going on?

He had been a fool in all segments of his life. His relationship with his wife had been a fantasy fathered by his own psyche. He had convinced himself that he had made the reconciliation work. In reality, he had simply been treading water until something arose that did not meet Annette's parameters. Parameters that he had been unaware existed.

Annette loved him? Don't think so. Brent became infuriated with himself. He had been deceived. By himself, not Annette. Her life had been doing just fine. She had not been the one walking around anticipating when something at work would be over her spouse's line. Why should she? He recalled the nights he really needed to work late but had not, so as not to worry or upset her. The times he should have been touring stores that he hadn't in order not to worry her. She had no appreciation of how he had altered his work life to keep his promise. But why should she? She never saw it nor had he discussed it with her.

He loved her and this should not be the way to get repaid for that love. He walked over to Annette. "How can you turn down that offer? It's no risk."

"It's not viable. That's it."

Brent led Annette over to the edge of the bed, sat her down beside him and looked in her eyes. "Annette I love you and I love the kids. I want you to be happy. I have never seen you this inflexible or unfair. Please tell me. What's your agenda?"

"No agenda," she said. "I love you, too. But this GM job has the characteristics of the one that almost ruined us. Director of marketing's a big job. Don't dispute that. It's somewhat competitive because you want the division to be successful. But general manager. A quantum leap in responsibility and competitiveness. Marlene's record is formidable. I know my husband. Wouldn't rest till you beat it. Ben Voorhees hasn't achieved his success sitting idly by. Pushes, pulls and prods. If he's in favor of Kruger but defers to Marlene's judgment, that pushing, pulling and prodding will take a big spike upward.

"You like to make the world go round, Brent. Won't be able to resist the challenge. Not inferring that you're wrong in taking that challenge. Not at all. Simply saying you won't be able to accept it and handle your family responsibilities in a meaningful way. At least, in a way I would define as meaningful. I think I know myself. Shortly, I wouldn't be able to tolerate it."

"Annette, that's as intelligently as you've talked about this issue. That analysis is the wife I know. And I can see your point. Our difference is me believing I can keep priorities straight and you believing I can't. Well, I believe I can strongly enough I'll bet on myself in the manner we've discussed."

Brent put his hands on Annette's arms and looked deeply in her eyes. "I love you sweetheart and will do everything in my power to make you happy. But everything has to be within reason. Demanding I turn down a job I've worked my adult life for isn't within reason. Not in my book. I'm offered Marlene's job, I'm taking it. I know we can be happy but you have to decide that for yourself."

"What do you mean by that?" she said. "That mean there's no more discussion?"

"About taking the job or not, nothing else to discuss. We're at an impasse. Said so yourself. I can't accept your position. Think it's selfish and unfair. But it's your prerogative to feel as you see fit. I've been and continue to be open for discussion about the definition and parameters of a good family life within the context of the GM job."

"Guess there's nothing more to say," she said.

Brent looked at her. Her blue eyes looked back and made him want to devour her. Her black sheath dress fit her body perfectly. Did he want the answer to the next question? Of course not. But they could not go on like this.

"There's one more thing. Is there someone else?"

"You're crazy," she said. "Of course not. Why would you ask such a stupid question?"

"Because your logic's been so strange over this. So not like the way you think. There's got to be something."

"It's not my logic, it's your selfishness. So. Is Bolivar going to be there?"

"Yes."

"Sure you don't have someone else?" she said.

"I'll pretend I didn't hear that comment," he said. "I'm going for the babysitter and we'll get out of here."

Paul and Audra had finished dressing and were sitting in the den having a drink before leaving.

"Tonight goes as planned, Marlene's job's yours, sweetie," said Audra. "Get goose bumps thinking about it. What a marvelous time I'm going to have telling my vile father. Was going to call. But think I'll take a couple days off and go to Charleston. Want to see the look on the nauseating man's face."

"Remember your own advice, my dear. Don't celebrate till Voorhees makes the announcement."

The edge in her voice sharpened. "Unless you've been lying, can't be anyone but you."

"I haven't been lying. Just let everything play out, Audra."

"Ready to celebrate. With all that's happening to you, didn't mention some great news. I got a huge promotion, Paul. Senior account exec handling the company's two largest accounts. Salary went up thirty percent and in line for vice president."

"Fantastic," he said. Paul knew that Audra had been sleeping with her company's president. At least, it had paid off. Oldest profession in the world with his wife one of the highest paid in it. What an achievement to celebrate. Maybe he would get a Rolex out of it.

Audra asked, "You have Stuart ready to put the shiv in Shannon's throat? No screw-ups. Stuart's hesitancy with Evan would be a bad one."

"It's not a problem. He's going to be nervous around Evan but I can help lead the discussion."

"Don't let Evan get the idea you've got a ring in the guy's nose," she said. "Stuart comes off slow in the first place. You can't let him slip how much he hates Shannon. Would destroy his credibility. Roth has a high ethic quotient."

"Excellent point," he said. "I'll make certain it doesn't get steered that way. Make sure you have a drink with that mousey wife of Stuart's. And make sure Stuart sees you doing it. He has to believe if I get the job, he's on the team."

"Wouldn't think of keeping that brick, would you?"

"Of course not. Tonight he's working for a better severance. Just unaware of what's in the pot at the end of his rainbow."

"Okay. But I'm spending the time I need with Annette Shannon. She'll spill her guts. But, Paul, don't count on it. Handle the Roth, Stuart thing like it's your only chip."

"That's my plan. The affair has to be played out and accepted by Atlanta management. Set up Stuart's credibility with Evan. It'll be accepted and get Shannon dismissed. If we only have marital difficulties, he could land in Tom Carthage's job. That's unacceptable."

"Old Tom's stepping down, huh?" said Audra. "Nice gentleman. Not too many of them left. Got fucked with that marriage of his."

"He did," said Paul. "But his leaving is bad timing. Requires Shannon's reputation to be shattered. Nothing left to pick up. I'm not having the arrogant, overbearing man looking over my shoulder from Atlanta."

"I'll talk to Shannon's wife about the horrible rumors of her marital difficulties," said Audra.

"Be careful," said Paul. "Nobody can deduce these things emanated from us."

"Don't worry. Know enough people in Atlanta to throw down some names if she presses me. Doesn't appear to be the confrontive type. This'll set up a conversation with Voorhees. She might even confide in me. Never can tell."

"Don't understand how talking about rumors will set her up for Ben."

"Because, sweetie," she said. "Be willing to bet my new paycheck she doesn't think she's got marital problems. The only way she'll have problems is if hubby takes the GM job. No one's told me but I'll wager that's her mindset. When I'm through she'll think I'm her ally. I get finished pitching marital difficulties to her, she'll be jumping out of her skin to tell Ben Voorhees there're no marital problems if there's no GM job in her husband's future. Or something to that effect. Ben'll pick it up."

"Can't tell you how much you mean to me and my career," he said. "That's just brilliant."

"Just my guess but a good one, I think. I'm good at this and we'll go far together," she said.

"How're you handling the meeting with Ben?"

"The simple part," she replied. "Know damn well they want to talk to her. Voorhees wants you but's reticent to overrule Marlene's choice. Got to have a legitimate excuse to do it. He gets one, it's over.

"Ben Voorhees isn't different from other successful people. He's developed a formula that's worked for him. Part of his formula's having financial people run divisions. Worked in the past and he doesn't want to change. Not satisfied with Shannon because Shannon's outside his business comfort zone. If not, you'd be working for Shannon now. Marlene's a powerful influence with Ben. So, CEO or not, he needs a viable reason to dismiss her choice. All we're doing is making sure he's gets it.

"Probably tasked Ascutney to talk with Annette. Going to make sure that doesn't happen. Little miss housewife and I are going right to the main man. I'll avoid Ascutney like a case of flu. When Voorhees is free from hangers on, I'll get dear Mrs. Shannon in front of him. Reintroduce myself and ask if he remembers Annette. Say he must remember her husband, Brent. Mention he's the one that's done such a fabulous job on the division's marketing program."

Paul laughed. "Don't praise him too much."

"Won't. But good enough to get a conversation where business talk's acceptable," she said. "That doesn't do it, say I'm married to a homebody. Very little travel. Takes an understanding wife to be able to handle Brent's travel schedule."

"Please don't infer you couldn't handle it."

"Excellent point. I'll say me, being a career woman with no children, it would pose no problems. But with two children must be a hassle."

"Better," said Paul. "Should get it into Voorhees' court. Great. Shannon's wife will fry Ben and enjoy doing it."

"These two pieces go together, Shannon's toast," Audra said. "And that whore Bolivar is out the door with him. Incidentally, how're you going to handle things with your arrogant, uncultured father?"

"Been thinking about that," he said. "Think I'll invite them both to Charlotte. Come up with a reason my father can't resist."

Audra chuckled. "Maybe World Wrestling Federation's in town."

"Maybe," he said. "I'll have them come to the office. Come into that beautiful GM's office. I'll have a dozen red roses and a tennis bracelet for my mother. Expensive but mother's worth it. Tell her this happened because of her support. Tell my scum father, it happened in spite of him."

"Let's think about it," Audra said. "We could refine the approach to make the sorry jerk-off pay more. Be more miserable. Nothing would be too much for the animal."

"We have a few weeks to refine it," he said draining his glass. "Let's finish our drinks and get to the party."

Driving uptown to the party, Brent realized that his marriage could be over. He had been a fool to think he could please Annette. Their bedroom discussion thirty minutes ago proved it. She had a box that their marriage had to fit in and this week he had jumped out of that box. As a result, to meet her needs, she had to force him to choose between a job he had worked his ass off for and her.

She had been correct in assessing her own earning potential. She could start at a Charlotte law firm for about what he made now. He knew she had gotten feelers through her contacts at that church legal assistance program. She was an excellent attorney in the public administration practice area. Along with the child support he would provide her, she and the children would be able to live in their house quite comfortably.

If she had another man in her life, she would be more than adequately set up. Yeah, she certainly had options.

He had difficulty comprehending it. Being set up by his own wife. He realized that he had two Krugers. One at work. One at home. The actuality of it crushed him. God, what a mess his life had turned into in four days.

"Going to say anything or this the silent treatment," said Annette.

"No silent treatment," he said. "Just thinking what a disaster my life's turned into in four days."

"And wasn't it nice you dragged the family with you."

"Thought that's what family was. Through thick and thin. All that stuff."

"Don't get sarcastic or flip with me," she retorted. "And yes, that's what a family is for as long as there's mutual agreement."

Brent felt himself losing the battle with his frazzled nerves. His temper was on the edge.

"Please, let's not fight," he managed to say. "Would just ask for your support tonight."

"One more time," she said. "What does that mean?"

"Means don't torpedo me with upper management."

"How could I do that?"

"Simple. Tell them you're not happy and don't support me for Marlene's job. My chances evaporate."

"They don't care what I think."

"Don't be naive," Brent said. "They knew we had problems when we came over here. Marlene stood up for me because I leveled with her. She carried the day without a whisper because I reported directly to her and she knew we could work things out.

"This is different. Would be reporting to Ben Voorhees and it's his call. His strong religious beliefs make him ultra sensitive to family issues. Laudable attribute but a bit problematic in this instance. If he discovers, or surmises, that promoting me will split up our family there go my chances. Poof."

"Who said anything about splitting up the family?"

"Annette, there're several things that anger me. Being taken for a fool is chief among them. Don't go there. There's no missing the veiled threat issued with your position's inflexibility. Your refusal to discuss any alternatives.

"That's a discussion for the future. All I'm asking you is don't come unglued and tell upper management you're against me taking Marlene's job. That's all. You have complete control over this situation. You don't want me to take Marlene's job. Fine. Just seek out Ben Voorhees, walk up to him and tell him you think if I'm the division GM, there is a strong probability our marriage will be ruined. That's all you have to do. Issue is settled. You'll be asked. Count on it. Negative response ends my chances. I'm asking for your loyalty."

"I think this crap's as overblown as your paranoia over Kruger," she said.

"I can assure you it's not overblown."

"My stance hasn't changed. Quit badgering me, Brent. If I'm asked about the opportunity for you, I'll say it's an honor and I've always been proud of your accomplishments. They ask if I'm supportive of you taking that job, it's no. Hear me one more time. Won't lie for you. Period."

"Okay," he said. "That's the best you can do for me, so be it."

They pulled up to valet parking. The door was opened for Annette while Brent got out and took the parking ticket. As he took it, he thought that his own wife would be torching him in no more than an hour. It would be at least an hour. The vultures wouldn't swoop immediately. That wouldn't be polite. Damn, Annette looked gorgeous tonight.

Paul and Audra separated upon arriving at the party. Paul went to a bar station and ordered a Dewar on the rocks.

The company's preparations impressed him. Two bars flanked the main ballroom with a third in an adjoining room. Banquet tables with cut flower arrangements surrounded a hardwood dance floor. A band assembled a sound system opposite an elegant buffet with two carving stations and four ice sculptures. Yes, Marlene's send-off would be an event to remember.

He thought about the party he and Audra would host after his promotion. It would be at the country club with less attendees than this but no less lavish. More so, in fact. It had to communicate that the division would step up under his leadership. He might have to throw a small amount of personal money into it for the lavish appointments. Most of the cost could be expensed. It would be imperative that Shannon and Bolivar be gone by then. He couldn't afford dirty laundry. Also, their firing would say who was the person in charge and how disloyalty would be rewarded.

Enough of this, he thought. First things first. For all that to happen, the Shannon, Bolivar affair had to find its way to Voorhees. Paul looked around the room but did not see Neal Stuart. He had a brief moment of inner panic as he saw the Atlanta group arriving. He had to find Stuart. All he needed would be for the idiot to have come down with the flu. Paul could not afford to have Evan Roth speak to Stuart before Paul prepped him once again. Timing was everything in this plan.

Paul decided to check the small room adjoining the ballroom. On the way, Nadia Swenson intercepted him.

"Isn't this a great party, Paul?" she said, already slurring her words. "So glad I'm in town for it. Spend a majority of my time in stores making sales happen."

What an ass kisser, Paul thought. At least she had faced reality.

"So glad you could be here, Nadia. Maybe later this evening we could have a drink together."

Nadia smiled. "That would be super."

"Good. We'll make time for it."

So uncouth, Paul thought as he continued to search for Stuart. His policy would be that she travel at least ninety percent of the time. He would only have to deal with her by e-mail and phone. A steady diet of the woman would be more than he could stand.

He walked into the smaller room and immediately saw Neal Stuart and his wife sitting at a table. He breathed a sigh of relief and approached them.

"How are you two this evening?" Paul said. "Don't believe I've had the pleasure of meeting your lovely wife, Neal."

Neal rose from his chair. "Evening, Paul. This is my wife, Mildred. Mildred," he said looking at her, "this is Paul Kruger, the division's director of finance."

"Mildred, it's a pleasure to meet you," said Paul. "My wife Audra is floating around here somewhere. I'll make certain you two meet this evening."

"It's an honor to meet you, Paul," said Mildred. "Neal's told me so much about you."

This is so easy it is near sickening, Paul thought. He laughed. "Well, hope some of it was good."

Mildred smiled. "All good."

She leaned close to Paul and continued in a whisper, "Hope you get the GM job. Neal told me you would. Then things would be a lot better."

"Mildred talks too much," said Neal.

Paul laughed. "Nonsense, Neal. Sure like what she has to say." They all laughed.

Paul held Mildred's hand and looked into her eyes. "Mildred, could you forgive my rudeness if I borrowed Neal for a few minutes? Won't be long at all."

Mildred blushed at Paul's touch and look. She stammered, "Oh, not at all. You two run along. I'll be fine right here. Might even try the buffet."

"Thank you so much, Mildred," Paul said. "I'll have him back in a jiffy."

Paul led Neal to the room's bar station. Paul ordered another Dewar and a rum and coke for Neal.

Paul asked, "Anyone mentioned Shannon and Bolivar to you?"

"No. Really nervous about the whole thing."

"Understand completely. I'd be nervous, too. But there's no need. If something is said, tell the truth. Nothing more, nothing less. What you told me was the truth, wasn't it? No embellishments?"

"Absolutely," said Neal. He was quite emphatic, which comforted Paul. "Not nervous about what to say. Just never had anything to do with these Atlanta people. Except to say hello a couple of times."

"Neal, I'll bet they'll talk to you. Relax and tell the truth," said Paul.
Fall in line you boob, he thought. Don't be such a sniffling whiner. Stuart

was pale to the point of transparency.

"Would you be more at ease if I were there when you were questioned?"

Relief spread across Stuart's face. "That possible?"

"Maybe."

Paul led Stuart into the main ballroom and scanned the room for Evan Roth. He was nowhere to be found. Where was the guy? He had to get this over with before Stuart self-destructed.

A voice in back of them boomed, "So, how's the financial wizard of Charlotte?"

Paul and Neal turned together to face Ben Voorhees. Paul thought Stuart's knees were going to buckle on the spot.

"Hi, Ben," said Paul. "Nice to see you. A marvelous send-off for Marlene. You folks outdid yourselves."

"Thanks," said Ben. "She's an important part of our success."

"Without question," said Paul. "Ben, forgive my rudeness. You had the pleasure of meeting Neal Stuart? He's the division's excellent director of advertising."

"Haven't had the pleasure," said Ben shaking Neal's hand. "Neal, an honor."

"Thanks. Same here," said Neal.

"Neal's a power behind the scenes in the division's success formula," said Paul. "Not a more stand up, honest, hard working person in our operation."

"It's a pleasure to meet those who make Richmont a success," said Ben. He smiled and continued. "Speaking of that, better move around to see the others. Good to see you both," he said moving off.

Paul thought that the gods must be looking over him. This was meant to be. Ben Voorhees would not have known Neal Stuart from the garbage collector. Now he thinks he is one of the cream of the crop. A hard working, honest employee. When Evan tells him about the affair and his information source, Ben will attach the highly circumstantial evidence to this hard working, self-effacing man. What a stroke of luck. Sorry he had not thought of it. He would have some answering to do when he fired Stuart. But, first things first.

"Glad I could introduce you to Ben Voorhees," said Paul. "He makes the company go."

"Goodness, what an honor."

"A wonderful human on top of being a great business person. Neal, you've gotten past the CEO. Anyone else will be downhill."

Neal laughed nervously. "Guess that's right."

The little fellow still looked like a deer in headlights. Then he spotted Evan Roth at one of the bar stations.

"Like to introduce you to one more senior manager," said Paul. "Hope I'm not disturbing your plans for the evening but like to get to know you better and introduce you to the people who can help your career."

"No. I'm enjoying myself and appreciate meeting people from Atlanta," said Neal.

Walking toward Evan, Paul thought that Neal seemed to be relaxing a bit. At the bar, Paul ordered two more drinks. He handed one to Neal and looked over at Evan. "Hi, Evan. You're looking great as always."

Evan walked toward them. "Thanks, Paul. Great party."

"Sure is. Evan, you ever met Neal Stuart? He's the division's superb director of advertising."

"Haven't had the pleasure," said Evan shaking Neal's hand. "Paul's told me what an asset you are to the division."

"Pleasure to meet you, Evan," Neal said. "Paul was being kind."

Paul thought that the dimwit was getting the idea. Way to go. He's relaxing.

"Evan, got a few minutes to sit down and visit? Haven't had a chance to catch up and I'd like you to get to know Neal better."

"Sure," said Evan. "Off duty tonight."

Paul led them to an empty table in a far corner of the ballroom. He made certain he and Evan were sitting with their backs to the room. Anyone who looked would see Neal Stuart's face. It would not draw interest.

After they were seated, Paul looked at Neal. "Any success I've had with Richmont, I owe to Evan Roth."

Evan beamed. "Paul's been successful because of his superior talents not me." He looked at Neal. "Neal, you report to Brent Shannon?"

"I do."

"Just For You has a successful marketing program," Evan said. "You should be proud of your department's achievements."

"Very proud and hope to have a bigger impact in the future."

"Certain you will." Evan looked at Paul and asked, "Be appropriate to talk a little business during this festive affair?"

"Fine. Long as I don't have to throw away my drink," said Paul.

Evan laughed. "Let you get away with it this one time."

"If you have business to discuss, I'll excuse myself," said Neal.

"Not at all, Neal. Please stay. You may be able to help," said Evan. "Concerns a sensitive issue. One which Paul might feel uncomfortable discussing." He looked over at Paul. "But no need for you to leave."

"Don't know the subject but I'll leave if it becomes necessary," Paul said.

Evan said, "Neal, you report to Brent Shannon and spend a good deal of time with him."

"Yes."

"This's highly confidential. Not to be repeated," said Evan. "Do you understand, Neal?"

"Certainly."

"Not certain but Shannon might be on a short list to replace Marlene Wolff," Evan said.

"Heard that," said Neal.

Paul pushed his chair back from the table until out of Evan's field of vision. He nodded to Neal, pointed to his own chest and mouthed not to bring up his name. Neal nodded that he had gotten the message.

"If you could, Neal," said Evan, "like you to put something to rest. At least, in my mind. Something that, if true, could have a negative impact on the company."

"If I can, be glad to help," said Neal.

"Nasty rumor's been swirling around. About a year now," said Evan. "Concerns your boss and Patricia Bolivar. The HR Director, I believe. About them being intimately involved. If true, would be disastrous if Shannon's promoted to head up the division. You can appreciate that."

"Absolutely," said Neal. "Would tear our division apart."

"Know you work with Shannon as closely as anyone. Also, your work ethic and integrity are above reproach. I'll be satisfied to forget this rumor if you say there's nothing to it. Assure you I'm no gossip advocate. Simply want to put this to rest for the company's good."

Neal looked Evan squarely in the eye. "Sorry, but can't give you that assurance."

The guy is going to pull this off in magnificent fashion. It could not have been scripted better, thought Paul. Evan might have set this conversation up to get the answer he wanted but who cared.

"Beg your pardon," Evan said. "What do you mean can't give me an assurance?"

"Sorry to say I've seen Brent and Patricia in social settings, drinks after work and dinner when traveling," said Neal. "To my standards, afraid they've exhibited inappropriate behavior."

Evan sat straight in his chair and leaned toward Neal. "How're you defining inappropriate?"

Neal never hesitated. "Seemed too intimate. Too much in each other's personal space to be just business associates." He gestured toward Evan with his open palms held close together.

Paul smiled to himself. There goes the garrote around Shannon's neck. Now squeeze the life out of him, little man.

"This's extraordinarily serious," Evan said. "You confident in your assessment?"

"Not looking to get anyone in trouble," said Neal. "But feel strong about it. No place for any of that in business. Couldn't say anything to Brent. He would've taken offense at the implication. Don't want to get on the bad side of Brent Shannon. Can believe me on that score. Got a dictatorial leadership style. Vindictive if you cross him. Hope this can remain confidential, Mr. Roth."

The idiot finally woke up to the reality that he had just crucified his boss, thought Paul. He was getting worried about his own survival. Paul almost laughed out loud. What Stuart did not realize was that he had screwed himself as much as he had Shannon.

"You can rest assured this conversation's confidential," said Evan. "Paul can vouch that I'm a man of my word."

"Absolutely," said Paul.

Evan stood up. "Well, better mingle with the other guests or Ben'll have me on the carpet tomorrow. Neal, a pleasure to visit with you. Certain we'll see each other in the future."

"Pleasure was all mine," Neal said. "And my comments will remain confidential?"

"Certainly," said Evan. He nodded to Paul and walked away.

Visibly unnerved, Neal looked at Paul. "Hope I didn't say anything out of turn."

"Not at all. I've got to run down Audra or get sued for divorce. Why don't you find Mildred and attack the buffet?"

"Okay. Hope we can meet Audra this evening."

"We'll make it happen," responded Paul as he patted Neal on the back.

Paul watched Stuart walk away, his inner soul dancing the victor's dance. He wanted to go outside and shout. Shannon was a dead man walking. Just didn't know it yet.

Annette had finished a conversation with Tom Carthage and stood alone with a gin and tonic in her hand. What a wonderful guy, she thought. He had been dealt some devastating blows in his personal life. It was a shame his marriage had not worked out. From all accounts, his ex-wife was a wonderful woman. Some things just were not meant to be.

Out of the corner of her eye, she saw Audra Kruger walking toward her. A visual reconnoiter confirmed there to be no avenues of escape. She did not need this. She had vowed to avoid political games this evening and Audra Kruger heightened political games to fine art.

Annette had always held the opinion that Audra was a beautiful woman and this evening did nothing to lessen her opinion. She would kill to have Audra's hips. The problem with Audra – one could not have a five-minute conversation without hearing about her old south heritage, prominence of her family or how well her husband did his job. She became boring quickly.

Audra reached her. "Hi, Annette. How're you? Been a while."

"Christmas party, I believe," said Annette.

"Week's been turmoil with Marlene's eminent departure. Paul's a wreck getting ready for the turnover."

"Yes. Brent's pretty upset about Marlene leaving. Liked working for her."

"Paul feels the same. He came over here with Marlene. She's special to him. Keep telling him she'll only be in Atlanta." She put her hand on Annette's arm. "Paul's certain Brent will be his next boss."

Annette laughed. "Brent's story's the opposite. Paul's the new GM."

Audra leaned toward Annette smiling, "Ought to get their stories straight."

"Agreed."

"Brent's been with Richmont what, about eight years?"

"Correct."

"Came from Chicago?"

"No. Brent's firm was based in Chicago but we lived in Minneapolis."

"Paul's always respected Brent," said Audra. "They've had their differences. I've heard about them. But they're both big boys."

Why would Brent be paranoid about this guy, thought Annette? Unless this woman proved to be a bold-faced liar, Paul and Brent should be able to work together. Strange, she thought. Brent had always been an excellent judge of people but he missed this one.

"You know, Brent has been the only business issue Paul's ever enlisted my aid for," Audra said.

"That right? What issue?"

"Helping to quell those ugly rumors about marital difficulties between you two. Nonsense, of course," said Audra. "All you have to do is be around you two for five minutes to know that."

"Well, I hate rumors but Brent and I had some marriage problems before we came to Richmont."

"I would have never guessed it," said Audra. "Everything must have gotten back in order because you've got a lovely family."

Quite a comment, Annette thought. The woman would not have given me the time of day before tonight.

"Oh, Brent and I still have issues from time to time. All couples do, I guess."

"I can tell you Paul and I do. Good everything's in order for you two. Brent takes the GM job, there'll be travel and late hours. Thing I like about Paul's job is he's a home body. Very little out of town work."

"If Brent got that job, my world would change. No question."

At first this conversation seemed to be the age-old bonding routine in case Brent got the job. But as it continued to develop, Annette became less certain of its motive.

"Would be hard for me, too," said Audra. "Could cope better because I've a fulltime career and no children."

"No question it's easier under those circumstances," Annette responded.

"You still do that pro bono legal work?"

"Sure do."

Suddenly, Annette got a feeling that this discussion could be calculated and rehearsed. But she still had no idea of motive. Why don't we change directions and try to make some sense out of it.

"Tell me," Annette said, "would you have any problems with Paul in the GM job?" Audra's sudden change in expression from one of total confidence to anxiousness gave even more credence to Annette's feeling of uneasiness.

"It would be difficult but I guess I would support Paul in his career," Audra replied. "Paul respects Brent so much. Was interested in how I could help you when Brent became GM. Soulmate maybe. Would be an honor."

This is way past weird, Annette thought. Her interactions with Audra Kruger over the past four years as well as others' past comments were diametrically opposed to Audra considering a soulmate role to anyone but Audra Kruger. Something is very wrong with this picture.

"How sweet and thoughtful of you." Annette smiled. "Such a dear. Those types of jobs tend to put a tremendous strain on a marriage. Many times self-inflicted strains. Don't know if I could cope by myself."

Audra's body relaxed with Annette's answer. Annette hadn't studied the law for nothing. This meeting had been timed and rehearsed. She still had no idea of exact motive but, whatever motive, it would be for Audra and her husband's benefit. Audra had always been known to be a manipulating shrew and Annette doubted a change in character now.

"Let's go fix our makeup and find our husbands," said Audra.

"Super idea."

Walking to the restroom, Annette knew she could not support Brent taking the GM job. But one thing was sure. If this drama being played out between she and Audra had the purpose of in some way hurting Brent's chances, she would not allow herself to be the pawn for these people. This Kruger woman had always been known as a ruthless tramp. Annette could only imagine her husband. Maybe Bolivar's warning to Brent was not just a concocted fairytale to get him in bed.

Annette still thought Brent and Bolivar were an item but she admitted it was conjecture. Her brother had been correct about that. What was not conjecture was this bewildering and questionable conversation with Audra Kruger. Annette could not live under the GM working conditions. Regardless, she cared deeply for Brent. If this turned out to be an underhanded strategy to destroy him through her, it was loathsome. Just reprehensible. In the world of the Krugers', loyalty might be something to be overlooked in the name of self-interest. Well, not where she grew up. Okay, Annette Shannon, keep your wits about you. If little housewife Annette is about to be led into a Black Widow's trap, let's see who's the Black Widow.

Brent had lost Annette. She was not hiding behind his coattails to prevent a verbal assault by the powers that be. Her behavior got stranger by the minute. She had never been a big party person. She had always been much more attuned to smaller, more intimate gatherings with people she knew well. Venues like this evening made her uncomfortable. She normally stayed with him as much as possible. Not tonight. She blasted off to the races daring the legions to attack. The woman confused him more with each act of this drama.

The hell with her. She was on her own and he needed a drink. At the bar station, just as he palmed his Wild Turkey, a hand fell on his shoulder.

"How you holding up, my man?"

Brent turned to see Tom Carthage standing behind him.

"Understand it's been quite a week so far," Tom said.

Brent smiled. He had not associated with anyone in his business career for whom he held more affection than Tom Carthage. Brent came to Richmont a traumatized human being. Tom guided him back to business health through a loose-tight leadership style that Brent could only hope to emulate. Tom always considered Brent's relationship with Annette. It had been a tremendous learning experience. He was a truly remarkable man.

"Hell, don't sell the week short," said Brent. "Got couple more hours."

"Come on, Tiger. Let's have a seat and talk."

Walking to a table, Brent noticed Annette in an animated conversation with Audra Kruger. He concluded that he did not care to hear that discussion.

Sitting down, Tom said, "Seriously. Making it okay?"

"Yeah, I guess. What've you heard?"

"Couple of conversations with Ben. First, he told me you were on the short list and asked what I thought. Let's say I didn't let you down. Second, after the Faulkton speech, Ben couldn't understand why Marlene continued to stand behind you. Think I put some perspective to that mess. Told him to have Marlene talk to Faulkton. Smart move, I thought. Hell of it all is Theodore Faulkton's a great business person."

"Know that. Guy's driven some numbers from that chain."

"Off the subject, Faulkton's suffering from a serious heart condition. One that might not be fixable," said Tom.

"No matter what the guy thinks of me, that's a shame."

"He's got to slow down. Probably'll spend more time on board work. He and Ben relate well. Same basic business philosophies. Impress him when the opportunity presents itself. Best way to bury the hatchet."

"Thanks for the heads up."

"How's Annette doing in all this?"

"A primary thorn in the briar patch," said Brent. He gave Tom a rundown on her position and their confrontations over the past four days.

"You're looking at the last person on earth who should be giving relationship advice," said Tom. "But think I can see why you two wound up at loggerheads."

"Enlighten me."

"You're in a power struggle at work," said Tom. "You might call it survival but it's about power. Power to get things done. Make a difference. To succeed. That's how guys like us self-actualize. You're involved in protecting yourself from a guy trying to go one up and have his way with you. Trying to avoid being pushed out and experiencing failure. An unacceptable end result. Nothing wrong with that, right?"

"Don't see anything wrong with it."

"Neither do I. But we're men. The one-up gender," Tom said. "Annette looks at it differently. Has nothing to do with her being a lawyer or working for the government like you mentioned in your recap a minute ago. Women want to connect. Get consensus. Not her nature to understand why you and Kruger can't get along. That you can't achieve a connection that allows you to work together. She sees the Just For You organization as a community where members should search for connection. Where members should acknowledge, welcome and foster dependence on one another. Not independence from one another.

"If she worked in a business organization on a daily basis her nature would be tempered by the realities of organizational life. Think we agree Marlene's had her female instincts tempered. But still marvelous at getting people involved and working together. Much better than most male executives in this company. These instincts are why insightful women who can grasp and adapt to the realities of organizational life make such effective managers. Glad I'm old. They'll replace us all before it's over.

"I'm telling you this, Tiger, because the primary cause of my marriage's failure was that I didn't understand those dynamics."

Tom Carthage continued to amaze him, Brent thought. A fantastic human that didn't deserve what the marriage gods dealt him.

"I'm afraid our relationship might have passed critical mass."

"Sorry to hear that cause I'm about to complicate your life more."

"Why not. But might have to get in line."

"I didn't want you to hear this on the gossip circuit. I'm taking early retirement the end of this quarter."

Brent was shocked. "Why?"

"Time I devoted myself to some things I've wanted to do for years. Going to teach marketing at Georgia State and try my hand at writing a book on market planning for small business. Looking forward to it."

"Tom, that sounds exciting. You'll make a marvelous contribution in both."

"Thanks. Now to complicate your life. My job's yours for the asking. You're best in the company. Everyone knows it. Ben would put his approval on it in a New York minute. Haven't talked to him because didn't want to give him an excuse to eliminate you from the GM job if that's what you want. You'd be successful at either."

"I'm honored you think that highly of me."

"You've earned what I think of you," said Tom. "Job would be a big step. Relocation back to Atlanta. Much more time commitment and travel. You're aware we're doing more international marketing. If you're interested, might make a difference in your personal situation. It's yours unless something I don't know." Tom laughed. "Like embezzlement, lying, falsifying documents, screwing the help. Stuff like that."

Hmm. Make sure you don't talk to Annette, Brent thought. "Think I'm cool on that list," he said.

Tom laughed again. "I know that, Brent. Well, I'd better circulate or Ben won't let me expense the trip. Think about it. Let me know Monday morning." He put his hand on Brent's shoulder. "Has to be no later than Monday morning.

Earlier the better."

"I will. Thanks again, Tom."

Brent watched Tom walk away and shook his head. Come on Richmont Corporation dangle that carrot. Come on Brent, sweetie, take a bite. Let me seduce you. He needed another drink. He went to the bar and ordered a Turkey. Come to think of it, he could use a flock of Turkeys. Waiting for his drink, he felt a hand on his arm. Okay, who's the messenger this time? he thought. He turned to see Patricia Bolivar standing next to him. Naturally, she looked ravishing and wore the perfume that drove him nuts.

"Isn't this a stupendous send-off for Marlene?" Patricia said.

"Certainly is."

"Asked me to introduce Ben Voorhees to make a presentation to Marlene. I've got to hurry," she said. "Wanted to tell you I talked to Marilyn Beamon. Heard nothing but if she does she'll try to defuse it."

"Great," said Brent. He decided not to mention his conversation with Tom Carthage.

"Seems Todd and Marilyn Beamon think I had something to do with saving his job when I worked in Atlanta. Feel they have a debt to pay," she said. "Think we have a good contact there." She squeezed his arm. "Have to run."

Brent thought how nice it would be if Annette saw the arm squeeze. Yep, that would about wrap it up. Brent headed for the buffet to do some mingling of his own.

Annette and Audra walked out of the women's room together. Annette noticed Ashley Weedon. She made a mental note to visit with her before the evening was over.

“Let’s get a glass of champagne,” said Audra.

“I’ll join you but make mine a gin and tonic,” replied Annette. Where is this drama taking us? thought Annette. The only way to find out is to have it run its course. At the bar station, Audra said, “We have to get to know each other better.”

“Think that would be mutually beneficial,” responded Annette. “Haven’t done enough together. Either the two of us or as couples.”

“Oh, I agree. When Brent gets Marlene’s job, hope I can be an outlet for you when he’s traveling. Can get pretty lonely.”

“Well, Brent hasn’t gotten the job. And he has to decide whether to accept it if it is offered.”

“Certainly he’d accept it,” said Audra.

Annette recognized a subtle smugness on Audra’s face. What a self-serving snob, Annette thought. “We’ve talked about it. We know it could put a strain on our marriage. He’s got to decide if it’s worth it.”

“Can’t believe he wouldn’t take it. It’s become Richmont’s plum job.”

“We’ve not decided,” said Annette.

“You’ll support him in his decision, won’t you?” said Audra.

The angle cometh, thought Annette. Audra was baiting her to reveal Brent and her disagreement on the GM job. What a trollop.

“You play tennis, Audra?”

A confused look covered Audra’s face. “Yes, I do. Why?”

“We’ve a lively tennis group at Raintree. Love to have you join us sometime.”

“Would be fun. Just need enough notice.”

“We’ll plan on it. Isn’t this a lovely party?”

"It is. Annette, it must be tenuous if you and Brent don't agree about him taking the GM job."

"Tenuous would be accurate."

"Just our brief conversation tonight makes me know I like your company. Hope this thing hasn't affected your marriage. That would be frightful."

"Hasn't helped," said Annette. "Hope we can get through it."

"Would be dreadful to be lasting damage."

"Audra, isn't that Ben Voorhees over there?"

"Where?"

"Left of the buffet."

"Why, yes it is," said Audra. "With Terry Thomas and Stan Ascutney."

"I remember Stan. He was helpful when we moved here."

"Ever met Ben?"

"Think in a receiving line at one of the New Year's Eve parties. But never talked to him. Have you?"

"Yes. A great guy," Audra said. "Come on. I'll introduce you.

"No. Don't want to disturb him."

"Nonsense. He'd love to meet you."

Annette and Audra walked over to the group.

"Hi, Audra," said Ben. "Nice to see you again."

"And you, Ben. Like to reintroduce Annette Shannon to you."

"An honor, Annette," Ben said. "My pleasure to introduce two of my associates, Terry Thomas and Stan Ascutney."

Ben Voorhees had the most beautiful, charming southern accent she had ever heard. She could picture him and Peter Ludlow drinking mint juleps on the veranda.

"You ladies are married to primary movers and shakers not only in this division but the whole company," said Ben. "Delighted you came over. Like to thank you for your support of our business efforts. Know I steal your husbands far too much. Appreciate your patience."

Annette looked at Audra. Audra's eyes had the look of a barracuda about to strike. Annette warned herself not to be lulled to sleep by these charming southern gentlemen with their self-effacing demeanor. Piranha swam in warm waters.

Annette looked into Ben Voorhees' eyes and realized he might have a hidden agenda but he had been sincere in his comments. Well, no time like the present. Time to end all the speculation.

"I've always been impressed with Richmont's treatment of employees who get things done," said Annette.

"Richmont prides itself on doing that," replied Ben.

Everyone in the group except she and Ben Voorhees were craning their necks so hard they would be stiff in the morning, thought Annette.

"Ben, I know I'm out of line. Brent'd kill me if he were here," said Annette. "But I have got to tell you, whatever the final decision, I appreciate the company thinking highly enough of my husband to consider him to replace Marlene. Please don't feel badly of me for saying that."

"Feel badly?" said Ben. "Consider it a compliment to the company."

Terry Thomas smiled and stepped between Audra and Annette with his back to Audra. He said, "Think I know how Brent feels about the opportunity. What're your thoughts?"

Annette felt the intensity of Ben's scrutiny. Stan Ascutney looked at the dance floor but was obviously listening.

"Terry, big jobs bring huge challenges. Chief among them is to keep one's priorities, to maintain a semblance of life balance," said Annette. "Brent and I have worked together for balance that includes family while not detracting from his job. Guess we would have an opportunity to do it again."

Ben Voorhees turned to separate himself, Terry Thomas and Annette from Stan and Audra although Annette knew that both of them could hear the conversation.

"Forgive us, Annette," said Ben. "Only reason Terry asked you the question was you and Brent had some past difficulties. Didn't want to make a decision that would exacerbate any issues you might still have. Weren't trying to pry."

"Hope everyone learns from experience. Brent and I continually do," said Annette.

"Honored you felt comfortable enough to share your time with me," said Ben. "Hope to see you many times in the future."

"Ben, hope so," Annette said. She turned to Audra. "Think I'll join you for champagne now."

"I've a presentation for Marlene shortly," said Ben. "I'd better get moving."

Annette and Audra walked the perimeter of the dance floor. Annette stopped, touched Audra's arm, and said, "Don't want any champagne. Would like to share something with you."

Audra looked at her glumly. "What's that?" Annette saw that the woman was boiling.

"I'm sure you know I grew up in a small Minnesota town. But please, please don't let that make you think I just fell off the proverbial soy bean truck."

Audra's face took on a shocked expression. "Whatever are you talking about?"

Annette leaned close to Audra and whispered in her ear. "Don't ever try to use me against my husband, you no good, arrogant, blue blood witch. Doesn't work. Never has, never will."

Annette drew away and continued. "Don't know who's getting Marlene's job. Don't care. But anything I can do to derail you, you conniving wench, consider it done. One more thing. Never want to lay eyes on you again."

Annette smiled sweetly, turned on her heels and went to have a few more gin and tonics. Maybe more than a few. On the way she decided, on second thought, she liked her own hips quite nicely. Audra could keep hers.

Sitting with Ashley and Dina, Brent thought that life could be quite a trip. The corporate cannibals had him in the pot and Tom Carthage had pulled him out. Annette would jump for joy. Unless she had other plans of which he had no knowledge.

"Hey, boss. Still with us?" said Ashley.

"Sorry, ladies. Preoccupied."

"No problem," said Dina. "Seem deep in thought."

"Thinking what a great party and presentation they had for Marlene," Brent said.

"Was super," Dina said. "And glad to see a woman make it big."

"Dina, she's the best business person I've had the privilege to work with," said Brent.

"She's great," Dina said. "Well, folks, past my bedtime. I'm outta here."

"About had it, too," said Ashley. "Night, boss. See you Monday."

"Good night you two. Drive carefully."

Brent sat alone and his mind returned to his wife. What's her scheme? Did she have a scheme? Damn. He had been schemed out. Kruger's got a scheme. Annette's got a scheme. He felt like a Spartan at Thermopylae. Eventually somebody's spear would get him.

Taking Tom up on the VP marketing job could force everything into the open. Kruger would get the division GM job. That would get the jerk off Brent's back. He could not figure out what he had ever done to the little worm.

It would be a significant promotion with a hell of a salary increase and include the senior executive perk and incentive package. However, it would not have the time commitment or stress of a general management position. The travel could be an issue. Programs to penetrate foreign markets would come with a pretty hectic travel schedule. At least, initially. However, it would be something Annette could deal with, he thought. The move back to Atlanta would not be an issue. Although she loved Charlotte, she enjoyed Atlanta, too.

Yep, old Tom had pulled him out of the cannibal's pot. But did he want out? He had worked tirelessly for a general management opportunity. Here was one looking him in the eye. Marketing VP would be challenging and right in his zone of expertise. The function needed serious work. Tom would admit that evaluation to be accurate. Tom had never been the same after Margaret left him. Ben's loyalty had kept him in the job. Tom probably mentioned some other things he wanted to do with his life within Ben's earshot and got a push toward early retirement. He bet it would be one sweet deal.

The problem was if he put both jobs on the satisfaction scale, the general management job won hands down. The only reason he would accept Tom's job would be to maintain peace with Annette. What would happen the next time he had to maintain peace and no white knight named Tom Carthage came riding out of the sunset?

Tom had not complicated his life. He would not waver from seeking Marlene's job. Annette would have to deal with it in her own way. He loved her and wanted her. But he could only go so far in helping her deal with her fear if fear was her problem.

Brent mentally returned to his surroundings and noticed the ballroom emptying out quickly. He saw Ben Voorhees and his entourage leaving after congratulating Marlene again and saying goodbye. Brent stood and decided to have one more Wild Turkey before the bar closed. He got his drink and sat at the table next to the bar station.

He was thinking of nothing in particular when he felt a hand on his shoulder. Brent looked up to find Marlene standing over him.

Brent smiled. "What a marvelous send-off Marlene. And an appropriate presentation. Without sounding solicitous, I think you're one hell of a person."

"Thank you, Brent. It has been the work of everyone that has made this division successful."

She had a sad look, Brent thought, and looked despondent for the finish of a great evening.

"Something wrong?" said Brent. "Look down and out."

"Been a long evening. Hate to interrupt Sunday, but I need to see you in the office tomorrow."

"That's okay," replied Brent. "Some problem I can prepare for? Learned my lesson last time."

Marlene smiled forlornly. "Don't worry. Discuss it in the morning. Would nine be okay?"

"Fine. See you then."

"See you in the morning." She put her hand on his shoulder again. Then walked away.

Brent followed her with his eyes. He had never seen a look like that in Marlene's eyes. As he got up to find Annette, he wondered what tomorrow would bring to the three ring circus known as Richmont's retail division.

Brent tipped the valet parking attendant and pulled the Audi away from the curb.

"Brent, party was lovely," said Annette. "Company went out of its way to provide Marlene a nice send-off. One that the Charlotte employees could be part of."

"Was superb. Ben Voorhees is sensitive to that sort of thing."

"Had a nice conversation with Tom Carthage," she said. "Such a kind man."

"Tom's taking early retirement. Told me tonight," Brent said. "End of the quarter."

"He's young to be doing that," she replied. "Couldn't be more than fifty-five or six."

"Guy's never been the same since the divorce. Ben probably encouraged him," he said.

"Yes, that's what happens," Annette said.

"Hey. If we knew the deal Ben worked up for him, could only pray for the same treatment some day," Brent said. "It's a hell of a company and I want a long career with it. Ben is fifty-eight or nine. Retire in the next five years. Marlene'll become CEO. Going to be an exciting, dynamic company."

Annette looked at him. "I can understand that. Problem is, people like Paul Kruger will succeed, too. Wherever there're peaks, there're valleys. He and that serpent he calls a wife are a deep valley."

Brent turned into the driveway, hit the garage door opener and said, "What're you talking about?"

"Take the babysitter home," she said. "You get back we'll have a drink. I'll tell you about it."

Brent packed up Nancy and drove her the eight blocks to her home. The ride was long enough to hear about the tragedy of her current love life. Honey, let me tell you a story, he mused.

After dropping her off, he thought about Marlene. What could be so important to drag them both in on a Sunday morning? Talk about out of character. Sunday had been the one day in the week Marlene had not violated people's personal time. Brent could not get her sad look from his mind's eye. He hoped nothing was wrong. She looked radiant at the party. Especially during Ben's presentation of her promotion gift. It had been a sterling silver and light tan leather desk set. It was the most elegant office accessory Brent had ever seen. God knows what it cost. Her obvious sadness was troubling. One of Marlene's personal characteristics was her inability to hide feelings and she had been sad. What the hell. He could not figure anything else out this week. Why start now?

Brent parked the car, went in the house and found Annette sitting on the den sofa sipping a B&B. He could not imagine anyone liking that sweet, syrupy stuff but she seemed to be fond of it. He went to the bar, poured a cognac and sat on the sofa with her. He wondered if he just sat on his bed for tonight.

"So, the Krugers," he said.

Annette told him the details of her lengthy encounter with Audra.

Brent laughed. "Woman didn't know who she was messing with. Bet she gave Paul old boy an earful on the way home."

"You think the whole thing's funny?"

"Think it's hilarious. You set the ogress on her figurative ass. Tell you though. Having trouble comprehending the Kruger's evilness."

"It's boundless," she said.

"Also, having a difficult time understanding your reaction to Audra considering our confrontations over the past few days," he said.

"Don't get mixed messages. I didn't take on Audra Kruger for you. Make no mistake about that."

"Why then? You were presented with a perfect time to end the issue."

"First. Yes, it was. But it wouldn't have settled any long-term issues. Would've only exacerbated our problems," she replied. "Second. Nobody treats me like Audra Kruger tried to do and gets away with it. Nobody. Regardless of our problems, no one has the right to take me for a fool and use me to destroy you. I hold a high degree of loyalty to the father of my children."

"Sounds like a back away from our relationship."

"Not exactly how I meant it but we need some soul searching about our future. The way it is won't work. We both admit we're at an impasse."

"When talking with Tom tonight he said his job was mine for the asking."

"Would be an excellent job for you to exercise your skills. Would it mean going back to Atlanta?"

"It would. But it's a moot point. I want the GM job."

"You doing this because it's what you want or taking Tom's job would say you're giving in to me?"

"Don't think that's it. I've worked hard to have an opportunity to run a business. Get this opportunity, I'm taking it. These opportunities don't come along every day.

"Our relationship, Annette. Can't say more than I have. One thing I've learned from this is you can't will someone to trust you. Trust is intrinsic. All I can do is behave in a manner that earns it. Obviously I've failed in that respect."

"I'm tired, Brent. Think I'll head upstairs. You're welcome to share our bed."

"Thanks. Be up shortly."

Annette stood, said good night and left the room. There was no physical contact between them.

SUNDAY

Some sadist must have designed that sofa, Brent thought rubbing his hip. He had slept downstairs for the second night. Pushing his luck with Annette might prove fatal. To argue with her would have been futile and the way she had looked, he would have come on to her. Would not have been a wise move.

Brent left a note for Annette and pulled out of the garage a little after seven. Perfect timing. The first time in a while, he thought. He had some time to kill before meeting with Marlene. The Kopper Kettle was closed on Sunday so he decided on Shoney's.

He stopped at a Petro Express, bought a Sunday paper and drove to the Shoney's on Carowinds Boulevard. After ordering the breakfast buffet, he stared at the paper without reading a word. Annette had to be leaving him. All signs pointed to it. His opportunity for Marlene's job had not been the precipitator of her departure. Only a convenient, plausible excuse she could use to justify her actions to her family and the kids. He had been such a fool these last eight years. He had lived in a make believe world of his own making. They had revived their relationship in his mind but not in the real world. What a crock. He had no one to blame but himself. He thought that would be a good topic to concentrate on for a few minutes. A little self-flagellation would be good for the soul. What an imbecile he had been. His own worst enemy.

Brent filled his plate at the buffet. Returning to his booth Brent contemplated what Annette would do. If she wanted no more of the south, she would move back to the Twin Cities. The children in tow, of course. He could fight that but what the hell. Why? It would do nothing but complicate the situation and make it more difficult for the kids. People with children who get divorced possess amazing thought processes. They extol their love for the children and then proceed to hammer the hell out of each other for the kids to witness. Naturally, the hammering is under the guise of protecting their rights. Even better, to protect the children. You betcha, the world is inhabited by some prodigious folks. If Annette went back to Minnesota, they would have to develop some arrangement for him to see the kids without tearing Erik and Tawney apart. Now that would be a trick.

If she went back north, maybe it would not be because of a love fest with the land of ten thousand lakes. Maybe someone would be waiting for her. If so, it did not matter what he did or did not do. Eventually, she would have found an excuse. Her hormones calling for whoever he might be could have reached a critical stage in conjunction with Marlene's promotion. Stranger things had happened this week.

On the other hand, she could be convinced he would take them into hell on earth again and wanted out. If so, she might stay in the house and go to work for one of the Charlotte law firms. This would be a scenario that would simplify logistics.

On his third cup of coffee, the thought struck him that she might go back north but did not want the kids. Now there would be a monkey wrench. The chances of that had to be next to zero because of Annette's devotion to the kids. Or did she have that much devotion? Nothing else had been as it seemed this week. Why would the concept that Annette had become tired of being held back by the kids be any stranger? She was a young woman. Maybe she wanted her career again. A fulltime career unencumbered by curtain grabbers. She could do that and stick it to his career at the same time. Why not? Kruger zapped him in pairs. Why not sweet Annette? What would he do? First, he would not fight it. But there would be no GM job in his future. If he got the kids, he'd better have a good reputation at Richmont. He would need it. Brent nearly broke out in a cold sweat thinking about it. Annette left, sans kids. He could not take the GM job. Kruger got it by default. Kruger would have mercy on him because he was a single parent. Yeah, right. Not in this lifetime.

He paid for breakfast, returned to the Audi and began the short drive to his office. His energies were being defused across too many issues. One thing at a time, please. What a debacle. There were three cats fighting in the gunny sack. No time to throw in a fourth. Enough of Annette right now. What was Marlene's problem? She looked terrible at the end of the party. She seemed to be torn up about something. He hoped she had not gotten some terrible news about her physical condition or something on that order. That could not be it. She would not involve him. The Faulkton thing had been conquered. Terry Thomas had been mollified. Annette had held up her end last night.

His mind wandered back to Annette. She had to be leaving. She would not have diced up Kruger's wife if that had not been the plan. Get off Annette. Keep the brain on the issue at hand.

Why would Marlene want him on Sunday? It was close to nine. He would know soon enough. Suddenly, the affair speculation crossed his mind. Did Kruger somehow get that idiotic accusation into play? That could not have happened. Marilyn Beamon would have warned Patricia. Or Todd would have said something to him or Patricia last night. Although they did not speak, Brent had seen Todd several times during the evening. There would have been a warning. An affair could not be the subject.

A more logical scenario would be that he had gotten the job and Marlene wanted to discuss the turnover free from distractions. That made more sense. He rewarded himself with a smile. But then why so sad last night? She had been down. Leaving? That could be it. She had poured her heart and soul into this business and it was starting to roll big time. She had been around for the resurrection but would not be for the ascension. Leaving had to be it. Brent could sympathize with her. It would be a bummer. But she was heading to a much bigger payoff. In the next few years, she would be the first female CEO of Richmont Corporation. She could deal nicely with a piece of nostalgia.

He parked his car, went in the side entrance and walked to his office. He had about ten minutes and he wanted to check e-mails. There was nothing of importance and at eight fifty-five, he approached Marlene's office.

Brent saw her office lights on and softly tapped on her open door.

"Good morning, Brent. Please come in and shut the door."

She motioned him to a chair in front of her desk, which Brent thought was strange. They normally sat at the conference table.

"Marlene, the party was great last night."

"Was wonderful," she said. She looked at Brent with disheartened eyes.

"Brent, there's no easy way for me to say what I have to."

Brent felt the most sinking feeling of his life. No one had ever said those words to him but he had to others. What followed would not be congratulations.

"Marlene?"

"I find it necessary to withdraw my support for your candidacy to replace me."

Brent knew if he didn't talk he was going to become ill. "Why're you doing that? Thought all negatives were put to bed."

"They were before last night and the conversation I had with Ben before he left."

"Kruger's financial background won out, huh? Nothing I can do about that." Thank God for Tom Carthage, he thought.

"Wasn't it. We'd gotten past that. I thought it was a done deal."

"Then what?"

"Seems last night it came to light that you and Patricia Bolivar may be involved in an inappropriate relationship," she said.

How did that despicable psychopath Kruger manage it? The lying, no good lowlife. He didn't mind losing fair and square but to make up things that destroy other people's reputations is unconscionable.

"Marlene, I can assure you Patricia Bolivar and I are close business associates. She's the best HR manager I've seen. But intimate involvement? No. Not now. Not ever."

"Ben informed me he came upon the information from a very reliable source."

"Don't care if he heard it from the Pope. Bolivar and I aren't having an affair. Ridiculous accusation not to mention destructive."

"It's certainly destructive. And I've no proof that it's either true or false."

"My word's not good anymore?"

"Look at it from my standpoint, Brent. Remember our conversation about the aggregate effect of multiple negatives. The incident with Terry Thomas. What caused your behavior? Was it Paul not being complete with his message? Was it your marital issues? Was it me leaving? Was it you hiding an office love affair? The Faulkton accusation suddenly comes up again because this revelation lends more credence to his assertions. Put all together, it's too much to pass off."

"Again, I swear to you I've had no affair with Patricia Bolivar," Brent said. "Ever. We aren't involved. But all I've got is my word. That's not good enough, I don't know what to do."

"In this instance, for this promotion, afraid it's not good enough," said Marlene.

Brent could feel himself lifting off the chair. He stood at the crossroads of devastation and fury. His mind searched for the road between the two.

"Anything I can do?"

"Afraid not. But we have to discuss the future. Paul will be announced as the division GM tomorrow afternoon. Ben and I will inform him tomorrow morning."

"Great. I'm screwed."

"An accurate assessment," she responded reinforcing her words with a piercing stare.

Brent was astonished. Marlene. The one he had counted on and had been in his corner until now.

"You saying I've no future here?"

"If I were Paul Kruger, I wouldn't accept two of my direct reports who were romantically involved. Would rip the organization apart," Marlene said.

"Marlene, we aren't romantically involved."

"You discuss it with Paul, not me. Be his call."

The abyss enveloped him. No way out. His thoughts turned to Patricia.

"What happens to Patricia in this corporate lynching?" he said. "An innocent bystander."

Marlene's eyes hardened. She obviously didn't like the corporate lynching comment. Fuck you very much, he thought.

"She'll leave the division," Marlene said. "Paul's never been enamored with her work. But Stan Ascutney thinks she walks on water. He'll protect her. Be a job for her in Atlanta or one of the other operating divisions if she wants it."

"What about me? Kruger'll kick me to the curb. How about other options?" Brent said. "Tom Carthage talked to me last night. Told me his job would be mine for the asking."

Marlene gave him one of her patented stares and laughed tightly. "Use your brain. That job would be a huge promotion, reporting to Ben. Your current reputation. That job's on a distant planet."

"I'm a big boy. What're you saying?"

"Nothing's been decided except Paul's promotion. His thoughts will drive this division's people decisions."

She took on a despondent look. "If I were you, I'd start exploring other options. Ones outside Richmont."

"Dammit," he said. "This's unfair. Given my best to this company, in general, and you, in particular. To be summarily dismissed based on untruths and hearsay isn't the leadership I've learned from you."

Brent saw she had been shaken and angered by his retort. She said, "May be unfair but the way it is. Look. You're no sales associate complaining how the big, bad company is against you. This's the big leagues, Brent. Voorhees doesn't need a reason not to promote you. Tried to school you in the dynamics of corporate politics. But what were your words? You didn't have time for all that political crap.

"Wait–"

"Don't interrupt me, Brent. That political crap, as you called it, just destroyed you. You didn't realize the downside risk of not guarding your backside and flanks with the players involved and you're a fool for it. If you got romantically involved in the workplace, you're somewhere south of an imbecile. I can't think of anyone making up a story as despicable as the affair. Ben isn't prone to exaggeration. He said a reliable source with an emphasis on reliable. Now this might not be the leadership you've learned from me. But it's your behavior that ran me out of options. So be accurate where you point your 'holier than thou' morality finger, Brent. If I were you, I'd look in the mirror."

She was right. Brent had been defeated because he had been ill-prepared for this fight. Hell, he didn't even know he had been in a fight. At least, not like this one. Kruger would roast in hell someday but that was of little consequence now. Prior to that roast, Mr. Kruger would be the division's GM.

"Want my resignation?"

"Not what I'd recommend. Come in, work and let things settle out," she said. "We'll get everything settled with Paul and discuss your and Patricia's future. Mid-week Paul will meet with you. By then, he'll have thought things through and gotten Ben's input. Sorry, Brent. But have to be honest with you. I were you, wouldn't count on opportunities at Richmont."

"Guess there's nothing else to say," he said.

"Guess not," she replied. "Sorry it had to end this way but hope you see my position."

"I don't have much choice, now do I?" Brent stood. "See you tomorrow."

He left and went back to his office where he sat and stared at the ceiling. In the span of a little more than one hundred hours, his life had been destroyed.

His marriage over. His career ended. Ben Voorhees would never give him a reference. And Kruger? Forget about it. When he woke up last Wednesday he had the world right where he wanted it. But that world had been an illusion. One that, when reality surfaced, destroyed him with a vengeance and vanished. Life as he thought it to be existed only in his mind.

Paul Kruger arose early, got the Sunday paper from the end of the driveway, made coffee and sat on the deck. He reviewed last evening. It could not have gone better. The affair strategy had been perfectly executed. His assessment that Neal Stuart should be the messenger had been correct. Stuart had destroyed Shannon without a backward glance.

After Stuart's near flawless performance, Paul realized he had to develop an airtight reason for firing him. It could not happen right away. He might have to promote Stuart for the short-term. If Shannon goes immediately, he could make Stuart acting marketing director. In a few months, certain things could happen to prove that Stuart had not been up to the task. It had not been Richmont's policy to demote a manager but to give an excellent severance and recommendation. That might be the most efficient way to eradicate Stuart.

The affair revelation would assure that Shannon's fate would not be as benign. He wondered if the contemptible drudge had been dismissed yet. Paul could do nothing now but wait for Ben Voorhees' call. He would not be comfortable until that call but it was probably a done deal. Shannon's reputation had been so damaged recovery would be impossible. He had been trapped and dying—or dead.

Paul's thoughts turned to Annette Shannon and her outwitting of Audra last night. When everything had been settled he would anonymously send her a flower arrangement. He could not remember when someone had bested his dear wife to that degree. It had been amusing to hear Audra rant and rave on the way home. She got slam dunked and knew it. It took all his willpower to keep a straight face. Concern for his own well being helped him stifle the urge.

"Morning," Audra said as she opened the sliding door from the den.

"Hi, baby. Coffee and croissants on the server."

"Thanks." She poured a cup of coffee, buttered a croissant and sat next to Paul.

"Still pissed off about that Shannon bitch," she said. "Knowingly embarrassed me with senior management."

"No reason to be embarrassed."

"You're right. They didn't pick it up."

Paul thought he might as well have a little fun. "Better hope they didn't."

"They didn't. Can't figure how she knew. Played it over in my mind. Can't see where I tipped her off."

"Happened. It's over. If that's all we had, we'd be in trouble. Luckily, the affair strategy went extraordinarily well. Stuart was phenomenal. I'm sure Evan literally went running to Bible Ben."

"Great," she said. "Should do the trick. Sorry the marital thing blew up but who'd think the Shannon woman had any guts."

"Know that now. Hopefully, won't have any more dealings with her."

"Just pisses me off. Don't like surprises."

This was getting tiresome, he thought. "It's over. Forget it, for god's sake."

She looked at him with eyes reduced to cold marble. Paul wondered how deep the disease of egomania dwelled within her. She was infuriated. Enough to lose her perspective.

"Speaking of surprises," Audra said. "Best get this promotion, sweetie."

"That declaration means?"

"Don't be naive. Our marriage has been about bringing complimentary talents to the partnership. You gave me the chance to stick it up my father's ass. I provided you the social expertise to be successful. A bonus has been your ability to satisfy my sexual desires. In return, I serviced your sexual appetite beyond your expectations."

"Dear, Audra. Such a succinct way of putting things."

"Well, sweetie pie, don't get this promotion, you don't hold up your part of the partnership."

"Wait a minute. Something unforeseen happens, something out of my control, be other opportunities," he replied.

"Don't want other damn opportunities. Want this one."

This wicked, blue blood bitch was backing him into a corner. There were times when he loathed her. One of them now.

"This is as good as a done deal," he said.

"Hope it is. It falls through, don't think of talking to me about moving back to Atlanta. I've a great career and this's where I'm staying."

You keep spreading your legs, little whore, the sky's the limit. Paul smiled. "Audra. Honey. You threatening me?" He thought the question should bring a caustic response. She didn't disappoint.

Her eyes became venomous. "You know better. Not my style. Simply for our relationship to stay solid better get this job." A smile appeared, unmasking the lecherous soul living within his wife. "You're aware I've other options."

Paul almost laughed at her. Instead, he calmly said, "More aware of your options than you imagine. And your tactics for keeping them open."

"What the hell you mean by that," she hissed.

Paul returned to reading his paper. Without looking at her he said, "Draw your own conclusions, dearest one."

"If all you're capable of is degrading me and my accomplishments, I'm going to take a shower and dress," Audra said with as much aloofness as she could muster.

Paul did not respond but watched her storm into the house. He married the wicked witch of the south. He had known her self-indulgence when they married but its depth continued to amaze him. It kept getting more pronounced with age and a modicum of career success. No wonder the men in her family detested her. Hell, he should have been set up for life when he took her off their hands.

Well, nothing would go wrong with this promotion. Except for Audra being outflanked, all had fallen into place. But the waiting was agonizing.

Brent stood up from his desk. One place he did not need to be was the offices of Richmont's retail division. He could feel nothing but shock. What in the hell would he do?

Without divine intervention, his marriage would be over and his business reputation destroyed. He had guarded both over the years. They would be gone. The situation had become so gruesome it was difficult to visualize his life in its aftermath.

The office building became suffocating. He left by the side entrance, went to his car and sat silently. He noted that Marlene's car was gone. She had come in to deliver the verdict. Once accomplished, she left to enjoy her Sunday. It had been years since tears of heartache and despondency filled his eyes. Brent Shannon silently cried.

After gaining some measure of self-control, Brent steered the Audi out of the parking lot and up Westinghouse. Heading nowhere in particular he eventually found himself at the entrance to Raintree Country Club. He concluded that no one he knew would be here. He could get a peaceful cup of coffee. He would prefer a Bloody Mary but thought better of it. A couple of them might cause him to blow his brains out. He'd better pass on the idea.

Entering the Grille Room, he heard a voice say, "Hey, heavy hitter. Wait up." Brent turned to see George Barnes walking toward him.

"Called you for an early tee time," George said. "Annette said you'd gone to the office. What's this Sunday work schedule?"

Before Brent could answer, George said, "You look terrible. Who shot your dog?"

"Had a life reversal. Appears it won't be long till I'm out of a job and a marriage."

"That really lowers your responsibility level," George said. "Sorry, buddy. Was uncalled for. Let's go have a couple of Bloody Marys. You can unload if you've a mind to."

"I'll stick to coffee."

"Might be a good idea."

They sat down and Brent said, "Life's a bit worse than the holocaust."

"Not good. Any morbid details you care to share?"

Brent brought George up to date on what had happened. "Lost on all counts. I'm fucked."

"I'd say you're having a shitty week. No doubt about it," George said. "Annette told you she's leaving?"

"Not been that explicit but it points that way. Especially her reaction to Audra Kruger and our conversation after we got home.

"Work. That's over. My future's up to Kruger. Do better with Bin Laden. Shame is, the bastard's getting Patricia, too. All she tried to do was help. Not a damn thing I can do. Grandmother told me it's a great life if you don't weaken. Think she's wrong on that one."

"Friend. Wish I had a slick answer. Truth is, there're no slick answers."

"Can't find any. Losing everything. How could my wife perpetrate this facade for eight years?"

"Not sure it was a facade. Possible she thought this was your station forever. Not pretty to consider but she might've been holding you hostage with the kids."

"What're you talking about?"

"Happens, buddy," said George. "Left you once and took the kids. Took you back if you sang her song. Your loss if you don't sing? Not just her. Kids, too. Happens more than you think. You cave cause you don't want to sell the kids to her."

"Pretty brutal," said Brent.

"Why so?" George said. "She's got you by the balls and knows it. Forego a bunch of ambition in favor of her life style requirements. In turn, she honors you with the kids. Damn smart. Tell you, they're taking over the world. Mark my words. Should've never given them the vote."

"You agree she's leaving?"

"How the hell am I supposed to know?" George said. "But doesn't look like she's ready to hunker down with good ole Brent. Sorry buddy."

"Okay. She goes, she goes," said Brent. "But work. Don't know what I'm going to do."

"Know I'm not much into big corporate stuff. A shame you got screwed when you didn't. Screw Patricia, that is," George said. "She's a looker. Getting fired anyway, shame you didn't get some."

"Not the logic I need."

"Sorry, Brent. Think Patricia might be able to help?"

"How?"

"Might have more credibility than you. Maybe she could talk to Marlene."

"Don't want to drag her into it."

"Drag her into it," said George. "Are you kidding me? She's already in it up to her cute ass. Don't give her a jingle to say you think your demise might be equally shared by her, you're a jerk. She's got to have the chance to defend herself. Times like these cause good people to retreat to self-preservation and dismiss the fate of others. Don't let that happen to you. She's given you everything she's got. Maybe her job. Owe her big time, friend."

"You're right."

"You two worked together till now. Don't let the bad guys divide and conquer," said George. "I have to get out of here or we'll be in divorce court together. Call me if you need to talk at somebody. Just remember, I don't know corporate politics. We're friends with Annette, too. All out of advice on the former and don't feel comfortable giving advice on the latter. Good luck, Brent."

"Thanks."

Over another cup of coffee, he reviewed their conversation. George's angle on Annette had been different but it did not seem relevant at this juncture. He had been right on target regarding Patricia. Brent had to talk to her pronto.

George's parting had been a politically correct way of telling him that Brent's world had become too complicated for him. He wanted no part of it except observing from the bleachers. Hell, he would think the same way, Brent thought. He was on this ride all by himself. Maybe how it was meant to be.

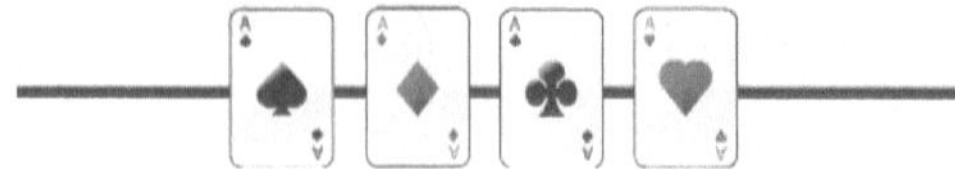

They hadn't been home from Sunday school and church for more than ten minutes until Erik and Tawney left to play with friends. Brent had not come home yet. What could have been so important for Marlene to want him on a Sunday? Sunday meetings had never been called in the entire time they had been here. Even in the darkest days of the division. And this one was taking a long time.

Annette thought about last evening. What an experience. She thoroughly enjoyed her time with Audra Kruger. Minnesota must have provided her a sheltered life. She had never witnessed that level of venal behavior. It had confused her thinking. In truth, she did not know what she thought. But one thing had become clear. Paul Kruger should not be given responsibility to lead other humans. If she felt that way did it mean that de facto she supported Brent's promotion? Absolutely not, she concluded. The realization that Kruger defined an abominable creation was as far as she could go. If she supported Brent for the job, it would mean the end of their marriage. It would lay waste to their family.

Regardless, her feelings had been rendered irrelevant. Brent had been dogmatic in his decision to compete for the job. His decision required her to make one. She could try to work something out with Brent. They could use the guideline method he advocated. Or she and the children could leave. What a monumental decision, she thought.

The children adored their father and he returned that adoration tenfold. The GM job would fracture that relationship. This would be the first job since their reconciliation with the dynamics to plunge them into the nightmare of eight years ago.

If she left Brent, would she stay in Charlotte or go back to Minnesota? She had developed contacts in Charlotte. She could get a decent offer from one of the better law firms in the city. However, her heart had always been in Minnesota and she missed her friends and family. She would go back.

She and Brent had fourteen years together. Some good, some bad. Should she throw them away? What would she be throwing away? A self-obsessed man. But the father of her children.

Annette's thoughts were interrupted by the phone ringing. It would be Brent to tell her he would be tied up for the rest of the day, she decided. Answering the phone, Charlie Radford's voice startled her.

"Charlie, been so long since we've talked," Annette said in a lighthearted voice.

"I've not slept since we talked." His tone foretold a serious call.

"I didn't mean to upset you, Charlie. Just looking for support."

"Avoided me for over five years. Suddenly call when you need a little support."

"I understand you could feel put out but I needed your input."

"Okay. Fine. May I then conclude I can look forward to you moving in and out of my life based upon your needs at the time?"

"That's not a tasteful way of phrasing it."

"Truth isn't always tasteful, Annette." The voice she heard bespoke a heavy heart.

"Charlie, what do you want of me?"

"At one time, Annette, we cared deeply for each other. I thought it was love."

His anguish was palpable and it put Annette on edge. Where was this going?

"We did care deeply for each other," she said.

"Did you love me?"

"I did."

"Still love you," said Charlie. "Still love me?"

Annette found herself sinking into a wash of memories. "Charlie, you're complicating my already complicated life."

"You called me first."

"I know."

"Remember the wonderful moments we had together?"

Annette got misty eyed. "Of course, I remember." She began to cry. "I felt so secure." She knew the destination of this journey and god, her heart wanted to go there.

"Why are you trying to tear my heart out again?"

"Don't want to do that."

"Annette, listen carefully," Charlie said. "I love you with all my heart. Have since three weeks after we met. I've dated but never found anyone to compare with you. I can't go on like this. Was almost resigned to my fate of never seeing you again and ready to get on with my life. Then you appear again."

Annette became tearful. "I never wanted to hurt you. Never. Ever. You're so special to me."

"Let me finish. I love you and want you. Want you more than anything else. But I've got to have closure or my life will be one of could've, should've. There're e-tickets for you and the children on Northwest Airlines' Monday afternoon flight to Minneapolis."

"Now wait—"

"Asked you to let me finish. Can't handle another call from you. I'll be at the airport to meet you. Can't wait to hold you in my arms, darling, but you have to make a decision by Monday afternoon.

"You decide to stick it out with Brent, God's speed. I'll harbor no animosity but communication between us must end."

"This's ridiculous, Charlie Radford," Annette said. "I can't make a life-altering decision that quickly."

"Know it's sudden," said Charlie. "For my own mental health that's how it's got to be. You called me with a problem. I'm calling you with a problem and a solution to make things right for us. And probably Brent.

"Tickets are on the airline's system in your name. Love you, darling. We can have a marvelous life together. Your move. Hope we're having dinner tomorrow night in Minneapolis." He hung up without waiting for a response.

Annette sat at the kitchen table in utter shock. Nothing got easier. She had called Charlie to get help and what she got was another problem. She could not react with Charlie's speed requirement. Things had to be discussed with Brent. He might not get the job. That would give them a chance to keep their family together. If he took the job, that would present a different set of issues. Regardless, none of this would happen on Charlie Radford's timetable.

The idea of him giving her an ultimatum. He knew better than that. She did not react well to that treatment. It had been close to an ultimatum by Charlie when she went on the cruise vacation with Brent. He learned then it was not a viable tactic with her. He must have forgotten. Tomorrow he would learn it again when he was driving home alone from the airport.

Annette was separated from her thoughts by the sounds of hungry children coming through the patio door. Where was Brent?

Brent was driving. Nowhere in particular. Estrangement gripped him. Marlene had told him that she had to wash her hands of him. She had not used those words. However, all she needed was a purple robe to be Pontius Pilate. Annette was in space. The outer galaxy. All she had been capable of was making accusations of self-deception. Yeah, he thought. All these lies and innuendos had been figments of his imagination.

His buddy George had told him to stay arm's length. George had his own life to lead. Signing up to play golf with a guy should not be a sign up to carry the weight of a guy's life dilemmas.

He turned into an empty parking lot, put the Audi in park and leaned back against the headrest with his eyes closed. How had life come to this? He had not always been the best example of a good human but he had not been the worst either. What had he done to Paul Kruger to cause this attack on his character and reputation? It appeared the man would stop at nothing to destroy him. And destroy him he had.

Marlene had not been interested in listening to his defense. It came down to the cumulative effect she discussed with him on Friday. The accusations and political traps targeted him to the point that she could not hold her argument for him without endangering her reputation with Ben and the board. Hell, she was becoming Richmont's chief financial officer. Even a whiff of emotion taking precedence over objective thinking and analysis, she could kiss her career bye-bye. She had worked hard to break through a thick glass ceiling. She would not blow it on a guy who might be dipping his wick in the company inkwell. How did Kruger pull off the affair lie? There might be some circumstantial gossip floating around but who would take advantage of something that malicious? It would have to be one low life bastard with a big time upside to Brent's destruction. Kruger had to have had help. Way up the organization help. Both being candidates, there was no way Kruger could tee all this up himself without looking like a self-serving schlep.

Suddenly he realized he had not warned Patricia that the cannibals had water in the pot and the fire lit. If she distanced herself from him as much as possible, she might survive. He felt terrible. The woman's support might cost her dearly.

He turned off the engine and called directory assistance for Patricia's home number. Don't be unlisted, he thought. Yeah, an affair. He did not even know her home number. Brent dialed and heard a feminine hello.

"Patricia, its Brent. Our mythical affair has seen the light of day."

"How did it get past us?"

"Don't know but sorry I dragged you into this."

"You didn't drag me anywhere. Came of my own free will. I thought, still think, you're best person for the job."

"You don't understand. Your job's in jeopardy."

"I'm a big girl. I can take care of myself."

Patricia, do not try to be so macho, he thought. "Fine. But you have to protect yourself. Ascutney's your best bet. Believe me, Patricia, these folks're playing for keeps. I've put you in their cross hairs."

"Might be right about Ascutney," she said. "But he won't chance his credibility with Voorhees."

Brent felt helpless. This woman put herself in harm's way for him and he had been rendered powerless to help her. She had been selfless enough to risk her career with Richmont for him. He could do nothing to protect her from these swine. God. His marriage. His career. His influence. His friendships. Everything crashing. Kruger was beneath contempt. He had included this innocent woman in his Machiavellian espionage. A woman that had only been trying to do what she thought to be right.

"How about you?" she said. "You're further down the slippery slope than me."

"Beyond help. Believe me," he said. "Only option's to let this soap opera play out. Pick life up on the other side."

"That's defeatist," she responded. "Got to be a way to combat this. Everything in Kruger's subterfuge are lies and innuendos. Got to be a way to expose him."

"Time's gone," Brent said. "Decision's made. Kruger got the job. I got the ax. I'm imploring you. There's nothing to be done for me. Protect yourself. And your career. You've worked hard, Patricia. Don't forfeit that work. Time to cut and run."

Brent heard her begin to cry.

"Don't want to cut and run," she lamented through tears. Then her voice hardened. "This should please your wife."

"Believe that relationship's over," he replied. "That's my problem. Patricia, I've got to go. You've got to talk to Ascutney and separate yourself from me. A hint of an alliance between us could be fatal to your career at Richmont. Never know how much I've appreciated your support and friendship. Best of luck."

"Sounds like you don't plan on me seeing you again," she said.

"You can't afford to see me again," Brent said as he pressed the disconnect.

Patricia hung up and collapsed on the sofa in tears. It had all fallen apart. Brent would have been an inspired leader. The division would have soared to new heights and been a dynamic, exciting place to work. Everyone would have continued to pull together as they had under Marlene's tutelage. But now, she bemoaned, the dark ages were about to descend.

Paul Kruger was a diabolical, unprincipled scoundrel. He would stop at nothing to assure his personal success. The last few days had been a testimony to that. He was so well connected in Atlanta that he would be immune from criticism emanating out of the Charlotte office unless there would be a dramatic fall in profits. He would pistol whip people to make certain that did not happen.

Through her tears, she thought that going to another company might be wise. Even in Atlanta she would not be insulated from witnessing the decimation of the division. Through her father's eyes she had observed what a person like Kruger could do to a business organization. Her father had been crushed by such a person. He never recovered. His experience provided ample verification that Kruger's impact to this organization could not be overstated.

Adam Jordan came down the stairs from taking a shower and changing clothes after his drive from Knoxville.

"What's wrong?" he said.

Patricia reviewed her conversation with Brent and the terrible predicament he found himself.

Adam sat on the sofa, put his arm around her and said, "This's going to sound cruel. But live by the sword, die by the sword. Guy got outflanked. Nothing else to say."

"If you want to classify lies and deceit as being outflanked, you could say that." Her voice did not contain a friendly tone.

"Not my point. Can be outmaneuvered by whatever means. It's a fact of life."

"A good, decent man's being ruined. All you can muster is, it happened?"

"Honey, not trying to be crass but the guy lost the war because he was ill-prepared to play tough. Happens. To good people. All the time."

"Marlene can't favor Kruger becoming GM. She's simply run out of options."

"Take Brent's advice," he replied. "Stay out of it. Protect yourself."

"Hear me, Adam. I'm not letting him be destroyed by the devil's disciple."

"Dammit, Patricia. You owe the man nothing."

"You're right. I don't. But I'm not standing by watching him be decimated."

"Nothing you can do. You've gotten involved too much already."

"Wrong, Adam. Marlene's boxed in by Kruger's tactics. Needs an avenue back to the fray. Going to see her. Explain there's no affair. That Brent's been set up by Kruger. What's to lose?"

"Just what remains of your credibility."

"So what? Don't want to be there without Brent anyway."

Adam faced Patricia with questioning eyes. "Patricia. I'm getting this uneasy feeling Shannon means more to you than just a business associate. Maybe more than you care to admit."

"I'm very fond of him."

"More than fondness, isn't it? You in love with him?"

Tears began to form in Patricia's eyes. "Sorry it came up under these circumstances. You deserve much better. Tried to suppress and deny my feelings but it's no use. Yes, I think I'm in love with Brent. Not to tell you would be terribly unfair. You're entitled to someone who can give your life the meaning it deserves."

"Patricia, don't be foolish. Please. We have beginnings of a wonderful life together. Don't let the emotion of this ruin that for us. Got to be something I can say or do to make you see what you're giving up. To see how happy we can be. Something to make you reconsider." His voice began to crack. "Besides, the man is married."

Patricia could see the pain in his eyes. "I could be walking off a precipice. But I can't deny it anymore. Won't deny it anymore. I'm in love with Brent Shannon. Very much in love. And yes, I know he's married."

His tone turned cold. "Am I supposed to thank you for your honesty?"

"You have every right to be angry with me. You're a marvelous human being and deserve a happiness I could never give you. Search for and find your soulmate, my dear Adam. Now I've got to find Marlene and talk to her. Right now."

Adam stood. "Patricia, if that's your final thought, I'll pack up, leave my key on the counter. Come to your senses, you know where I am."

Patricia stood, kissed him on the cheek, and whispered, "You're a wonderful guy."

Adam brushed her aside and began walking upstairs. Hunched shoulders signaled him to be barely under control.

Patricia walked out the door without looking back. She had to find Marlene. She wondered what else she might find in this world gone mad. Patricia shivered although it was not cold.

Paul Kruger left the grocery store after picking up snacks. He and Audra invited two couples over for drinks before going to the club for dinner. Audra was playing tennis. God knows what else, he thought.

Driving home, he became anxious. He had tried but failed to convince himself that there would be no need to worry. Everything had gone as planned except for Shannon's wife sticking it to Audra.

Everything would be fine. He had to convince himself of that or he would have a seizure. But he had been a worrier his whole life and this would be his first critical step to the corporate pinnacle. To his destiny. What could go wrong? There might be something.

Marlene would have to back off. The last hurdle. It had been a masterful plan. What could be tormenting him?

Paul pulled into his driveway. Audra had not arrived home yet. As he got out of the car his cell phone rang.

"How're you today?" Wilson Rachet's voice said.

"Going crazy. Last night went as planned." He thought it best not to tell Wilson about Audra's fiasco. Wilson hated her as it was. "Hope it's enough. I've never been so anxious in my life."

Wilson laughed. "Stop worrying."

Paul's heart leapt in his chest. "What do you mean?"

"It's over. Got called to the office this morning to look over and finalize the compensation package for the new GM of the retail division. One Paul Kruger."

Paul felt weak. He sat back down in the car barely able to breathe. "Wilson. Are you certain?"

"Am I certain? Was there and blessed your package," Wilson said. "Ben, Todd Beamon, Stan Ascutney and myself. It's a done deal. You're the new GM. Announcement's tomorrow afternoon. Marlene'll meet with you first thing in the morning. You're it, my man. Congratulations."

"You've made me a happy man. Can't believe it's over. Everything worked to perfection."

"Lucky we kept working our plan. Until late last night, Ben had decided to defer to Marlene's judgment. You'd have been outside looking in."

Paul shuttered. That picture made him ill. "Well, we don't have to worry about that anymore. Anything said about Shannon?"

"Nothing from Ben. But Ascutney cornered me after the meeting and said there was a sensitive issue in Charlotte. Wanted to discuss it tomorrow morning. Has to be Shannon and Bolivar. Asked Stan how sensitive and he said the termination kind. Mention nothing about this. You're told, act shocked and dismayed. Say you were so anxious to have them on your team but these circumstances make that impossible. Back out no matter what your gut tells you. Ole Bible Ben'll take care of it. They're history."

"Wilson, I can't thank you enough. To say this made my day would be a gross understatement."

"I'll think of some repayment down the road. Just relax and bask in the glow of the moment."

"Thanks again, Wilson." Paul disconnected.

He went into the house, built himself a Dewar and water and went to the deck. He sat looking at the lake with tears flowing down his cheeks. The demeaning and personal humiliations by others were over. His hard work had been worth it. The necessity to put up with Audra's indiscretions and disrespect for him. The challenge of pulling himself out of the cesspool that was his father's world. The requirement to withstand the verbal abuse of Audra's pompous, contemptuous family. All the pain had paid off. All had been worth it. Just for this minute of triumph. He cried tears of joy and thankfulness.

This would be only the first step. His plan had two more. When Marlene was promoted to CEO he would follow her career path to Richmont's CFO. Finally, CEO at Richmont or another company of like or larger size. It would happen now. He needed a successful track record in general management. This promotion assured that record and anyone in the division found not contributing to his record would be summarily replaced.

He smiled. His clear mind could see all his past demons scurrying to Brent Shannon's body to protect him. They were too late. They would be cremated with Shannon's destruction. Next would come the disownment of his father and the rescue of his mother from the brutal Neanderthal. Shannon would burn tomorrow by Ben Voorhees' hand. Shortly thereafter, his father, by Paul's own hand.

A contented, fulfilled Paul Kruger went into the house to build another drink and await the arrival of the resident whore. His wife.

Annette became more worried about Brent by the minute. Normally, he would call when this late. He had been gone since before she got up this morning. The meeting with Marlene could not have taken this long.

It was mid-afternoon. Annette sat in the den alone. He must be good and angry with her, she thought. His feelings had been obvious when he did not sleep with her and snuck upstairs to get fresh clothes and toilet articles. The inability of their marriage to withstand this strain had become apparent to her. A divorce would likely be the viable solution. Brent wanted a life she could not abide. She could not restrain him for the rest of his life. They would consume each other.

The whole mess had been complicated with Charlie Radford's asinine ultimatum. If he thought for one moment that she would abide it, he was mistaken. The very idea. Pushing her for a decision. When she checked with Northwest, there were three tickets for Monday afternoon's flight to Minneapolis.

What a horrible state of affairs. Annette had been in love with Charlie Radford. Deeply in love. He had been the most caring, considerate man she had ever known. In retrospect, she had done everyone a disservice by reconciling with Brent. She had wanted the children to have their father. A selfless reason but in hindsight, not a wise one. Nonetheless, they had eight good years before the repulsive head of ambition once again emerged.

In the final analysis, marriage had to be a union with faith and acceptance as its bedrock. It could not be a partnership of two humans built through control and behavior modification. The man was what he was. Her idiotic belief that she could change him was the result of selfishness and a measure of cruelty. She had wanted her way and punish him at the same time. She was ashamed of herself.

Her brother had been correct. Brent could not satisfy her insatiable need for constant attention. Not if he was to realize what his self-actualization need drove him to achieve. It was an unworkable union. She should have been bright enough to recognize that eight years ago. Of course, she hadn't been. God, what was she supposed to do now?

Charlie's wish would not come to fruition. At least not on his timetable. It was a matter of principle. Where could Brent be?

The phone rang. Brent, it's about time, she thought. She picked up the phone and said hello.

"Annette, how are you? Katie Lockhart."

"Katie. My goodness. Been ages," replied Annette.

When they moved to Atlanta and Annette passed the Georgia bar, she had done some part-time legal work for a mid-size law firm in East Cobb County.

Katie had been three years out of law school and a junior associate in the firm. They worked together and became close professional associates. Katie specialized in corporate law and eventually secured a position with a large Atlanta corporate law firm. The one that handled Richmont's legal work.

"Been a long time," said Katie. "Ever get back to Atlanta?"

"Only when Brent and Erik drag me to a Braves game."

Katie laughed. "Shopping excursion's in order next time the boys feel athletically starved."

"Best offer in a long time."

"Let's do it."

"You're on. Katie, great to hear your voice. Why the call?"

"Something on my mind all weekend. Couldn't shake it. I had to call."

"You sound concerned. What is it?"

"Know this is a personal question from someone who hasn't kept in contact but how's your marriage holding up these days?"

Stunned and defensive, Annette asked, "That would be a concern of yours why?"

"Know it's personal. Regardless. Why so defensive?"

"I'm so weary of anyone having an association with Richmont Corporation so freaking interested in my marriage all of a sudden," Annette said.

"I sure understand your feelings. Annette, Brent ever mentioned the name Wilson Rachet?"

"Not that I remember."

"If Brent knew Wilson, does he talk enough shop at home he would have mentioned him?"

"More than just a casual business associate, I've probably heard the name. Brent doesn't talk confidential stuff but he's pretty open who he deals with."

"Not trying to talk in circles. I'll get to my point. Please stay with me."

"Not making a lot of sense so far."

"Humor me. Brent knows a guy well enough to take career advice from him, think you'd heard his name?"

"No doubt. Katie, what's this twenty questions game?"

"Pretty hefty competition going on over there for Marlene's job, huh?" said Katie.

"You bet."

"Who's on the short list?"

"I'm not in the company," said Annette. "But if you're to believe Brent, it's him and Paul Kruger."

"That's what I was afraid of. My career's right down the drain."

"What are you talking about? You're speaking in tongues."

"Annette, I'm certain Brent is being sabotaged by Kruger. Big time sabotage. High level sabotage. The highest."

Annette heard warning bells in her head and felt apprehension creeping through her body. "How do you know this?"

"Had lunch with Wilson Rachet on Friday," Katie said. "He seemed all concerned about your marriage. Wilson handles all the labor law issues for Richmont and I work for him."

"Why would he have questions about our marriage?"

Katie laughed. "You've been out of the game too long. To be the little birdie on Ben Voorhees' shoulder, to put a knife in your husband's heart to assure the promotion of Kruger. That's why."

"Are Rachet and Kruger friends?"

Katie laughed harder and longer than before. "Annette, you've got to be kidding. What a marvelous job in clandestine maneuvering. You people in Charlotte don't have a clue, do you? Damn, they're good. Annette, Kruger and Rachet are an item."

"What do you mean?"

"What do I mean? Annette, they're lovers. They're gay. They've obviously kept it real quiet. For survival reasons. Can you imagine what Ben Voorhees would do to a couple of gay lovers with hidden agendas in his company? Buy a freakin used electric chair. That's what he'd do.

"Only reason I know is I saw them in our parking garage one night demonstrating how much they love each other. Everyone was supposed to be gone. But not little Katie here. Tell you. Two girls and it would've turned me on. Quite a show. I almost died."

Annette's stomach began to churn. "I can't believe this. Kruger's married."

"Better believe it. And honey, ever heard of the closet?" said Katie. "This promotion's huge to Kruger. He's the ambition-run-amok poster boy. Do whatever's necessary to ruin Brent's chances. Trust me. Take what I'm about to say very seriously. These are two ruthless men. They'll stop at nothing."

"I'll tell Brent as soon as he comes in but what can he do now?"

"Not sure. But it'd be real helpful if my name could be kept out of any discussions or confrontations."

"Do my best," said Annette. "Thanks for sticking your neck out, Katie. We'll get together and lunch's on me."

"Good luck to Brent." Katie Lockhart hung up.

Annette fell into aftershock. She had faced information she did not know how to process and act on but this state of affairs had become surreal, and this phone call represented a bizarre turn. This predicament had developed a life of its own and spinning out of control. Brent had been correct about Kruger but he only knew half the story.

She started to jot down some notes from Katie's expose. Where could Brent be? She tried his cell phone again but no answer. She hoped he had not done something stupid. His absence began to frighten her.

Driving aimlessly around the city, Brent checked his phone and saw that Annette had tried to call him several times. Screw her, he thought. She would not be bringing anything positive to his quandary. Let her plan the rest of her life. His resentment rose by the minute. It had never been his nature but this catastrophe warranted a little resentment.

He had to do something to help Patricia. Her predicament weighed on his soul. How could he help? Where could he go? He had lost the last fragment of influence in the Richmont Corporation when Marlene bailed on him. She had administered the *coup de grace*. The only person who might talk to him would be Tom Carthage and with his current string of luck, Tom would probably be out on his speed boat.

Brent speed-dialed Tom's home number and was surprised by his hearty hello.

"Tom. Brent."

"What the devil you gotten into, Tiger?" said Tom.

"What've you heard?"

"Nothing good. Seems you're damaged goods around Richmont."

"That's nice," said Brent.

"No one's talked to me. But that Lear's not the biggest thing in the air. Could listen in on most of the conversation. Seems Annette acquitted herself well but what's this affair with the HR director?"

"I'm not having an affair with Patricia Bolivar. I have no idea how that rumor started."

"Don't know. Evan Roth was the bearer of the bad news. Sounded convincing to me. Ben was more than convinced."

Evan Roth. How convenient, thought Brent. Kruger's mentor in Atlanta.

"Damn, Tom. I'm getting tarred and feathered by Paul Kruger. And it's smoke and mirrors built on lies, deceit and innuendo. Know I sound like I should be committed but it's the truth. For some reason, the guy's trying to destroy me."

"Brent," said Tom. "Kruger's not the informant regarding the affair. He had nothing to do with the accusation."

"Then who?"

"Might be better I don't say."

Brent could feel his relationship with Tom Carthage slipping away. His last resource in Richmont.

"Tom, I need your help. Not for me. For Patricia Bolivar. She shouldn't have her career ruined because Kruger wants me out of the company."

"Brent. Again. It wasn't Kruger."

"I'm going to sound neurotic but Evan Roth is Kruger's mentor. Bet my last dollar Kruger's tentacles are behind this."

"Okay, Brent. Tell you what I know. Only to stop your unfair accusations toward Paul Kruger. The affair was uncovered through a conversation between Evan Roth and your advertising manager, Neal Stuart."

Brent came close to swerving off the road. "Neal Stuart. Can't be."

"Those're the facts. Your competition with Paul Kruger's over. There's no evidence of wrongdoing by him. He didn't instruct you to have an affair."

Tom had been his last hope and sounded as distant and detached as the others. The conversation on the Lear last night must have been a persuasive one. "Okay, Tom. Forget me," said Brent. "But Patricia and I never had an affair. Can't you intercede in some capacity to save her career?"

"I'm sorry, no," said Tom. "I want to believe you. But there's credible circumstantial evidence considering it's one of your direct reports that has respect for you."

Dumbfounded, Brent could hardly hold his tongue in check. Kruger was masterful at this game. If he ran the division with the ruthlessness he displayed in getting the job, there were going to be some miserable people working in a highly successful business. At least successful in the short-term. Just long enough to get Kruger promoted again.

"Brent, like to help. But my hands are tied. You wouldn't believe the retirement package Ben worked up for me. Can't afford to put that in jeopardy. Would screw up the rest of my life."

"You're right. Can't ask you to do that."

"I'll talk to Stan Ascutney," said Tom. "Off the record. See if Stan can help her. But that's as far as I can go."

"Thanks, Tom. What'd you think's in my future?"

"Can kiss the GM job goodbye. Kruger will be announced as the new GM tomorrow. For you, I think it's still in the air but not by much. Ben's not a happy camper and you have no friend in Terry Thomas."

"No surprise there," said Brent.

"Marlene's out of the loop," said Tom. "Her position became untenable and

I think she capitulated before we left Charlotte last night."

"We talked this morning. Withdrew her support," responded Brent.

"She had no recourse. Considering what's stacked up against you. You haven't asked but want to level with you. Can't recommend you as my replacement given these circumstances. Sorry but I'd look like a fool. Ben'd laugh me out of his office."

"Wouldn't expect you to. So where do I stand?"

"Not sure. But I'd mend fences with Kruger," said Tom. "Ben's infuriated but in the end, Paul has the call. If Paul thinks he can work with you, you're on the team. Bolivar will have to relocate within the company or leave. If Paul thinks your presence would be disruptive, you'll be asked to leave. And I wouldn't count on another job at Richmont or a juicy recommendation. Sorry, Tiger. That's the way I see it."

"Tom, appreciate your candor. Best of luck in your new ventures."

"Don't let this end our friendship," said Tom. "Hope you appreciate my position."

"I do. Counting on us staying in contact. Thanks, Tom." Brent disconnected. Well, there goes the ball game, Brent thought. No time on the clock.

As he finally headed home, there was nothing more to do. Just lay back and let the vultures pick his bones bare.

Annette heard the garage door open and breathed a sigh of relief. Brent had arrived. He came into the kitchen and flopped down at the table with his head in his hands.

"It's over," he said. "Marlene's withdrawn her support. The job's Kruger's."

"Meeting take this long? I worried about you," said Annette.

"No. Was driving around making calls. You'll feel some vindication the fatal blow was an accusation about Patricia and I having an affair. No substance, of course. Yet untruths seem to bother no one but me."

"You think I leveled the accusation, you're mistaken," said Annette. "I'm first to admit it to be supposition on my part."

"Know it wasn't you. At least not to Atlanta management. That distinction goes to Neal Stuart."

Annette leaned over the table, her eyes blinking in astonishment. "Can assure you I didn't talk to that little snail."

"Also be interested to know my mentor backed away from me. Ole Tom couldn't put his retirement in jeopardy. You know what Annette. I should consider that Louisiana leper colony."

"I don't know how to admit this and not look like an idiot," said Annette. "You might've been right about Kruger."

"I'll be damned. Better take your temperature," he retorted.

Brent didn't have a clue about the Kruger, Rachet relationship. She smiled to herself. She bet neither did Audra Kruger. Audra would kill the squirrelly little twit.

Annette leaned over the table again, her blue eyes sparkling with mischief. "He's been one step ahead of you during this whole thing."

"You wouldn't kid me, would you?"

"Interested how?"

"Annette. Games don't interest me right now." Brent stood. "I'm getting a drink."

"Don't. Not yet. Sit down and hear me out."

Brent returned to the table, sat down and said, "Okay. All ears."

Annette saw Brent becoming agitated. Agitated with the whole world in general and her in particular. At the present moment, she couldn't say she blamed him.

"Got a call from Katie Lockhart. Brent, Kruger's a closet gay. His lover is Wilson Rachet."

"Who the hell's Wilson Rachet?"

"Attorney with Richmont's law firm. Works on the Richmont account. Specializes in labor law. Means he handles all HR issues. Guy's part of Richmont's inner circle. Kruger had a head start because he knew about the promotion as soon as the decision had been made."

"Now we got Wilson tied down, who's Katie?"

"Used to work with her when I did legal work in East Cobb. Became pretty close professional associates. Works in the same firm as Wilson Rachet now. Does a lot of work for him."

"She reliable?"

"You betcha. First, she's put her career on the line telling me this. Second, Rachet talked to her Friday about our possible marital problems. It had been bothering her all weekend so she called."

"This is nice to know," he said. "But not sure what I can do with it."

Annette could not believe it. She was trying to help this man and he had turned her off. Her husband had been defeated and awaited his execution.

"What do you mean?" she asked. "You know where all the lies and deceit have been emanating from. Plus, the man is gay. How fast you think it'll take Bible Ben to skewer him? As well as his bedmate lawyer friend. I believe in freedom of choice, including sexual orientation. But the way these animals screwed you, send them both to hell."

"Okay, counselor. Give me advantage of your thinking. How am I supposed to pull this off?"

Annette became perplexed. She stood and sat on the edge of the table. "You get in your car and go talk to Marlene."

"You bet, counselor. Great idea. Just for fun let's play out that conversation," he said. "Been accused of everything but embezzling company funds. Who knows, that might be next on the menu. Just to make sure I'm dead. So with my impeccable credibility and untarnished reputation, I barge in on Marlene Wolff and say, 'By the way. Got some hot info that the guy you're about to make GM is gay. And his sleepover friend is an attorney who represents Richmont. Pulled some dirty tricks on me over the last few days and I want to report all this to you. They're bad guys and Ben should know. And as long as I've got your attention, think I ought to have the GM job. At the least, Carthage's job.' How's that for a speech? Cool, huh?"

Brent stood up and headed toward the den. "Get real, Annette. It's over. Plain and simple. It's over. I'm getting a drink or seven. Join me if you want."

Annette sat in shocked silence. These despicable humans should not be allowed to succeed but there was no way to stop them. Brent's sarcasm-laced assessment had been correct. The process was past the point in which information this damaging could see the light of day. It would incriminate the messenger much more than the perpetrator.

Although her life had been turned upside down and most likely would never recover from this debacle, she felt terrible for Brent. For all his narrow focus and job consumption, he was a decent human being. It was terrible that he would be forced to endure this wretched outcome that was now a foregone certainty. She put her head on the table and wept.

Marlene might still be at the office, Patricia thought, as she pulled out of the townhouse complex. She called her direct line but got no answer. She decided to go to Marlene's condo. She would not call first. She did not want to get dismissed over the phone. Senior management had to know the truth about the horrid things that had gone on and Marlene happened to be the one available.

Marlene answered the door and her eyes shot up in surprise.

"Sorry to barge in but need to speak with you," said Patricia.

"Sorry, too," Marlene said. "But I've guests coming. I have no time now. Arrange an appointment tomorrow."

"This is urgent." Patricia stepped across the front door's threshold. "Brent Shannon and I are not having an affair."

"How'd you find out about this?"

"Received a call from Brent telling me to protect myself and my reputation."

"Excellent advice."

"The only way I can, Marlene, is state to my boss the accusation is ludicrous and untrue."

"Sorry. This's neither the time nor place to discuss it."

"Might not be the time," said Patricia. "But Paul Kruger's ruthlessness is ruining the lives of some fine people."

"I'm not interested in hearing a frantic counterargument. This'll be sorted out in the coming weeks. Brent Shannon gave you sound advice. If I were you, I'd concentrate on work and keep a low profile. Would be the most efficacious strategy to salvage your career at Richmont."

Patricia became incensed. Her message had not been granted the magnitude it deserved. "You're not interested in truth or fairness, are you? Only interested in getting this mess behind you so your promotion's secure."

"Patricia. Better leave while your boat's still afloat. See you in the morning and be more than happy to discuss your future. However brief it may be at Richmont."

Marlene took Patricia's arm and guided her to the door and opened it. "Now, please excuse me. I have to finish preparing for my guests." Marlene closed the door in Patricia's face.

Patricia walked to her car, overwhelmed with sorrow. It was over. Marlene's support for Brent had dissolved. The last respected link to senior management had been taken away. No one would listen.

Patricia realized she had destroyed her career at Richmont due to her support of Brent. Her career. The segment of her life that she had always held at the zenith of importance. Odd. For some reason, she suddenly became buoyed by an inner calm. She would do it all over again without a moment's hesitation.

Annette came downstairs. She worried about Brent because his despondency had reached a dangerous level.

"Brent, I have to go out," she said. "Please stay here. Don't go out."

"Going nowhere. On my fourth Turkey and planning to add to the flock."

"I'm going to the church for a legal assistance board meeting. Probably couple of hours. Watch the drinking. Kids'll be home shortly. Got my cell phone."

"Nothing to worry about here. Go right ahead. Thought I'd indulge in a little self-pity. Good for the soul at times. Appropriate right now, don't you think?"

Annette drove toward the church. She had never seen Brent this depressed. He had always succeeded without having to dip into the cesspool of corporate politics. Although bright, he had been ill-prepared for the evil that bubbled to the surface with Marlene's promotion. Even after it appeared, he had not recognized its power. The man was defeated and alone.

She could rally to him but it would be false support. Support emanating from pity not devotion. Just as the children had not been a reason to reconcile eight years ago, pity would not be an acceptable reason now. A short-term solution which, in relationships, was the worst kind.

The compatibility foundation for a successful marriage did not exist for them. It had taken a long time for her to recognize that fact. Some wonderful people had been hurt by her lack of insight. This would not be the time to elongate the pain but to let healing begin. She had been ignorant of the environment that Brent had walked into last Wednesday which made her a liability to him. However, she knew she was correct regarding their marriage.

The board meeting was short. Shortness was the singular advantage to having meetings on Sunday afternoon. Annette had been so anxious about Brent that she remembered little of what had been discussed. She had facilitated this darkness that now enveloped her husband. During the meeting, she could not purge her mind of that realization. It tore at her inner soul causing her to question whether to be around him or stay away.

She felt terrible about it but even with this sympathy for Brent, she understood that she could not abide an absentee husband. She would not change. She needed to be well within the central focus circle of a relationship. Always. Never out of it. Also, she had made her children an inseparable extension of herself. They must be in that circle as well. Always. Her needs allowed her mate to have a job but not necessarily a career. Her relationship with Brent had the singular objective of meeting her needs while caging a free and striving human. What a miserable relationship failure she had precipitated.

Walking out of the conference room, she felt a gentle hand on her shoulder. She turned to see Peter Ludlow standing behind her.

"My dear, this is probably rude and uncalled for but you looked quite despondent and preoccupied during the meeting," he said. "Were you opposed to something we decided?"

"Oh, no. Sorry to be mentally on another planet, Peter. Has nothing to do with the board's actions. A personal issue."

"Seems to be bothering you quite a bit. You know things usually work out for the best." He smiled. "Known as faith in some circles."

"Thanks for the encouragement, Peter. But don't think that's the case here." Peter took her hand. "Oh. Someone critically ill?"

"No, nothing like that. Just something with my husband. I can't talk about it but thanks for your concern," Annette said. She hoped she used a dismissive not rude inflection in her voice. Peter defined a sweet man.

"I apologize for my intrusiveness," said Peter as he began turning away.

Annette took his arm. "No, Peter. I owe you the apology. For my rudeness. Just terribly upset. Have difficulty grasping how evil some people can be."

"The case sometimes. The Almighty blessed us with free will and some use that gift to mock him rather than praise him."

"I'm just a homemaker but it strikes me as heinous when people can use lies and deceit to achieve their personal goals at the expense of good people who are only trying to realize their own dreams."

"Regrettably, it happens. How does all this affect your husband?"

"Really don't feel comfortable discussing it," she said. "He's just been terribly hurt for the self-serving reasons of others. Makes me ill."

"That's terrible but sometimes we have to face those situations. Hope things work out for him."

"They probably will. Isn't it awful villainous people succeed in this world and good people suffer because of it?"

"I'll pray for your family, Annette."

"Thank you so much, Peter. You're a kind man."

She left the church, got in her car and pulled out of the church parking lot. She drove home as distraught as her life had ever experienced. She decided her best course of action now would to be home to make sure Brent remained sane and keep the children at bay. My god, what dark hole have we fallen into? she groaned.

MONDAY

Paul and Audra left the house together.

"How long have we waited for this day?" said Audra. "Took the day off to be around for the good news. Going for some things at the store but be back shortly."

"I'll call as soon as I get the word," Paul said. He gave Audra a kiss on the cheek, got in his car and pulled out of the driveway.

He drove to the freeway entrance and merged into the early morning traffic. He wondered how the announcement would be handled. Obviously, Ben Voorhees would make it. Paul debated whether Ben would fly over or have Marlene do the Charlotte honors. It would be much better if Ben came to Charlotte. It would be testimony to the importance of the position and the person who held it. Yes, he concluded, Ben would likely fly over.

Paul could hardly contain himself with his first taste of the sweet fruit of vindication. He had triumphed over the barbarians that tormented him. Those that persecuted him in his earlier life. That dreg of society who sired him. The vermin he had to endure in those military post schools. Each and every one of them would now be embodied in the sub-human, Brent Shannon. Their resolve would be to protect him. His body and mind their last Bastogne. They would fail and Shannon's destruction would be their crucifixion. He smiled. Retribution. So intoxicating.

If it had not been for that astonishing person, his mother, he would have perished. The only man who ever befriended him had been his Tai Kwon Do instructor at Fort Bragg. Paul had felt a magnetic closeness to him that had frightened him at times. There were no other men who chose to be close to him until Wilson. Dear Wilson.

Paul remembered it like yesterday. One Friday evening, they had met for drinks and decided to go back to Wilson's apartment. Wilson said he would scare up some pasta and wine.

It had been raining heavily that evening and they got soaking wet. Paul almost became sexually excited remembering it. Wilson had thrown him a towel and bathrobe and told him to get a shower before he caught the death of cold. He had been enjoying the steaming water cascading over his body when Wilson stepped in the shower. Paul had been shocked but strangely excited as Wilson pulled him close. He had melted into Wilson's arms and felt his masculine body against him. In that instant of bliss, Paul remembered his closeness to the Tai Kwon Do instructor and realized it had been his first feelings of physical desire. Wilson had gently led him to bed and they made beautiful love. They had been lovers since.

Their current plan assumed that Ben would retire in two or three years, Marlene would become CEO and Paul would be promoted to CFO. Under Marlene's leadership, the organizational culture would change. As a social liberal, she would be shocked but not vindictive toward a gay CFO. He and Audra would divorce amicably and he would finally be with the person he loved. The preface to their plan was his promotion to general manager of the retail division. Now accomplished, nothing could stand in their way.

Paul parked the Jaguar, went into his office and began to check his accumulated weekend e-mails. His phone rang and Marlene asked him to come over to her office. What a marvelous day he thought as he left his office. These were his first steps toward the pinnacle of corporate power.

Brent pointed his Audi south on Park Road heading to the office but with no sense of urgency. Maybe he could have a seven-hour breakfast at The Kopper Kettle. He left the house early only because he had little desire to shoot the bull with his wife. Also, he had never seen as large a flock of Turkeys as he had yesterday afternoon which still intermittently kicked him in the back of the head. He figured being hung over at work would be the least of his worries today. Of course, he had no colossal urge to see the coronation of King Paul of Prickdom either.

He had learned a bitter lesson from this experience. If he would be fortunate enough to be given another opportunity in another company, he would master the political game. He would never be decimated again by some contentious worm like Kruger.

The ending had arrived for his marriage. He had come to that conclusion all by himself. He had always been a forgiving guy but Annette had crossed the line. She had played him like the proverbial fiddle for eight years. He had jumped through hoops while she had a grand ole time. Well, enough of that. It would be a long time before he got mixed up with another woman. However, he would be as good a father as time, distance and the courts would allow.

One thing had come out of his demolishment. He had found out who were his friends. His grandmother had told him that people could count their friends on one hand. Hell, it didn't take that many fingers. He had his sister Cory and Patricia Bolivar. After that was said, it was all said.

Last Wednesday he thought he had his world by the tail. Actually, the last four days proved that his world had him by the balls. Just incredible. His support crumbled like a house of cards. Annette, Marlene, George, Tom Carthage were all illusions. When crunch time came, self-protection and convenience trumped good ole Brent.

He parked and went to his office. Ashley intercepted him on the way. How early does she get here? Brent thought.

Ashley followed him into his office. "Boss, think there'll be an announcement today?"

"Believe so, Ash."

"Terry going with Marlene to Atlanta?"

"Who?"

"Terry. Marlene's admin assistant," said Ashley.

"Don't have the faintest. Why?"

"Like to apply to be your admin assistant when you're GM."

"We'll discuss that later, Ash. Please shut the door when you leave. Some things I need to get done immediately."

As Ashley turned to leave, Neal Stuart stuck his head in the door. "Brent, got a few minutes?"

"No, I don't. Ashley, shut the door."

Brent sat staring out his office window. As he watched the southwestern sky beget storm clouds, he knew that company had to be the last thing he needed now.

Paul's stride and bearing to Marlene's office transmitted power. Long and quick with head erect and shoulders back. He wanted to communicate that here walked a man of purpose and power. Paul's intellect visualized him walking through a great doorway. Behind him his personal age of tribulation. A dark period of repudiation but preparation. The great doorway became the threshold to his fulfillment. An age of self-gratification, happiness and retribution. Yes, sweet retribution.

Everyone he passed smiled and warmly greeted him. The word had obviously been leaked. Probably by Marlene's assistant. Paul returned their greetings professionally but with slightly more aloofness than usual. He must establish presence and demonstrate gravitas. No one could doubt who was in charge. No better time to start than now. He could not wait to call Wilson. It would be his first call, of course.

Marlene's assistant waved him into Marlene's office. Marlene looked up from her desk and motioned to one of the armchairs in front of her desk. "Paul, have a seat."

"Wonderful party Saturday night," Paul said.

"Yes, it was. Paul, do you know Wilson Rachet?"

Paul was taken aback by the question but recovered. He probably had to coordinate with Wilson regarding the employment termination of Shannon and Bolivar.

"Sorry, I don't," said Paul. "Oh, wait. Isn't he an attorney? Works for the firm we use in Atlanta."

"That's correct," said Marlene. "Do you know him socially?"

Paul became concerned. His underarms turned from dry to damp. This line of questioning had what purpose? Wilson and he had been extraordinarily discreet with their relationship. That could not be it. Paul studied Marlene. She had a relaxed look on her face, not the piercing stare she exhibited when troubled.

"Might have seen him at some company functions. That would be it."

Marlene's sudden change in demeanor overwhelmed him. She sat forward in her chair and burned two holes in his face with her eyes. Paul felt himself becoming stunned and unnerved. Something had to be terribly wrong.

"Paul, I'm going to ask you one more time and you'd best think very carefully before answering. Ready? Do you know Wilson Rachet socially?"

Paul became terrified to a degree he had not felt since occupying the same house with his father. Obviously, Marlene thought she knew something about him and Wilson. But that would be impossible. No one could tell her anything except for him or Wilson. That would never happen because it would be career suicide for them both.

"Marlene, I'm not certain what you want from me but I don't appreciate this treatment. These interrogation tactics. Other than at a company function, I've not met the man." Paul mustered a defiant look. "Am I supposed to have?"

"All I want from you, Mr. Kruger, is the truth. I wish to inform you, as we're speaking, Ben Voorhees and Anthony Markham, the law firm's senior managing partner, are meeting with Wilson Rachet. Given the options they'll present to him, I'm confident it will be confirmed that you and Wilson have been involved in an intimate relationship for many years. You've been lovers."

Paul's throat closed making it painful to breath. His mouth became so dry he could hardly open it to talk.

When he spoke, it sounded like a rasp. "Where did you come up with that nonsense?"

"Where's unimportant. Truth's what's important," Marlene said.

Marlene's assistant stuck his head in the door to say that Mr. Voorhees was on the phone.

Marlene nodded. Picking up the phone, she looked at Paul. "Don't leave. We're far from finished."

Paul Kruger, his nerves in shambles, listened to a one-way conversation in which Marlene's contributions were nods with an occasional, "I see." She concluded the conversation with her assurance that she would take care of things on this end.

She put down the phone and looked at Paul. "Interesting. Seems you and Wilson became lovers before we hired you. He got you the interview with us, in fact. Wilson has passed his lover privileged information for years. Most recently, giving you ample lead time to the announcement of my promotion. Seems he also helped you construct a web of deceit about Brent Shannon to assure that you, not Brent, was selected to run this division. From marital difficulties to the bogus affair with Patricia Bolivar."

Paul's mental faculties shut down. He was close to tears and disintegrating in a fit of rage. How could they have gotten Wilson to tell them all this? The threats had to be horrific. The malicious primates had hurt the love of his life.

"This is ridiculous," he said. "Defamatory and preposterous. I've never been subjected to this type of unprofessional behavior. The company should be ashamed of you as a senior executive." He could see by the look on Marlene's face that he had crossed a line.

"What I see as unprofessional is your covert attempt to destroy Brent Shannon through innuendos and lies."

Paul sat straight in his chair and stared at Marlene. "I'm being discriminated against because I'm gay."

"Only professional propriety prevents me from laughing in your face. Your employment isn't being terminated because you're gay, you arrogant fool. It's being terminated because you're a liar and perpetuated a series of events that were detrimental to the health of this organization."

Paul's voice became a shrill screech. "What do you mean, terminated? You can't possibly think about firing me. Not after all I've done for this company."

"Yes, your employment with the Richmont Corporation is terminated, effective immediately," Marlene said. "You will leave these premises upon the conclusion of our discussion. Give your office keys to my assistant. He will assure their security and the security of the personal effects in your office. Please be here at six this evening. An attorney from Atlanta and I will cover your severance arrangements and supervise your removal of personal items from the premises."

Paul's composure vanished. His eyes filled with tears and his voice became cracked and desperate.

"We need to talk about this," he stammered.

"There's nothing to talk about," she said. "Now get off of this company's property or I'll have you forcibly removed."

Paul stormed to Marlene's office door where he lost control of his volcanic rage.

"You fucking bitch. Roast in hell." He slammed the door and left.

From a sea of despair, Brent heard his phone ringing. Patricia was on the other end.

"Do you have the foggiest notion what's going on?" she said.

"Other than I'm screwed, no."

"Don't be too sure of that. Just got off the phone with Todd Beamon. Know Randall Norton?"

"No. Is he accusing me of something now?"

"You better pull yourself out of funkville," Patricia said. "Norton's the catalog division's director of finance. The guy you mentioned Wednesday night. One you thought might get Marlene's job. Todd just finished a compensation package for him. He's coming to Charlotte as the new GM."

Brent sat up in his chair. "You sure? Can't be, Patricia. Kruger's got the job locked."

Patricia laughed. "Seems not."

"All well and good," he said. "But doesn't solve our problem."

"Doesn't. But we'll have a more objective hearing than from Kruger."

"True. Thanks for the information, Patricia."

"You all right?"

"No. But talk to you later." Brent hung up the phone.

He fell back into his personal world of doom when his office door burst open. A wild-eyed Paul Kruger stormed in.

"Christ. What the hell, Paul," Brent said. "You damn near shattered my door."

"You unmitigated demon," screamed Paul. His eyes were crazed. "You've ruined everything. Just everything. Suppose you're quite satisfied."

Paul inched toward Brent while Brent looked for something to throw at him if the need arose. The man was stark raving mad. Brent had never seen him like this. Kruger had always been controlled.

"What the hell you talking about?" Brent said.

"You villain," Paul literally shouted. "You know what I'm talking about. Everyone has a right to a private life without being exploited by narrow, bigoted people."

"Don't have any idea about this private life business. Can assure you anything exposed about your private life wasn't exposed by me. Don't give a rat's ass about your private life. Now settle the hell down," Brent said. He was trying to be as measured and calm as possible but the guy was over the edge.

"You did it. Yes, you did," wailed Paul. "Or at the very least, engineered it. Was right about you. Just like the scum I grew up around."

Kruger was hysterical. Brent tried to be the adult in this exchange but felt himself about to have to revert to the schoolyard.

"Don't know what your problem is and I don't give a damn. Got enough on my own plate, thank you. Generated by you, incidentally. But you're not coming into my office screaming and demeaning me. Now get the hell out."

Paul clenched his fists but kept them at his side. "This isn't over. I'll get you. Better look over your shoulder for the rest of your natural life," Paul pronounced.

"Get the fuck out of here before I kick your ass," said Brent.

Paul turned to walk out. He picked up a magazine from a side table, threw it at Brent and disappeared out the door.

Brent walked around the desk to pick up the pencil holder and its contents that were hit by Paul's flying magazine.

Ashley ran into the office. "What was that all about?"

"Don't want to know," he replied. "If it's still on its hinges, shut the door on your way out."

Shaking his head, Brent sat down at his desk. The phone rang again. Wonder if it's a bill collector, Brent thought as he picked it up and said hello.

"Brent. It's Marlene. Would you be in my office at two-thirty this afternoon?"

"Do I have to prepare anything," Brent said.

"No. Just be prompt."

Brent hung up the phone. So sweet and to the point. Ought to walk around the outside of the building. See which tree they had selected to hang him from at the appointed time.

Paul's Jaguar roared out of the parking lot and up Westinghouse considerably exceeding the speed limit. How could Shannon have gotten the information about him and Wilson? They had been so careful. Denying themselves to each other in favor of absolute discretion. Oh, that scum Shannon. That evil, bigoted man. He used Paul's deep love for Wilson against him. What a vile tramp. Oh god, poor Wilson, he thought. What ordeal had they put him through? Paul speed dialed Wilson's cell phone and greeted with a gruff hello.

"Wilson. My god, how're you doing? "

"How am I doing? Oh, I'm doing just fine. Let me tell you just how fine, sweetie. Ever told you the firm has a small office in Macon, Georgia?"

"Don't think so. What's that got to do with us?"

"Nothing to do with you, baby. Just me. Was told I could discuss my relationship with you and receive an excellent severance and recommendation. Or could decide not to and be reassigned to the firm's Macon office as a paralegal. With the appropriate remuneration adjustment, of course. If I took the Macon assignment and decided to leave the firm in the future, there would be no positive recommendation."

"I assume you took the severance," said Paul.

Wilson laughed. "That's a good assumption, you idiot."

"I got fired, too," said Paul. "The world's in ruins. But something good comes out of everything. Can be together getting our careers back on track."

Wilson laughed. Almost a controlled scream. A sound Paul had never heard from him.

"Don't think so, self-indulging bitch," Wilson said. "Think I'll get my dignity and life back solo. At least not with you."

"What do you mean? Don't talk like that. You mean everything to me."

"Not enough to keep your stupid mouth shut. Unmitigated bitch. Been fun at times, Paul. You were a pleasure to bed. So complying. So submissive. But time to start over. Frankly, you've lost appeal. Friends told me not to be involved with a closet. Nothing good would come of it. Should've listened."

Frantic, Paul said, "Wilson, I said nothing. To anyone."

"Don't have time to argue, you groveling fool. Do wish you luck." He laughed. "You'll need it. I'll be leaving for west coast in the next two weeks. Don't contact me. Ever." The phone went dead.

Paul felt faint. Bright dots appeared in front of his eyes. His world tumbled. Madly in love with Wilson, Paul could not, would not, let him go. He had to develop a plan. This had been a major defeat but he could recover. He had fought off the demons his entire life. This battle had been lost but not the war.

Of course. Audra could be the answer. He could not hide his dismissal from her, of course. She would be distraught and brutally angry but she would recover. They could still reach their socio-economic objectives. She did not want to go to Charleston as a failure. No, it would not be easy but he and Audra could still help each other achieve their goals. When they did, Wilson would not be able to resist him. Life would be fine. He would land on his feet.

Paul pulled into the circular driveway behind a car he did not recognize. Paul realized he loved this place as he looked out at the lake. Until he got himself reconnected, Audra's promotion would allow them to maintain this lifestyle. As he walked through the double front doors into the foyer, his breath suddenly left him as his body absorbed the weight of something heavy striking him. Stunned momentarily, he looked down at his feet and saw his Tumi three-suiter on the floor. It had been hurled at him. Paul looked up to see a livid Audra across the foyer.

"Pick up the fuckin' suitcase, go upstairs and pack enough things to get your faggot ass out of here," she spewed.

Paul was stunned.

"Whatever are you talking about?" he managed to reply.

"Don't play that bull shit game with me, you queer son of a bitch," she said. "Didn't know I'd been living with a fuckin' three-dollar bill all these years. Get upstairs, pack some clothes and get the hell out of here before I hit you with something that hurts."

"Must've heard I got terminated. That's because our strategy got found out."

"I'm going for another drink," Audra said. "Then I'm going on the deck to drink it. By the time I'm finished I want you gone."

"Audra, please."

"You sniveling excuse for a man. Don't even try. I got a friendly call from Marilyn Beamon a while ago. The bitch never liked me and couldn't wait to announce all the sordid details to me. She had just a fucking good time. Should send you a thank you note. Maybe catch you at the local steambath. You filthy, queer asshole.

"Best thing you can do is shut the hell up and get out of here. Take the Jaguar.

It's all you'll get when I'm through with you." Audra turned on her heels and disappeared into the den.

Paul walked upstairs. His mind had imploded. He had no intelligible thoughts of where he was or what he was doing except packing to exit life as he knew it. Along with a few clothes, he managed to pack the five by seven picture of his mother and the one elegant gift his father had given him.

Paul went downstairs. He put down his suitcase and looked for Audra with tears in his eyes. At least he wanted to tell her goodbye. He stood at the door to the den, looked across the room and through the double glass doors. He saw her on the deck handing a drink to her boss. He kissed her on the ear and softly caressed her buttocks with his hand. They looked out at the lake with Audra's head on his shoulder.

Paul left the house, threw his suitcase in the Jaguar's trunk and drove away.

Northwest Airlines Flight 1671 rotated off the Charlotte Douglas International Airport's runway 18R at two-thirty-five. Shortly thereafter, it began a slow climbing turn to the northwest to pick up its initial heading to Minneapolis-St. Paul International Airport.

The Shannon family, minus the man of the house, occupied three seats in row 11. Erik sat by the window and Tawney in the middle. They were both excited about seeing their grandparents. They had fought for the window seat when they boarded but the argument had been settled peacefully. It had been agreed Erik could see the take-off and Tawney the landing.

A lifetime could be crammed into a single day, Annette thought. Brent had barely left the garage when the phone rang. It had been exactly six-eighteen because she had looked at the digital clock on the bedside table before answering. The time of day bespoke that Brent had been in an accident, his car had stalled or there had been a family crisis. She remembered picking up the phone to begin the most inconceivable conversation of her life. It had played through her mind all day and she could recall it almost verbatim. She had said hello and the conversational trip of her life commenced.

"Hello, Annette, this is Ben Voorhees," a smooth southern voice had said. "Do you remember our visit Saturday night?"

"Certainly," Annette had responded and become instantly wide awake.

"Young lady, I received a call in the middle of the night from Peter Ludlow. You know Peter, I believe."

"I do. We're involved in a legal assistance group at our church."

"Peter and I've known each other for forty years give or take a month or two. No one in the world I trust more. Be on our board if he still wanted to work for a living."

"He's a nice man."

"Told me something was bothering him. That we had to talk. Said he thought there might be a serious miscarriage of justice about to occur at Richmont. And he thought I might be an unwitting party to it. Thought I should get a heads-up.

"Said there's a very bright attorney who worked with him that might be able to give me the particulars much better than he could. Seems he worked with her in a pro bono legal group. Said she gave her full energy to every issue brought to her as if she were getting two hundred and fifty dollars an hour. Felt her word was above reproach. Never known Peter Ludlow to be wrong about another human in forty years. Don't think he's going to start now.

"You're the person he was referring to, Annette. Sorry for the early call but you think you could tell me what Peter's talking about?"

She had almost fallen off the side of the bed.

"Mr. Voorhees, if you'll let me compose myself, be happy to tell you what I know."

"Take your time and the name's Ben."

"My information came from an attorney I know. Katie Lockhart. She works at the law firm representing Richmont's interests. Hope she won't feel any ramifications for confiding in me."

"Can assure you she won't."

"You know Wilson Rachet?"

"Of course. Handles all our human resource legal work."

"Wilson Rachet and Paul Kruger are lovers. They're gay."

"That's preposterous." From the tone of his voice, Annette had thought he would hang up on her.

"May be preposterous but it's true. You asked what I know, please hear me out."

"Go on."

"They concocted a plan to discredit Brent's and my marriage."

"Do you have marital problems?"

"We do. But the problems aren't of Brent's making. I hold that distinction. He's a good man, Ben. Don't feel comfortable going into the details but you can be assured Wilson Rachet nor Paul Kruger have any accurate knowledge of our relationship. They fabricated untruths to destroy Brent's chance for Marlene's job."

"I appreciate your sharing this with me. But you're talking about two respected businessmen. Find this impossible to believe."

His disbelief had infuriated her. He had been more than willing to believe those swine while calling her a liar.

"Mr. Voorhees. I'm not from the Paul Kruger school of ethics. Telling you exactly what I heard. From a source I respect who enjoys a huge downside risk by confiding in me. If you choose not to believe me, that's your prerogative. But know that you'll perpetrate an injustice that I don't think you want attributed to your company."

"Hmm. I see. Annette, I have to ask you a personal question."

"Go ahead. If I feel I can answer it, I will."

"Do you know anything about an affair between your husband and Patricia Bolivar, the human resource director?"

Annette had been taken back by that. She remembered thinking she should have had him define personal. However, she had recovered quickly. Good law training.

"Know nothing about that. Mind telling me where you came upon that piece of information?"

"Don't feel comfortable giving you that, Annette. Will say it came from a source close to your husband."

"Ben, going to guess wherever you got it, Neal Stuart was involved."

"Go on."

"Saw Kruger, Stuart and somebody I didn't know all huddled up Saturday night. I thought it was strange. Entire time we've been in Charlotte, never, and I mean never, seen Paul Kruger socialize with anybody at Neal Stuart's level. Not even his staff. Now I know why the huddle. Neal has resented Brent since the moment we got here. Naturally, thought he should've gotten the director job. But that's gossip. Not what you're looking for."

"You're as bright and perceptive, as Peter said."

"Pretty easy, really. Hatched the marital problems from the fact they were privy to information about our earlier issues. The ones we had when we first came to Richmont."

"Wilson would've had that information."

"Needed a patsy for the affair accusation. Stuart fit the profile to a tee. Resentment coupled with ambition beyond capability."

"Annette, certainly appreciate your willingness to share with me. Hope everything works out in your marriage."

"Things usually work out for the best."

"Normally the case. If you'll excuse me, I have some investigation and collaboration to do. If a terrible mistake is about to happen, thankfully it can be undone."

Still unbelievable, Annette thought, as the aircraft leveled off. Her thoughts turned to Brent.

They could not have a marriage where both achieved happiness. Their objectives were at complete odds. Brent needed to be free to achieve his goals. Annette knew that one of his goals was to have a full, fruitful family life. However, he needed a mate that defined full and fruitful in the same hemisphere as he. Regrettably, she could not be that mate.

Tears came to her eyes. Brent was a marvelous man but he would eventually drive her to drink and she him. Although she detested the term, she *was* high maintenance. That's the reason she found Charlie so comforting and caring. He had a job that he would occupy until the day he retired. Compensated adequately for the lifestyle he wanted, he worked diligently enough to hold his job. But nothing extra. His personal life always consumed the extra. The type of man she required for happiness.

It had been unfair to reconcile with Brent. But she had and there could be no turning back the clock. Now the only right thing would be to secure the future. Her future would be with Charlie and she could not wait to see his ruddy face and rumpled hair at the airport.

Brent would thrive. Initially he would be hurt but he would lose himself in work and make his world tick. She would always have a place in her heart for him but it would have to be from afar.

Her guilt concerned the children. The ones she had tried to protect all these years and now would hurt. But she and Brent could work out an arrangement that would give them some semblance of continuity. Also, she knew Charlie. He would foster as close a relationship between them and their Dad as she. She looked over to see Erik and Tawney staring out at the clouds.

Annette leaned back on the headrest, closed her eyes and as flight 1671 moved swiftly through the sky toward her new life, marveled at how much could change with a phone call.

Brent was having a tough time coming up for air. First, Patricia called to say some guy named Randall Norton from catalog was coming in as GM. Then Kruger came barging in like Berserker, the Scandinavian warrior of legend, called Brent every name in the book, threw a magazine at him and stormed out.

But the *coup de grace* had been Annette's call to inform him that she and the children were going back to Minnesota. Permanently. Oh and he didn't receive an invitation to tag along. He had told her there did not seem to be any hesitation in her voice and she responded, no, none. She said if she did not leave they would destroy each other. This would be the only way to salvage amicable parents for the children. Brent had mentioned the possibility of his moving back to the Twin Cities. He asked if that would help. The response had been a firm, no. She had said they could work out something for the children. Distance might be an advantage. At least in the short-term.

Brent had felt sick to his stomach. He had almost been forced to use his wastebasket. He had told her that he loved her deeply and he would always have a scar on his heart where she had been. Nonetheless, if she had made up her mind he would not stand in her way. Brent had said he needed to ask her one favor. If there was another man, please don't tell him. He was not sure he could handle that piece of information right now. Annette had not responded, which, of course, gave Brent his answer. He could be a dumb shit at times.

Annette had said she would always have a place in her heart for Brent and they would talk soon about arrangements. Brent remembered that he had thought, ah, arrangements? So that's what they call them. Brent had told her goodbye and to have a safe trip. She had said goodbye and good luck. She would talk to him soon. Brent had hung up the phone with silent tears making two paths down his cheeks.

The clock on his desk brought him back to the present. Two-fifteen and he was due in Marlene's office at two-thirty for the lynching. He had to get hold of himself. The hanging tree awaited and required dignity.

Brent arrived at Marlene's office at two twenty-five and her assistant asked him to have a seat. Marlene would be with him in a moment. Brent wondered if he would get a last meal. At least some microwave popcorn. What a dismal end to all of this. A horrid ending to something that began with uncertainty but promise. His wife gone. His kids gone. His career at Richmont gone. He wondered if his car would still be in the parking lot. Marlene opened the door and motioned for Brent to come in.

He walked toward her office hoping his execution would be mercifully short. As he walked through the door, he saw Ben Voorhees sitting at the conference table.

"Hello, Brent. Please have a seat. We'd like to visit with you," said Ben.

Brent walked across the office and sat at the table. The big guy came to do the lynching himself. He obviously didn't know his own importance, Brent concluded.

"It's come to my attention you've run quite an obstacle course the last several days," Ben said.

Strange comment, Brent thought.

"And what obstacle course is that?"

"We discovered you've been the target of untruths and deceitful behavior since the announcement of Marlene's promotion."

He couldn't handle anymore verbal calisthenics. Okay, what would be next, Brent thought.

"Ben, let's just say it's been an interesting week."

"I want you to know nothing that's happened since last Wednesday was known or sanctioned by this company. It was perpetuated by unprincipled individuals who are no longer associated, in any way, with the Richmont Corporation."

"Freely admit they put my life in turmoil," Brent said. "Turmoil that will have long-term implications."

Marlene leaned toward him. "Brent, we understand that. Can't begin to tell you how personally sorry I am that this type of thing went on under my watch and I became drawn into the subterfuge. Wretched behavior by persons I trusted. Can assure you I feel violated although certainly not to your extent. You have my deepest apologies."

"Marlene, that means a great deal to me," Brent said.

"Although egregious, we have to put this behind us and get on with life," Ben said.

Ben looked at Brent with understanding eyes. "Know that's easier said than done. I went through an ugly personal crisis. Found comfort in my Christian faith." He smiled and continued, "This isn't a sermon. Everyone has to find their own answers."

Brent returned Ben's smile but said nothing. He had an idea he would be awfully glad Ben Voorhees was known as Bible Ben.

After an uneasy silence, Ben coughed and said, "Well, let's get on to the second reason I wanted to visit with you, in person. Brent, don't want to lose you. You're a valuable talent who's done a tremendous job for our company. We'd like you to continue contributing to our success."

"I'd like to stay with the company very much," said Brent. "But both of you need to be aware that my wife and I have separated. My time and mind are going to be impacted by getting my personal life in order."

"I'm sad to hear that, Brent," said Marlene. "I like and respect Annette. Hope the separation didn't result from the unscrupulous persons we had among us."

"No. This mess simply brought the problems between us into clear relief," said Brent. "If it hadn't been this, it would've been something else."

"Thanks for bringing your personal situation up but it has no bearing on the company wanting you to stay," said Ben. "Only injustice I can't correct is, with all this conflict and its impact on the division, don't feel I can promote you to the GM position."

He understood Ben's thinking, thought Brent. But in the end Kruger accomplished one half of his objective. "Guess I can understand your decision."

"Brent, there's just too much turmoil," said Marlene.

"As close as you and Tom Carthage are, I'm sure you know he's elected to take an early retirement," said Ben.

"I do. Tom told me Saturday night. Sounds like he has an exciting life planned."

"He does. Think he'll be happy and I'm delighted for him," said Ben. "Well, to get to the point at hand. Brent, I would be privileged if you would agree to relocate to Atlanta and become Richmont's vice president of marketing. You would report to me and if you conditionally agree, like you to come to Atlanta tomorrow to visit about what I see as the critical marketing issues facing us. Especially in the international arena. And of course, Stan Ascutney and I will be prepared to cover the components of your compensation package."

"Ben, I'd be honored to stay with Richmont in that capacity," Brent said. "But going back to the earlier comments about my personal life. Going to be six months or so before I could devote all the energy needed to make Richmont's marketing effort sing."

Ben smiled. "Think I've got that covered. Spoke with Tom Carthage this morning. He's agreed to an amendment to his retirement package. He will be on salary continuation for six months. He'll officially retire after that. Will be able to get his new life started but be available to you anytime you need him over that period of time. Would only ask that you do everything in your power to have your life sorted out in six months."

"Think that's doable," said Brent.

Ben extended his hand across the table. "Then we've a deal, contingent on our mutual agreement to the company's marketing goals and your acceptance of our compensation package."

Brent grabbed Ben's hand. "Yes, sir, we have a deal."

"Brent, so glad you're coming to Atlanta. You've made me a marketing advocate and taught me more than Duke University ever did. Delighted I'll be able to continue my education," Marlene said.

Ben stood. "I'd better get back to Atlanta. Brent, Marlene has to come over tomorrow and we're sending the Lear over for her. Why don't you hop on?"

Brent stood. "Great. I'll get the flight schedule and be there."

"Ben, doesn't this make Brent and I peers," asked Marlene?

"Yes. Hadn't thought of it," Ben said.

"Wonderful," said Marlene. "Allows me to do something."

Marlene stood, threw her arms around Brent and kissed him on the cheek. "I'm so sorry about you and Annette but I'm ecstatic you'll be in Atlanta."

"That's very gracious of you," said Brent. "Thank you both for your support. See you in the morning."

Walking out of Marlene's office, the realization gripped Brent that in this struggle, there were no winners.

TRUMPED

Paul Kruger drove south on I-77. Once again, the evil ones had thwarted his destiny. What he had worked so hard for had been snatched away from him. Why? When would the torment stop? When would the demons leave him alone? His tortured mind held no answer.

The Jaguar crossed into South Carolina. Maybe he would go to the coast. He loved the seashore. Paul pulled into the South Carolina Welcome Center. Since most of the diagonal parking spaces in front of the building were occupied, he parked in the side lot. He turned off the engine thinking, yes, the shore would be nice. He could start over in Savannah. Or Jacksonville. Definitely not Charleston. Demons lived there.

Paul carefully balanced the picture of his mother on the beige, leather covered console between the seats. He smiled. What a magnificent woman. The rock of his life. He would make her so proud of him. An inspiration struck him. He knew how to destroy the demons. Yes, his mother would be proud of him.

He looked at the passenger seat to see his father's gift. A truly elegant gift. He and Audra had had to admit that when his father had given it to him last Christmas. Now he would be able to use it as he knew his father intended. Paul looked out over the South Carolina countryside. What a beautiful afternoon. He could relax here for hours but he knew the time to get started had come. He could not be sure how long the trip would take.

He had to admire his father's gift again. So appropriate, he thought. Paul had a doleful smile on his face. His thoughts were of his mother. His sweet, lovely mother.

As an elderly couple began to get in their RV for yet another leg of their trip to Florida, they both heard what they thought to be a car's backfire. Thankfully, they looked toward the freeway which spared them from observing the driver's side window of an immaculate, dark blue Jaguar parked in the side lot. A window suddenly soiled by a thick red spray of blood, bone fragments and brain tissue emanating from the exit wound on the left side of Paul Kruger's head. A wound caused by the .45 caliber bullet discharged from the nickel plated, military side arm given to Paul by his father. His father's gift had mercifully put to peace a brain torn asunder by the imaginary yet powerful demons dwelling within it.

Brent Shannon sat in his office without a clue what he should do. After he left Marlene's office, his major task had been to check tomorrow's flight schedule, which he accomplished with one phone call.

He had no reason or desire to go home. The empty house would do nothing for his psyche. He'd had that experience eight years ago. Once in a lifetime would be quite enough.

Brent's body felt paralyzed. It was almost too heavy to lift out of the desk chair. But his mind whirled in hyper-drive. His life had experienced category five winds of change and would never be the same again. Traumatized by the events of the past days, Brent knew that he did not have the luxury of despondency. He would be forced to quickly regain control of his life. Brent heard a soft knock and looked up to see Patricia's face peering around the door jam.

"Hear you're leaving town," she said as she walked in his office.

"Appears to be the case."

"You should be excited. It's a marvelous opportunity."

"It is."

"Is Annette enthused about it?"

"Annette's gone back to Minnesota with the children. On a permanent basis."

"I'm sorry, Brent."

"Don't be. It's for the best," he said. "On a different subject, want you to know I couldn't have survived this ordeal without your support. I'm forever in your debt."

Patricia laughed. "Owe me nothing. Told you I did it for selfish reasons. But hold you to your perceived debt when you're Richmont's CEO."

Brent smiled. "Hey, this isn't goodbye. We'll see each other when you're in Atlanta for business. Plus, I remember you and Adam go to Atlanta from time to time. The three of us could have dinner." He laughed. "I might even scare up a date."

"Adam and I have ended our relationship," she said.

"Oh, Patricia. My turn to say I'm sorry. Liked Adam the few times I was with him."

"Thanks but it was coming for quite a while. Adam wanted a commitment I wasn't prepared to give. I'd better go, Brent." Her eyes foretold coming tears. Brent stood and came around the desk with his hand extended. "Once again, couldn't have made it without you."

Patricia held his hand in both of hers and smiled softly. "How many times do I have to tell you I'm selfish?"

Brent smiled and looked in her eyes but said nothing.

She continued to hold his hand in hers. "Know it's dreadfully unprofessional but could I have a little hug."

It took all the self-discipline in his body but he said, "Don't think so, Patricia. A little hug would turn into a big hug and don't think either of us are ready for that yet."

Patricia let go of his hand. "Maybe you're right." The first tear softly fell from her left eye.

Brent took her hand back. "Would you like to go on a date with me? Dinner maybe."

Patricia's face displayed an equal amount of surprise and hope. "Think that would be marvelous."

"Great. Think it would be marvelous, too. When you get back to your office put it in your PDA. Friday evening, six months from last Friday. In Atlanta. Six months should give us both a chance to make some sense out of this crazy world we find ourselves in. And with your permission, I'd be ready for that hug then."

Patricia looked at him with fondness but said nothing. She smiled knowingly, turned and walked out of Brent's office.

ACKNOWLEGEMENTS

To Mary, thanks for hanging with me through "thick and thin" for 44 years.

To Margee and Scott, thanks for bringing the old Chinese proverb, "May you live in interesting times" to fruition in my life while you were growing up and beyond.

To "The Pusser", "Wingman", "Grunt" and "The Lizard", who make life more fulfilling everyday and prove the wonderful gift of being blessed with grandchildren.

To Carol Poissoit, thanks for the encouragement without which TRUMPED would not have come to pass. Also, many thanks for your help in seeing the story from a woman's point of view.

To Pete Lotruglio, thanks for being a great friend. Also, for taking the time to read the first and second really rough drafts and making valuable comments.

To Dick Justice, thanks for your comments and teaching me some basic English that I had forgotten.

To Bill Weitzel, who taught me how organizations really work.

To Nicole Smith, thanks for making TRUMPED a reality. I hope we can do some more.

www.ingramcontent.com/pod-product-compliance
Lightning Source LLC
Chambersburg PA
CBHW020300030826
48979CB00026B/1599/J

* 9 7 8 0 9 8 2 0 1 9 7 4 0 *